2019 draws to a close. V criminal lawyer Glenn Murray Cohen is stuck in a dead-end gig managing the career of Phil Funston, Bangkok's most talented guitarist and most obnoxious foreign resident. Glenn's sense of honor won't let him quit without finding a suitable replacement. His mysterious friend, the General, promises to make this happen if Glenn will represent him on a business negotiation. An American company has offered to buy an interest in the General's security business, but questions linger about the prospective buyers' motives. Glenn reluctantly agrees, and it isn't long before he and his NJA Club friends are again drawn into a web of intrigue and danger. When they discover the buyers are really foreign thugs tailing an American scientist, pieces of the puzzle fall into place. Glenn and the NJA gang must learn who is really behind this, and why, as they struggle to protect the scientist and themselves. Another exotic thriller from a master of the genre.

Five-Star Praise for *Bangkok Whispers*

"I read Bangkok Shadows and got sucked into the strange world of Bangkok. *Bangkok Whispers* makes you want to visit Thailand and see this for yourself. His description of the streets, alleys and tucked away stores in Bangkok is impressive. But it's the fully drawn out characters that really make the novel.... The full range of likable characters to despicable, all interesting and unpredictable."

—Larry L.

"A tangled tale of schemes within schemes nested like in a Russian Doll though no Russians here except in backcast references to *Bangkok Shadows*. Again, spot on capture of sensory feel, rhythm and pace of Thailand and its culture. And a page burner to boot!"

— Dr. Cal G.O.

"Loved the characters. Stayed up late reading this well-crafted novel. A great read."

—Mike C.

Five-Star Praise for *Bangkok Shadows*

"Stephen Shaiken gets Bangkok like only someone who has lived there can. He has craftily and subtly caught the essence of the mystery to westerners that comes so naturally to the Thai peoples. Let's get some more!!!! Please.

—Tom K.

"Awesome read ... Really enjoyed the character detail.Can't wait for his next work. Need a Thailand vacation in the near future for myself."

—Anthony

BANGKOK BLUES

STEPHEN SHAIKEN

2022

Copyright © 2022 by Stephen Shaiken

Cover design by vaughnsuzette

Text design by Shayan Saalabi

All rights reserved.

Print ISBN 978-1-7321474-5-4

Ebook ISBN 978-1-7321474-4-7

No part of this document may be used or reproduced in any manner whatsoever without written permission except in the case of brief quotations embodied in critical articles and reviews.

This is a work of fiction. Names, characters, businesses, places, events, and incidents are either the products of the author's imagination or used in a fictitious manner. Any resemblance to actual persons, living or dead, events, or locales is entirely coincidental.

Published by Crosswinds Press

Table of Contents

One	9
Two	14
Three	26
Four	34
Five	44
Six	54
Seven	63
Eight	71
Nine	74
Ten	83
Eleven	91
Twelve	105
Thirteen	112
Fourteen	116
Fifteen	123
Sixteen	131
Seventeen	138
Eighteen	145
Nineteen	153
Twenty	158
Twenty-One	166
Twenty-Two	173
Twenty-Three	183
Twenty-Four	201
Twenty-Five	213
Twenty-Six	225
Twenty-Seven	234
Twenty-Eight	244
Twenty-Nine	262
Thirty	270
Thirty-One	284
Thirty-Two	289
Acknowledgements	294
About the Author	295

One

Bangkok, Thailand, Late November 2019

THE MAN on the floor squirmed in the dark, his wrists and ankles chafing against the ropes that bound him. His eyes were wide open, but he couldn't see a thing. He stopped moving when he heard footsteps outside the door. *Probably coming to tell me again that if they don't get the money, they will kill me. Maybe kick me again to make the point.*

The door opened and an unseen hand turned on the light. The sudden brightness forced the man to close his eyes. He managed to comprehend the strong, mumbling Australian accent.

"Don't worry, my friend, I'm one of the good guys. I'm here to send you home."

"Home?" the man on the floor asked. "Who are you?"

The Australian recognized the clipped accent of an upper-class Englishman, the kind he didn't care for at all. He'd been told this one was the general manager of a five-star British-owned hotel, the kind that would never have a room for him. Not that he'd ever want to stay there.

"Like I said," the Australian said. "I'm one of the good guys. Stay still while I cut you loose."

The man sat up as soon as he was free.

"How long have I been here?" he asked. The Australian told him a week.

"What about the men that took me here?" he then asked. "They're all over this place. They won't let us get away."

His liberator smiled, flashing a set of uneven yellowing teeth. "There were only six, and they are all dead."

The Englishman took the Australian's hand and stood with his assistance. When his eyes adapted to the light, he saw a skinny man with long gray stringy hair tied in a ponytail, and several days stubble on his face. He reeked of something the Englishman thought either tobacco or weed, maybe both. The Australian was no more than five foot eight and weighed not an ounce above a hundred forty pounds.

"You killed six men?" the man asked. "No offense, especially if you're really rescuing me, but you don't look the type."

"They all think that just before they die," the Australian replied, a half-smile crossing his face. His eyes were red-rimmed, but the blue in their centers shined brightly. When the Englishman stood at his full height, he was a head taller than the gnome-like Australian creature.

"You still haven't told me who you are or why you came."

"I work for a man who owns the best security firm in the Kingdom," the Australian said. "When the firm you hired to protect you failed to do so and you were kidnapped, your lawyer had the good sense to call my boss. Now let's go. Your driver is waiting outside."

The two men walked out of the room into a short hallway. Two bodies lay at the end. The Englishman followed the Australian down a staircase, and they stepped over two more bodies on their way down.

"There's no blood anywhere," the Englishman said. "Are they unconscious?"

"Like I told you, they are dead. I don't use weapons, unless I am forced to grab one from the guy I'm killing. I prefer breaking necks. Quick and easy. And like you say, no messy blood."

They reached the bottom of the stairs and walked through one more door to the dark street. A Mercedes Benz sat by the curb thirty feet away. The Englishman recognized his car and driver. He brushed dirt from his suit as he spoke.

"Whoever your employer is, please extend my deepest gratitude. As for you, my friend, I don't know how to thank you enough." He glanced back at the building after they walked through the door. "I suppose the loss of any life is regrettable, though regret is not what I'm feeling towards them at this moment. Will all these dead bodies cause us any difficulties with the police?"

The Australian smiled.

"My boss will take care of that, rest assured. It's a full-service company. Like they say, 'you get what you pay for.'"

"From what I see, worth every penny, every one well spent."

Just wait until you get the bill, the Australian thought. *These rich Brits think they're entitled to everything. And they're incredibly cheap.*

The Englishman gave his rescuer his name and the name of his hotel. "If I may ever be of any assistance to you, please feel free to call."

Unlikely, the Australian thought. *But I could use a light for that joint I found in my pocket.*

He explained this to the hotelier, who had cleared his Saville Row suit of most of a week's worth of floor dirt. A terse smile appeared on his face.

"Never cared much for hippies, but then again, I've never owed my life to one. My driver smokes, cigarettes only of course, and not in the car or in my presence."

They walked to the Mercedes, where the driver handed the Australian a lighter. When the joint was lit, he walked away.

"I could give you a lift to the Skytrain if that helps. You'd have to put that out, of course."

The Australian exhaled a cloud of ganja smoke.

"No thanks. It's a lovely night, and I'd rather walk."

"You still haven't told me your name," the Englishman said as the Australian continued walking down the street into the Bangkok night. The latter turned and faced the hotelier.

"My friends know what to call me. And you're not my friend."

Then he was gone.

"Rather unpleasant fellow," the Englishman said to his driver as they pulled from the curb. "Though he did save my life, not to mention the hotel chain saved several million pounds. Who would ever imagine such a fellow so capable in the most difficult of circumstances?"

"He kept my lighter," the driver replied. "Do you think you can buy me another?"

⁓

THE AUSTRALIAN smoked his joint as he walked through the abandoned industrial area just off of Song Wat Road, a stone's throw from the Chao Phraya River. He smoked it so far down it caused a slight burn on a fingertip. He dropped it and kept walking. He was on the outskirts of Chinatown and there were bound to be open restaurants and bars and taxicabs if he decided he no longer wished to walk. *Some dim sum would hit the spot*, he thought. *Maybe they have Foster's, maybe even on tap.*

He thought how much he wanted to call his best friend, Glenn Murray Cohen, and tell him he was back in Bangkok for a while, so let the good times roll. The General told him not to contact anyone, not even Glenn, until he was fully debriefed. Once the General could positively identify the gang that was kidnapping wealthy foreigners in Southeast Asia, he could sell the information to law enforcement. He could also elect to charge prospective victims a small fortune to keep them safe, and even better, be able to handle actual kidnappings extrajudicially, which was certain to be more successful than working with the local police. The General never actually said any of this, but this veteran of Australian Special Forces had no trouble figuring it out. As long as he was well-paid and enjoyed himself, he couldn't care less. The General was an excellent boss. After he got debriefed on this assignment, he would be free to do as he pleased.

I'll bet Glenn will be shocked to see Sleepy Joe again. We'll get wrecked on good weed and watch The Big Lebowski *for the thirty-seventh time. See if one of us can trip up the other on knowing the next line.*

Two

GLENN MURRAY Cohen did not enjoy managing a blues guitarist in Bangkok. It was not Bangkok he minded, and certainly not the blues; to the contrary, he cherished both very much. What Glenn did not enjoy was Phil Funston being that Bangkok guitarist. There were well over ten thousand Western men in Thailand's capital, and Funston was the *farang* Glenn liked least. This made the many unpleasant hours a week they spent together even more difficult to bear.

GLENN SAT on a stool in the Starbucks on the third level of the massive Central World shopping complex, waiting for Phil. He watched the bustling concourse that ran from the Chit Lom BTS station directly into Central World. Phil was taking the BTS, or Skytrain, and would have to pass the stretch of the window where Glenn sat. Funston was already a half-hour late, and hadn't answered Glenn's calls or texts.

A half hour turned into fifty minutes late, and Glenn was fuming. Just as he finished his third cup of Ethiopian Highland, he spotted Funston's lumpy, shaved head bobbing past the window. Funston turned into the Starbucks towards Glenn.

"About time," Glenn snapped, as Funston took the stool next to him. "You were supposed to be here close to an hour ago."

Funston frowned and shook his oddly-shaped, lumpy head. The fluorescent lights above reflected off the crown, casting a butter-colored glow across his bald scalp. He didn't have the right shape for a shaved head.

"Glenn, it's not like the only thing going on in my life is meeting you to buy strings, picks, and a pedal. I don't even need you for that. What do you know about gear? I could go myself, on my schedule, and spare you some mental anguish."

"Except I can't trust you," Glenn replied. "The last time I gave you cash, you spent it all in sleazy bars along Soi 22, ruining your gut and brain drinking Mekong and SangSom and ran out of strings and picks at the next gig. I had to charm another band's manager into lending me a guitar. It's not like any of them would do *you* a favor. And you need one of those George Harrison pedals to make that great sound of his."

Funston laughed.

"It's called a wah-wah pedal. Harrison even wrote a song about it, admitting it made him who he was. Anyway, I'm a better guitarist than he was, wah-wah or no wah-wah."

"And I'm a better manager than whoever managed Harrison, because you're still alive and not in jail," Glenn said. "Now let's go and get those supplies."

"Like I just said, we call them gear. And you might want to consider that the Beatles' first manager committed suicide."

Central World did not cater to the poor of any nationality. While all were free to visit, gawk, and enjoy the chilly air-conditioning, only foreigners and affluent Thais could afford the mostly high-end stores. Central World was located in the heart of Thailand's capital, but the languages heard on the escalators and in the stores were as likely to be Chinese, Hindi, Arabic, English, or Korean, as Thai.

They mounted an escalator, Glenn ahead of Funston.

"Since when did a mere pick get elevated to 'gear' status?" Glenn asked as they moved upward. "I thought that was only for things like amps and stands."

"How about if you leave the music part to me, and you stick with the business end?" The escalator reached the next floor, and they walked.

•

"SPENDING MONEY *is* the business end," Glenn said as they neared the entrance to the music store. A display of expensive guitars, drums, and keyboards filled the window. A sign in English, Thai, and Chinese announced the availability of lessons for guitar, bass, and piano. All major brands were represented: Fender, Gibson, PRS, Ibanez, Yamaha. Most were actually made in China these days, but the American or Japanese brands they displayed carried the most prestige, especially American. The Chinese-made instruments were relatively inexpensive, at least for Westerners, but the few made-in-America options were quite costly, higher priced than in the U.S.

I ought to know, Glenn thought. He bought Phil a used American-made Gibson Les Paul, for almost four thousand U.S. dollars. It replaced an equally valuable Les Paul that was stolen from Phil in Patpong, which might be the sleaziest part of Bangkok. Phil's story was that he was returning from an audition and stopped to tie a shoelace. When he was bent over and using both hands, some street person grabbed it and ran off, probably selling it to pay for the next hit of *ya ba*, Thailand's version of smokable methamphetamine. No one at the NJA Club believed this, and all thought Phil was ripped off at a sleazy massage parlor or by a "freelance" prostitute, cheaper than those from the bars and clubs but more likely to steal. Glenn later checked the online prices in America and was pleasantly surprised to find he had actually paid slightly lower than the usual price. It was not as difficult to find a replacement as Glenn feared; every so often, a would-be farang rock star in Bangkok was forced to sell their axe to keep a roof over their heads and afford a plate of noodles for dinner, served street-side.

Inside, the sound of tasteful blues guitar flowed softly from a PA system. Glenn recognized it as Derek Trucks, one of his favorite contemporary blues masters. *Someone here has good taste*, he thought. The customers were mostly Thais, and affluent from the expensive clothing they wore and the costly instruments they examined.

"They sell all this stuff cheaper at MBK," Phil said just before they entered the store. "Even less at Chawtuchuek." Glenn frowned. MBK was a middle- and working-class department store, with a bargain basement. Glenn saw little reason for him to be that frugal in Thailand, already one huge bargain basement for people with dollars.

"The last time you bought strings over at MBK, they turned out to be cheap Chinese junk, packaged in fake Ernie Ball and D'Addario envelopes," Glenn replied, referring to two well-respected guitar string brands. "I don't mind spending money on quality, but what's the point of buying junk that makes you look and sound bad?" Glenn believed Phil had pocketed the savings for his drinking and whoremongering, but he could not prove it.

Funston's face and bald pate reddened. He recalled his humiliation when the strings popped, one after another, in the middle of a gig at the vaunted Saxophone Club. A Thai drummer explained the source of his problems, but it was too late. Even if Phil could find the exact little stall that sold him the counterfeit strings, it wouldn't do him any good. Bangkok did not have a Better Business Bureau. Fortunately, the other band playing that night was one of the few in Bangkok Phil had not fought with, and he was able to borrow a guitar without Glenn's intervention. The audience thought it was all part of the act.

"In Thailand, the farang always loses," the drummer explained to Glenn after the show, when he complained about being sold fake strings. Glenn nodded in agreement, having learned this over the course of his thirteen years in the Kingdom. He rarely argued with a Thai about any subject. Phil had not learned this and continually argued with Thai and farang alike about everything. It never got him what he wanted and alienated most people. Few had ever personally seen or heard a guitarist as good as Phil Funston, but Phil's personality and habits would preclude his audience from growing. The greatest impediment to Phil Funston's success was Phil Funston himself.

Glenn considered shooting down the Chawtuchuek idea as well but decided it was not necessary. Even Phil Funston understood the near impossibility of two farangs with minimal Thai finding the guitar supply section of a covered market the size of all the NFL stadiums in America combined.

As Glenn and Phil were about to pass through the sliding glass doorway of the store, a couple engaged in conversation passed through. The man was close to six feet tall and built large but not fat. The slight Thai woman was nearly a foot shorter. As they walked through the door, the woman brushed against Phil.

"Why don't you watch where you're going?" he called out. The woman started to say something which to Glenn sounded like the word "sorry." Phil grew more angry.

"Did I say you could speak?" he bellowed.

The man stepped toward Phil. He was a few inches taller and looked several degrees more powerful.

"It was an accident. She tried to apologize. Chill out." Glenn recognized a Swedish accent.

"A little early in the day to be paying a bar fine, isn't it?" Phil asked the Swede, referring to the fee a john pays the bar when taking a hooker, in addition to paying the woman. The Swede erupted and reached a hand towards Phil, seeking to grab him by the shirt. Glenn threw his left arm in the way to block the Swede's arm while pushing Phil into the open doorway with his right.

"I'll meet you inside," he told Funston.

When the doors closed and Glenn saw Funston on the other side, he turned to the couple.

"I am really sorry," he began. "My name is Glenn Cohen, and I manage Phil Funston, who you just met. Phil is a remarkable guitarist, plays with the best musicians, and is a really good guy, but he's had a bad week. Family member very seriously ill. He's not handling it well. You're seeing him at his worst, never like this otherwise. I know that's no excuse, but I hope you'll understand this isn't really who he is." Glenn reached into his pocket and withdrew a card case. He handed it to the Swede.

"Phil's playing this Thursday night at that new club just off On Nut," he said. "I'd love to have you two come as my guests, cover charge waived, two drinks apiece on me, and let me know what song you'd like the band to dedicate to you two. Just call me and leave your names and the song. I'll make sure the folks at the gate know about you."

The Swede took the card, studied it, and handed it to the woman.

"You seem like a nice man, Glenn, and I appreciate your kind gesture. We're putting this behind us. However, I don't think my wife or I care to ever see this boor again. I happen to be in the music business myself, promoting rock concerts anywhere in Asia I can. We live in Chiang Mai and we're catching the night train up there in a few hours. I was killing time seeing what stuff they have down here we don't see up there. I won't hold this against you. Next time I've got something going in Bangkok, I'll send you complementary tickets and you can come backstage after and meet people."

I'm hoping to get out of this business, but I appreciate the thought.

"Thanks," Glenn said. "I love listening to music when I'm not also working."

The Swede smiled.

"Don't we all? You're a good man. I know what jerks these artists can be. If it weren't for the money, I'd be gone."

What money? Glenn asked himself.

∽

WHEN GLENN caught up with Phil inside the store, he pulled him into an aisle with no customers browsing. Glenn and Phil were the only farangs in the store.

"Are you out of your mind?" he asked Phil. "Can you go more than a few hours without picking a fight?"

"Why are you blaming me?" Phil asked. "That whore ran right into me. I can't allow such disrespect in public."

Glenn gripped the edge of a shelf and leaned slightly towards the display.

"Phil, the only one showing disrespect was you. It was an accident. She was trying to apologize."

"She was playing games," Phil said. "It didn't sound sincere."

"I give up trying to persuade you what's right. I'll settle for a promise not to do it again."

A young Thai man dressed all in black turned into their aisle just as Glenn was finished speaking. The young man greeted Phil as soon as he saw and recognized him. He was short and wiry and for the moment crackled with an enthusiasm less restrained than Glenn was accustomed to seeing from Thais.

"You're Phil Funston, aren't you?" he asked, in lightly accented English. "I've seen you play over in Banglampoo and down on Thong Lor. I'm honored to meet you."

"Hey, dude, always a pleasure to meet a fan," Phil replied. "I'm playing at this new club over on Khao San this weekend, if you have the time. Give me your name and my manager over here will get the cover charge waived. You'll still get the drink ticket."

Glenn smiled. He liked it when Phil was gracious, especially to a fan. It was an uncommon treat to experience him being pleasant.

"I'm Glenn Cohen, Phil's manager. Thanks for the nice words, and we look forward to seeing you Saturday night as our guest. I just need your name."

The salesman said his name was Rong. *Easy to remember*, Glenn thought.

"Rong from the music store at Central World, and one guest, will be admitted free of charge and given drink tickets," Glenn said. "Now you can help us find what we need so I can get Phil back to rehearsal."

The order was promptly filled. Rong knew every inch of the large store. After Glenn paid, Rong mentioned that he was a bass player. Glenn assumed anyone working in a music store was a musician, just not successful.

"I can come by and sit in with Phil during practice," Rong volunteered as they walked to the cash register. "For free." It was not unusual for musicians to offer to play with Phil. Musicians know they improve by playing with artists like Phil. Bangkok was filled with wannabes who believed merely saying they practiced with Phil would get them gigs. Once they got to know him, their ardor faded quickly.

"Thanks, kid," Glenn said. "You never know when the need is there, and now I know where to reach you." Glenn told his brain to file a note to call Rong the following week.

"Hey, I'm going to bring a bunch of my friends Saturday night," Rong called to Glenn and Phil as they walked to the front door.

"See the benefit of being nice to people?" Glenn asked Phil when as they stepped onto the down escalator.

"Not really," Phil replied.

~

GLENN KNEW he was managing Phil as well as any farang in Bangkok could manage another, and Phil Funston was not just any farang. After nearly twenty years in the Kingdom, Phil still spoke and acted like a sexpat on his first delusional visit to Thailand. He frequented places Glenn refused to enter and treated Thai people and their culture with utter disdain. Both were glaring defects in Glenn's eyes, but the disdain and lack of respect for Thais disturbed him most. Glenn admired both, though in his soul recognized that he understood little about either. He knew enough not to do what displeased Thais: yelling, starting fights, ridiculing Thais in public, bragging incessantly, and most annoyingly of all, rambling endlessly about exploits in bars and massage parlors. Phil Funston was unrestrained by these considerations or any others. Glenn conceded that with Phil, it was nothing specific against Thais; Phil treated all peoples and cultures with the same disrespect.

Glenn tried to persuade Phil he would achieve greater musical success if he changed his behavior. His words fell on deaf ears and Glenn gave up, asking only that Phil behave when working and avoid the police. Phil agreed to these rules but regularly broke them. Glenn carried a roll of thousand-baht notes in case Phil's abusive language and attitude caused an offended Thai to call the boys in brown. Paying cabbies, hookers, and bars were the easy ones. It was more difficult when the Thai version of John Q. Citizen was the complainant. In Thailand, when a Thai citizen calls the police on a farang, there are but two possible outcomes: the farang pays the cop-and often the offended Thai as well—or the farang had better know how to ask for a lawyer in Thai. He'd lived in Thailand long enough to know it was cheaper and less painful to pay off the victim instead of the victim and the police. Glenn always tried to pay off an aggrieved Thai citizen before the law was called.

The times Phil insulted or assaulted a Thai were the most difficult, as some of the cops were torn between taking the money or making this obnoxious foreigner cool his heels in a Thai jail for a few days. Glenn upped the bribe when this happened. He twice succeeded in bribing Phil's way out of a Thai jail. The other two cost him more than he would earn from Phil in three months. Glenn prayed there would not be a fifth time.

I'm tired of being dragged out of bed at all hours to pay Phil's taxi fare, bar bill, or even more objectionably, his "bar fine," Glenn told himself every time it happened. Glenn never understood why the rent-a-girlfriend charge the bar put on top of her fee would be deemed a fine; fines were imposed for breaking a rule, and it seemed like the whole purpose of those bars was to sell sex.

∼

GLENN MET Phil years ago at the NJA Club, the Bangkok bar and bistro where Glenn spent more time than any place outside his condo. The crowd was a mix of Thais and Westerners, all of them amazed that Phil Funston had not yet been beaten to death by an angry mob. The English language newspapers regularly reported such encounters between an out-of-line farang and the family or friends of someone the farang was believed to have wronged. No one at the Club would be surprised to read Phil's name as one of them, nor would any be likely to shed a tear.

Glenn and Phil still had a major advantage over other foreigners: they could legally work in the Kingdom. Phil claimed permanent resident status, which seemed true, as whatever Thai government documentation he showed club owners or the occasional inquiring official worked. The NJA Club was rife with rumors about Phil holding permanent residence through a make-believe marriage to a Thai woman, whom he paid money each year to maintain the immigration charade. Glenn wondered whether any woman would want to be legally tethered to Phil Funston, no matter how much money he paid. "He'd be better off paying a fixer to get him his papers," was how Edward the Englishman put it. Edward was gay, and Funston was a homophobe, so the two hadn't exchanged many words in the dozen or so years Glenn had known them.

However Phil obtained his legal right to work, it meant Glenn never paid a single baht as a bribe to avoid immigration or labor violations. *Be thankful for that much*, Glenn sometimes thought.

Glenn's business visa allowed him to work as he wished. His Thai consultant explained that just about anything was covered by a corporation he had set up. The visa was arranged through Charlie, Glenn's gray-market lawyer friend in America. Charlie set everything up all those years ago, after Glenn had snatched a bundle of cash from a murdered client and decided to start a new life elsewhere. Since arriving in Thailand, Charlie contacted him twice; both calls led to Glenn and his friends being dragged into dangerous CIA business. The payments they received were most generous, but money was not Glenn's problem. Glenn placed the memories of those dangerous times in sealed boxes, to be opened only when there were no other options, as he did with memories of his fifteen years as a criminal defense lawyer in San Francisco. Otherwise Glenn thought about Charlie only every three years, when a Thai immigration consultant sent by Charlie came to arrange for a new visa.

At the time, I thought it was great. Who knew it would lead to Phil Funston?
How did I ever allow myself to be talked into this?

Three

Second Week of December 2019

GLENN BLAMED his old friend, the General, for his professional relationship with Phil. The General had pushed him hard to become Funston's manager when Phil contemplated returning to the U.S.A. after his guitar was stolen. The General told Glenn that with the excitement of international intrigue over, and his best friend, Sleepy Joe, off on regular secret assignments for him, Glenn needed something to occupy his time. This was a perfect opportunity for a music lover. The General not only persuaded him to become Phil's manager, but to also loan him four thousand U.S. dollars to replace the stolen Gibson Les Paul, a vintage model from the mid-seventies. Phil had yet to pay any part of that loan, and Glenn never expected to see any money.

The General and his son owned clubs throughout Bangkok, assuring Glenn of steady work for his irascible client. They didn't pay well and, adding insult to injury, demanded ten percent of any fee paid to Phil by anyone, anywhere. The kickbacks guaranteed that the General and son would assure steady work for Phil, and that other owners would follow suit and cut Phil all reasonable slack for his behavior. Since all of these clubs were under the General's protection, the new guitar was safe, and Glenn could smoke weed in the alleys behind any club without fear.

Under the General's umbrella, any problems within the confines of the venue where Phil performed would be resolved without the law, where the angry patron or employee could be bought off. Police were only called when Phil started fights in the streets, restaurants, bars, massage parlors, BTS stations, or twice on the grounds of *wats*, and those were difficult and expensive to resolve. *It's not just the waste of money,* Glenn often thought. *If I wanted this kind of stress, I could have stayed home in San Francisco and practiced criminal law. It paid a hell of a lot better.*

On the positive side, Phil worked regularly and honestly, and while he didn't live like a Western rock star, was in no danger of missing meals or living on the streets. Glenn's presence resulted in Phil avoiding most of the fights and arguments with band leaders and club owners that kept him from getting callbacks in the past. Glenn could do only so much to protect Phil from himself, and after three years, he still hadn't progressed beyond playing the better clubs in Bangkok. There were no offers to tour Asia or play on an album and receive credit. He wasn't even called to play at any of the numerous venues on vacation islands like Phuket, Koh Phangan, or Koh Samui. Glenn might be able to bail Phil out of jail and poverty, but he could not persuade other musicians to hire him. Glenn himself barely tolerated being with Phil, but as manager, he had no choice. His initial agreement was for six months, but for two years after that time, they continued to operate as if the contract were still in effect. *I could walk away any time I want, but that wouldn't be right,* Glenn had determined. *I would have to find a suitable replacement. Lawyers can't leave a case until the client finds someone else, so it ought to be that way with any professional responsibility.*

Glenn accepted his predicament was not entirely the General's fault, but without his urging, Glenn would not have this millstone around his neck.

Glenn and the General became friends soon after the American lawyer moved to Bangkok and wandered into the NJA Club because it was a short walk from his new condo. The bar and restaurant with the mysterious name occupied the ground level of a nondescript two-story building on an obscure soi off busy Sukhumvit Road, between the Thong Lor and Ekamai BTS stops. A farang in Bangkok is never in danger of starving, but once Glenn found the NJA Club, he rarely ate elsewhere.

The lower stretch of Sukhumvit, below Soi Sixty-Three, also called Ekamai, was long-ago dubbed "The Green Zone." There's great disagreement about the origins of the name, but no disagreement about it having the highest concentration of foreigners in the Kingdom. There's also disagreement about how far it currently extends, as many farangs now live beyond the traditional borders, even past what were once the outer limits, like the Phra Khanong and On Nut neighborhoods. Most bars, restaurants, and coffee shops in the Zone catered to foreigners; the Thais had their own places dotted among the Western businesses on the main street and on the side sois. The NJA Club was different, and the clientele was a mix of farangs and Thais. The General was the most senior Thai customer, in age and years of patronage. Glenn quickly learned how unusual it was for a retired Thai general, one with vast commercial interests and vast connections, to socialize primarily with farangs.

Glenn and the General were the closest of friends, and facing death together drew them even closer. Thus, the General persuaded Glenn to become Phil's manager despite the trial lawyer's sixth sense warning that it was a terrible idea. Now that he was proven right, and wanted out in an honorable way, the General had no ideas to offer.

Whenever Glenn brought up the notion of his quitting, the General reminded him that Glenn Murray Cohen was a man of his word, and he had promised to manage Phil so that he reached his full potential, and the job was not finished. The General understood his American friend very well. Glenn would not quit until he found a suitable replacement, but there weren't two qualified people in the kingdom willing to trouble themselves with Phil Funston.

And if I quit, Phil goes to hell in a handcart, and the General and his son lose a draw for their clubs, whom they rip off every time he plays anywhere.

~

As soon as Glenn entered the NJA Club, he spotted the General at his usual table in the rear, facing the door. His burly bodyguard sat behind him, automatic rifle cradled in his arms. Glenn was unaware of any enemies out to harm the General, but the General feared a violent revolution aimed at overthrowing the monarchy he'd served his entire life, and for which he would unhesitatingly die to protect. Ever since 2010, when the Red Shirts occupied the commercial district and burned down Siam Square, the General remained at the ready for an insurgent attack.

We're the safest people in Bangkok with him around, Glenn thought. Glenn did not fear communists or insurrectionists, but there were plenty of dangerous criminals out there, including government operatives from all sides. Several had tried to kill Glenn and his friends, and they had been forced to kill a few themselves.

I'm never doing that again, Glenn assured himself every time those thoughts pushed past the defenses his mind had constructed. *When danger calls, Glenn Murray Cohen will be missing in action.*

Glenn sat next to the General. The older man signaled the waitress, who scurried to their table. Her name was Kit, or at least that was the nickname she, like all Thais, used. Kit was young, no more than mid-twenties, and had been at the NJA Club for only a month. The Club's long-time waitress, Mai, resigned to take a job as an agricultural worker in Israel. Glenn found this ironic.

I'm the Jew, and she gets to Israel before me.

"Maybe she thinks that will win your heart," the General advised Glenn the day Mai announced her departure. Every NJA Club regular knew that Mai carried a searing torch for Glenn, who feared another disastrous relationship, this time at the Club, would ruin his life, so he refrained from sparking the fire. Being lonely often felt bad but being forced out of the NJA Club due to a messy breakup with an employee would be more than he could bear. He wished her luck in the Holy Land and was relieved to see that pressure leave with Mai's Korean Air flight to Israel.

"I hear your star is playing at one of my son's clubs this weekend," the General said. "Maybe I'll come by. My new *mia noi* likes American music."

Glenn frowned. The General was a married man with grown children who openly paraded an endless string of young women who served brief stints as his "minor wife," the best translation of the Thai term. Glenn grew accustomed to the General's endless campaign to set him up with a friend of the current mia noi, and once agreed to take the offer if he couldn't find a woman within six months. The General and his mia noi went their separate ways, and by the time the General had settled upon a replacement, the deal was forgotten. The hectoring, however, continued unabated.

"My offer stands, as always," the General added. "Just give me the word, and one of her beautiful friends is yours."

"Why would I want one?" Glenn snapped.

"Because you can afford one, the first and probably the only requirement. What good is your money if you are not enjoying it?"

The men realized that Kit was standing next to the table, waiting for them to place their orders. Glenn recalled how Mai would not countenance her time being wasted and would speak up.

Give this one a few weeks, and she'll be as pushy as Mai. She'll be telling us to give her our orders now or go thirsty. Kit took their orders and headed to the bar. In the old days, Ray would mix two martinis as soon as the General and Glenn were together. These days, Glenn often forewent his daily cocktail, since working in clubs with Phil provided his quota of alcohol. Glenn didn't like booze, preferred weed, but alcohol was readily available in places where weed could not be smoked, at least not indoors while watching the show. On days when Phil had a gig, Glenn reserved his solitary drink for that venue, and drank coffee, water, juice or diet soda at the NJA Club. Ray knew this, and if he didn't know if there was a gig, waited to see what Glenn preferred. The General ordered a martini, and Glenn a Coke Zero.

"Your son pays the lowest rate of any club," Glenn said. "We know when Phil is on the bill, the club is packed, and the bar sells booze faster than the staff can pour. You and your son are the only owners that make me and Phil pay for our own drinks. Sometimes when he takes drinks off the fee, after cab fare, we barely break even. And these clubs are always a long and expensive cab ride. I should get extra money just for having to spend all that time in a taxi with Phil. I know your son does whatever you tell him. How about ordering him to boost Phil's fee by fifty percent, and pour a few drinks on the house?"

The General smiled.

"If Phil didn't start out playing in our clubs twice a week for your first year as his manager, no one would know who he is. Make your money elsewhere today, but give us a break."

Like you've ever given anyone a break, Glenn thought.

"How can we make money elsewhere if you guys insist on taking ten percent off the top everywhere?" Glenn asked.

Kit returned with the drinks. She looked away when she eyed Glenn surveying her from head to toe.

"At least your eyes are still focused on the right things," the General said when Kit was out of earshot.

Glenn smiled and shook his head.

"Automatic response."

The General took a long sip of his martini.

"Exactly my point," he said when done. "Your natural state of mind is to crave a woman. Give in and let me bring you one."

"Isn't craving something Buddhists are supposed to avoid?" Glenn asked. "Shouldn't you be trying to persuade me not to give in to my sexual yearnings?"

The General shook his head vigorously three times in each direction.

"Glenn, I am to Buddhism what you are to Judaism. We choose not to practice any religion, but the religions we choose not to practice are those of our people. Call me a Buddhist, but don't expect me to be against craving. I'd certainly never try and talk you out of it."

Glenn stared into his Coke Zero while the General sipped a quarter inch off his martini.

"I guess that means you are not willing to drop the kickbacks or at least increase Phil's fees in your places?"

"When you tell me to bring you the girl, the fee gets increased," the General replied.

The General's phone vibrated. He picked it off the table and answered, speaking in Thai for a few seconds.

"I have to leave now," he told Glenn. "Business." He rose from his chair and headed toward the door, his bodyguard a foot behind. Then he stopped and turned to Glenn.

"We don't spend as much time together, like we used to," he said. "Maybe you're very busy with Phil Funston. I miss our talks. There's no one else quite like you, Mr. Glenn Murray Cohen, Esquire. How about you come by my house for coffee tomorrow morning? Around eight. We'll spend a few hours drinking good coffee, talking, maybe smoke cigars. See you then."

And maybe you'll tell me when Sleepy Joe comes back from this recent job you gave him.

Four

WHEN GLENN told Lek, his building concierge, that he was off to have early morning coffee with The General at his home, Lek's smile grew wider than usual.

"A great honor when a man like the General invites you into his home," he told Glenn. "Especially a farang." Then he looked at Glenn, his smile contracting to neutral.

"Sorry if I insulted you, *Khun* Glenn. I did not mean to." He clasped his hands to his heart and gave Glenn a deep *wai*, so deep, that at its furthest, Lek's back was almost parallel to the floor, as if he were in a yoga pose.

"No problem, Lek. It is true, and I'm honored." The smile returned to Lek's face.

Glenn loved his condo, and especially Lek as concierge. Lek was more than worth the monthly condo association fees. Over Glenn's many years in the building, their relationship grew from employer-employee to friendship. Glenn admired Lek's salt-of-the-earth Isan character: hard-working, kindness as the default mode, and most appreciated, loyalty. In over a dozen years, Lek had escorted a knife-wielding ex-girlfriend from the building, connected Glenn with his cousin, a police officer in the local precinct, explained to Glenn what he did not understand about Thailand—a great deal, actually—and never breathed a word about Glenn's endless weed-smoking, filing any suspicious odor complaints from other co-op owners into the circular filing cabinet. The ongoing cultural advice may not have turned a Jewish-American criminal lawyer from San Francisco into a Thai, but it prevented him from becoming a farang disliked by Thais, like Phil Funston.

Glenn had visited the General's house only once before, when Sleepy Joe was arrested with a few kilos of weed. Sleepy Joe was Glenn's closest friend and his weed dealer. Glenn met Joe around the same time he met the General. Glenn was looking for source of weed, and the first time he met Joe, the Aussie smelled like a stubbed-out joint. They were soon close friends. When Sleepy Joe was arrested, he used his phone call to awaken Glenn in the middle of the night.

The General used his connections to arrange a suitable bribe, and Joe was set free without charges. Glenn learned the General set up the bust, angry because Sleepy Joe bought from another source to save a few baht. The General neither smoked nor dealt weed, but had a finger in any extra-legal business in Green Belt districts of Klong Toey, Phrom Phong, Thong Lor and Ekamai, and Glenn had no doubt his influence extended to every part of Bangkok. Glenn was never certain of the General's actual involvement in illegal activities; perhaps he merely provided security or financing. The General talked in vague terms about his security business and his mia noi, but never about the mysteries of what he really did.

It was only after rescuing Sleepy Joe from the clutches of the Thai criminal justice system that Joe revealed his past as a member of the Australian Special forces. The skinny fellow with the long, stringy, graying hair dressed in Salvation Army–style clothing was a trained killer. Glenn witnessed several Russians, North Koreans, and Thais learn this final lesson of their lives when he was dragged into the intrigues and dangers he so studiously sought to avoid.

Sleepy Joe and the General patched up their differences, and the former Australian Special Forces turned hippie went to work for the General. His assignments were frequent and usually lasted one to three months. Sleepy Joe always returned, and when he did, he and Glenn spent days on end as before, smoking prodigious quantities of weed, watching their favorite movies over and over again, and listening to the best rock and jazz had to offer over the past seventy years. Glenn tried prying details of their work. After the second year of shoulder shrugs from Sleepy Joe and smiles from the General, Glenn stopped asking. *Probably better not to know.*

Glenn walked the mile to the General's house on a side soi off Soi 16. It was still early, but Glenn knew the General rose with the dawn, and an invitation for morning coffee meant no later than eight. He could have gotten a seat on the BTS at this hour, but the sun had not yet fried the streets of Bangkok, leaving a rare opportunity to stroll without crowds or stifling, humid heat.

The more enterprising food vendors were already set up for business. Some lorded over a few tables and chairs scattered on the sidewalk, while others simply handed the early customers their breakfast, to be eaten wherever they could find a place to enjoy their meal, which might mean leaning against a wall.

Glenn walked the even-numbered side of Sukhumvit Boulevard. The BTS Skytrain ran above him to the right blocked out the weak morning sun. He passed the Emporium, one of Central World's rivals. Next came Benjasiri Park, a welcome green space in the midst of an urban center of eighteen million people. The large gold coin near the entrance greeted

Glenn like an old friend. He'd visited the park countless times over the years, often for no reason other than to sit amidst its tall green trees, alongside a peaceful man-made lake. Within the park, it was several degrees cooler than the rest of Bangkok. Every time Glenn set foot in Benjasiri, it wrapped him in a cloak of calm. When he passed it, it sometimes lured him as the Greek Sirens lured Odysseus. Glenn figured that somewhere in the hollows of his brain lived memories of Prospect Park, before his family left Brooklyn when he was five years old. Most memories of youth and family were rough images, blurry photos suggesting a scene, but not clearly defined.

Small knots of people practiced Qui Gong around the lake. Others strolled the shore or sat on benches under the canopies of trees. A sleepy-eyed policeman stood solitary guard at the main entry, paying Glenn no notice. A middle aged farang walking the street at half past seven in the morning was hardly an odd sight in this part of town.

He turned right off Sukhumvit at Soi 16, passing the hulking Exchange Tower. Glenn once belonged to an expensive health club which occupied three floors of the building and had the best equipment as well as excellent sauna and steam rooms. Almost a year before, the club went belly-up without notice. When Glenn came to work out, the doors were padlocked. Just before the closure, Glenn chatted with a Thai woman on the next treadmill. He couldn't summon the courage to ask for her contact information. After the gym went under, he never saw her again, and his memory of her face was fading.

∽

Soi 16 is one of Bangkok's many irrational streets. Numbered sois are supposed to run perpendicular to avenues, and parallel to each other. Soi 16 did so for a hundred meters, then it suddenly turned right, running parallel to Sukhumvit, an avenue, in a way no numbered street should.

He remembered the correct place to turn, though his last and only visit had been over five years ago. He reached the property, approached the gate and pressed the intercom button. Glenn could have sworn the voice that snapped at him in Thai was the same he'd heard the last time. Glenn explained in English who he was, and why he was ringing the General's bell so early. The gate swung open. He walked to the large house.

A pretty young maid answered the door and led Glenn to the General's library, just as on his last visit. The room hadn't changed in the intervening years. Books, in English and Thai, filled the shelves on every wall. A silver coffee pot and two mugs sat in the center of the table, flanked by milk and sweetener in their respective silvers.

"Pour yourself a cup," the General said. "Nice, mild arabica from Panama, grown high in the mountains in Boquete." The General expected his fellow coffee connoisseur to know all there was to know about Panamanian coffee.

"I've been dying to try some but never see it anywhere. Not in Food Villa or Tops," Glenn replied, referring to two pricey supermarkets favored by more affluent farangs. "How did you get your hands on some?"

"I mentioned I'd like some to the Ambassador, and a few pounds appeared at my front gate not too long afterward."

Glenn considered the statement while he poured his coffee.

"The Panamanian Ambassador to Thailand, or the Thai Ambassador to Panama?" he asked.

"Both," the General replied.

"As you know, it is rare for me to invite anyone into my home," the General said. "Even more unusual for a farang to receive an invitation, and never has one been invited twice."

"Then this must be a most auspicious occasion," Glenn replied.

The General placed his empty cup on the table.

"Indeed it is, Glenn. To begin, I'm sure you will be delighted to hear that from this day on, you do not have to give a gratuity to my son or me, whether Phil plays one of our clubs, or anywhere else."

Glenn nodded slowly, but his mind worked quickly. Glenn understood that keeping the General happy was a prerequisite to a successful business in Bangkok; he also understood it was a way for the General to test loyalty. *Maybe I passed the test.*

"Almost like being family," the General explained, "except you can't be family, as you are a farang."

The General's words were like a bucket of ice water thrown in Glenn's face.

"I'm surprised to hear you say that," Glenn said. "You're always telling me how much you love America and what a good friend I am. Good enough for you to feel comfortable shaking out of me every baht you can. Now you're saying we're not good enough to be family."

The General laughed.

"No, no, Glenn, you have it all wrong. I say that because you need to be protected. If you were Thai, and knew about our family issues, you'd appreciate what I'm saying."

The General saw Glenn's confusion on his face.

"Trust me. When a Thai person feels about a farang the way I feel about you, or even better, the way any woman I find for you would feel, that farang can expect nothing but kindness, compassion, and being treated at least as good if not better than if they were Thai. But by not really being family, which you people in the West want and expect to be, you avoid many unpleasantries."

Much as Glenn disliked being told discrimination against him was for his own good, he remained quiet. He'd learned long ago to never criticize the Thai view of life to any Thai, especially their belief the farang can never be right, and in fact must always be wrong. He also knew the General was correct about the benefits of being spared "unpleasantries." Glenn was a firm believer in the adage taught him by the General many years ago: farangs must stay out of Thai-to-Thai matters. The end result could only be that all the Thais gang up against the farang.

The General interrupted Glenn's thoughts.

"Look at it this way, Glenn. I just gave you and Phil a ten percent raise. If you were truly family, and I tried to do the same, other relatives would demand something out of it, or be jealous of you, or create some other problem, so like a true Thai, I would just leave things alone, and no raise for you."

Glenn calculated the raise to be a few hundred dollars a year each for him and somewhat more for Phil, but he multiplied the sums by four to reflect their actual value in Thailand. From the General's point of view, this was an act of enormous generosity, especially for Phil Funston. *Maybe getting rid of the kickback will make it easier to find a new manager for Phil*, Glenn thought.

"Let's go out and celebrate your good fortune with a fine morning cigar," the General said. As always, the General did not consider the possibility that his suggestion would be resisted. He pressed a button on the desk, and the pretty maid came into the room. The General spoke to her in Thai and motioned for Glenn to follow him through a sliding door in the library that led to the garden.

∼

THE GARDEN was enclosed by eight-foot walls with barbed wire running along the top. Glenn suspected it was electrified as well, and that cameras recorded from every angle. The two men sat on wrought iron chairs around a small table. The maid appeared, carrying a tray with two cups of steaming coffee, cream and sugar, two cigars, a cutter, a lighter, and a large ashtray with a caricature of a smiling cigar. She placed them on the table and left without a word.

"You know, Glenn, I can't touch her with my wife around, but there's nothing standing in your way," the General said when she was gone.

Glenn was unamused.

"General, it's not my nature to take advantage of someone in her situation. She's a maid, and I'm a foreigner, a lawyer, a friend of her important employer. A totally unequal relationship where there's little choice for her, at least in this country. It's what we in America call exploitation."

"What are you talking about, Glenn? Nobody would have to force her to do anything. Maybe we'd have to force you. She'd jump into bed with you in a second. Or wherever you asked her to jump."

"Yeah, either because you made her do it, or she thinks there's money in it," Glenn replied.

The General laughed.

"Glenn, why do you have such a low opinion of our women? Not to mention an even lower opinion of yourself?"

"Let's smoke the cigars with our coffee," Glenn said. The General nodded and cut a small hole in the cap, the end that goes into the mouth. He did it with such speed and elegance that Glenn never saw it happen.

After Sleepy Joe began to disappear for months on end, Glenn found himself alone most of the time and began to experiment with life, trying new experiences. He jogged in the early morning, but it bored him. He took golf lessons, tried to learn guitar, even went to Jewish religious services a few times. None of them lasted very long. One of the more out-of-character experiments was cigar smoking, which did not captivate him as weed did, but to his surprise, as with alcohol and his martinis, he found he could tolerate a fine cigar even if it did not titillate him. Since he did not smoke them very often, a cigar gave a buzz not completely different from weed, and there was something soothing and satisfying about slowly and intermittently drawing in smoke, holding and savoring it for a moment, and breathing it out without inhaling. The mild cigars actually left a pleasant aftertaste, which slowly grew on him. He did not consider himself addicted or habituated, and he could go weeks without a puff, but to his surprise, he found himself occasionally reflecting upon how pleasant it might be to light up a cigar and take a break from the world. He favored the Romeo y Julieta 1875 above all other mild cigars, and while they were quite expensive in Thailand, a few cigars a month meant little to Glenn's finances.

"Romeo y Julieta," the General said. "1875, your favorite." He handed Glenn a cigar and a guillotine cutter. Glenn inserted the cap of his own cigar into the hole in the center of the small rectangular cutter, pushing it in no more than a sixteenth of an inch, and squeezed the ends of the little rectangle with thumb and forefinger. Stainless steel blades emerged from each side and cut off a slice, leaving a small hole to draw smoke. Glenn looked at his handiwork with approval and handed the cutter back to the General.

"Mild enough to smoke any time of day, from morning coffee to nightcap," the General said as he lit his cigar. He skillfully held the foot, the end to light, a half inch or so from the flame, and slowly rotated the cigar as he drew the fire closer. After a few light puffs, the General examined the lit end, blowing as he studied. Glenn saw a bright cherry red tip after the fourth blast of breath. The General then took a deeper puff, leaned back, and slowly exhaled a plume of smoke into the soft morning light. Glenn did the same, and the two men spent the next five minutes sipping coffee, taking intermittent puffs, and savoring the relative cool of early Bangkok as they made small talk.

This is what I like about cigars, Glenn thought when they took a break from their chatter. Then the General spoke up.

"Now for the other matter I wished to discuss."

Five

THE GENERAL liked Glenn Murray Cohen immensely. He reminded the General of the smartest Americans he knew in America, when he was a military attaché with the Embassy in Washington, D.C. The smartest ones were almost always Jewish, and many were lawyers, which the General understood required a skillful application of their intelligence. As a soldier, the General was in awe of the Israeli Defense Forces, and despite Glenn's revulsion towards violence and battle, the General knew that Glenn's ethnicity belied that posture.

The instant Glenn walked into the NJA Club one evening almost thirteen years before, the General recognized him as one of those men he admired. The way he carried himself, the clothing he wore, the fine haircut, and of course, the fact that Glenn ordered a vodka martini. The General watched Glenn as he sat at the bar, thinking whatever thoughts possessed smart American Jews when sitting at bars in Bangkok. When Mai the waitress passed his table, the General told her to have Ray the bartender mix another martini and deliver it to the General's table. Mai was then to invite the farang to join him. He mentioned he was an American.

"How do you know he's an American?" Mai asked. "They all look the same. The white ones, anyway."

"I know an American when I see one," the General replied. "Just do as I say."

"Well, whatever he is, he's handsome," Mai replied.

"Maybe you'll be lucky," the General said as Mai left to deliver the messages.

∽

HE APPEARS *to have no hesitancy or fears about a Thai, a total stranger, buying him a drink and inviting him to sit. Americans can be that way. Especially Jewish Americans. They aren't afraid of anything. Like the Israelis. Like good Thai soldiers. Europeans are different. They have a lot more fear, a lot more uncomfortable when they are not the ones in charge. Americans have self-confidence. Europeans have attitude.*

"Thanks for the drink, and for the invite," Glenn said when he was seated. "I'm fairly new in town and live nearby. I was getting a little bored, and a little lonely too, so I decided to give this place a chance."

Americans love to tell you all about themselves. That's good, because then there are few surprises. Not like here.

"You're very welcome," the General said. "Why did you assume I spoke English, and on your level?"

"Why else would you invite me for a drink?" Glenn replied.

It was, as Claude Raines said to Humphrey Bogart in *Casablanca*, the start of a beautiful friendship.

∽

GLENN WAS drawing a healthy puff on his cigar when he decided he would bring up "the other matter." He blew the smoke out so quickly, it looked like a fighter jet had performed maneuvers in front of his face. When the smoke cleared, he spoke.

"We've been close friends for thirteen years, General. In that time, I have been to your house exactly twice. The first time, almost six years ago, was from your end, a business matter. Would I be correct in assuming this visit also entails some business of yours?"

The General lifted his cigar from the ashtray, holding it between his thumb and forefinger and third finger. He studied the glowing foot for a few seconds, then placed it back in the ashtray.

"Notice how it keeps burning, and evenly, even when not drawn upon. That's the sign of a really good cigar. I don't blame you for being partial to the Romeo y Julieta, though I'm a Montecristo man myself. Robusto Largo."

"I'd expect nothing less than the best out of your humidor, General, and the Montecristo is a great cigar. In fact, it's my second choice," Glenn said. "But what is this other business?"

The General studied the ash on his cigar, and Glenn wondered whether he would take a puff or keep talking. The General chose the latter.

"Glenn, I know that you miss your dear friend Sleepy Joe when he is on assignment for me. I can see how much pleasure it brings you when he is home between assignments. You two are like brothers. You look and sound completely different, but in all other ways, you are so similar. Love the same music, movies, and food. Neither one of you can find a girlfriend, so it's for the best that you have each other."

That was the first Glenn heard about Sleepy Joe not having a girlfriend. As far as Glenn knew, Joe was still involved with Nahmwan, a beautiful woman who was Joe's match when it came to offense and defense in any fight. She worked for the General in Chiang Mai, and had fended off the North Koreans when they ambushed Glenn and company on a road outside that city.

"What happened to Nahmwan?" Glenn asked. He was concerned.

The General laughed.

"Don't worry about Nahmwan. She's still working for me, still up in Chiang Mai. She just realized after a while that Sleepy Joe just was not relationship material. She understood he'd rather be hanging around with you, smoking ganja, watching *The Big Lebowski* one more time, listening to blues and rock. I think your friend understood that as well. Apparently no hard feelings, and if need be, they can work together."

"He's a better man than me," Glenn said. "I could never be in the same room as an ex."

The General took a puff, and Glenn followed suit. The smoke clouds from their cigars merged about three feet above their heads. Glenn stared at the General

"But I wonder why he didn't say anything. I've seen him a few times since the breakup."

"He didn't think it was important enough to occupy the time he spends with you. Proving Nahmwan was correct."

Glenn took a deep draw on his cigar and blew out a series of smoke rings.

"But what's this got to do with the other matter?" he asked the General.

The General sipped his coffee. Glenn checked his own cup to confirm it was still hot enough before he sipped. He believed he had developed sensitivity in his fingertips and could usually rely on the touch of the cup to inform him if the temperature was suitable. Glenn hated cold coffee and found even warm coffee disgusting. He felt the heat come through the ceramic walls of the cup.

"Seems to me you really miss being with your best friend, and he feels the same. I think both of you will be better off spending more time together. Sleepy Joe is one of my best men, and you are my closest farang friend, closer to me than most Thais. My goal is to see that both of you are very happy and most productive."

Glenn did not understand what the General meant by "productive."

"I'm retired, if you want to call it that," Glenn said. "I spent fifteen years being productive as a criminal defense lawyer in San Francisco, and the past dozen plus years, except for the troubles Charlie caused me, have been utterly unproductive, and that's how I prefer things." Glenn and the General understood that managing Phil was a hobby and a nuisance, not a real job.

The General put down his coffee cup and grinned.

"Glenn, I'd say you have been remarkably productive. In the past few years, you've kidnapped a dangerous Russian gangster so he could be brought to trial in America, and you exposed a North Korean drug and spy operation reaching into both our nations. I'd say that is very productive."

Both men grew silent. They knew the General saw those two events as matters of courage, skill, and patriotism, while to Glenn they were senseless acts of violence, motivated primarily by money. Glenn was the only person in either incident who acted out of concern for others. In the Russian gangster operation, the CIA pressured him into doing their dirty work when they dummied up criminal charges against the Thai woman he loved, dismissed in exchange for Glenn's participation. In the second case, Glenn tried to save the life of Gordon Planter, an old acquaintance, even though he brought danger to Glenn and his friends. Gordon Planter was revealed to be a North Korean agent, and was eventually killed by the CIA after a failed escape attempt. Glenn felt much anger at his government, although he'd killed three North Koreans who tried to kill him, which he could not forget. Unlike the General, Sleepy Joe, and the CIA agents, Glenn could not reconcile himself to killing, not even when it was the clearest instance of self-defense.

"Consider me retired then," Glenn said. "And to be honest with you, Sleepy Joe should do the same."

"You're retired from danger," the General said. "But you are never retired from being a lawyer, as I am never retired from being a general. We don't have to wage violent battles. We can fight in other ways. Safer ways. That applies to you and me, and Sleepy Joe as well. I remind you that in your two dangerous escapades, they were your stories, not mine, and it was you who brought me into the fight. Not that I minded, of course."

Glenn remembered that in the Russian kidnapping plot, the General had provided advice and a bodyguard who saved Glenn's life when a CIA agent decided to eliminate any witnesses to the kidnapping. The protection sent was not just anyone; the General sent Wang, the cook and owner of the NJA Club, an Isan native who had been the General's adjutant when they fought communists in the Northeast in the late seventies. The second time, the General put on a uniform, strapped on an assault rifle, and did battle with the North Koreans. He's right. He didn't mind it at all. Enjoyed it, as a matter of fact. But that was almost three years ago. He might be more inclined to leave the violence to younger people.

"General, it's an honor to be a guest in your lovely home, and an even greater honor to be your friend. Having said that, my General, there is no way you or anyone else is dragging me into doing anything I don't feel like doing. That definitely includes anything to do with whatever your business might be at any moment."

The General shook his head.

"It doesn't sound like you're very happy with what you are doing now. We all thought being in the music business, even as Phil's manager, would be good for you. We knew how much you love music, especially the blues, and how much you love hanging out in clubs. I'm sorry it didn't work out. I really am."

Glenn needed a full half-minute to respond. This is the first time I've ever heard him apologize for anything, he thought. Whatever he wants from me, it must be very important.

"I'm looking for a way to get out of my deal with Funston," Glenn said when he could compose his words. "I know either of us could walk away at any time right now. Our contract expired long ago, and we're on a month-to-month basis, but I feel responsible to make sure he at least has someone to take my place. Phil may be a first-class jerk, but he is a wonderful musician, and his career could go further with the right person."

The General studied the remaining length of his cigar, then set it down in the ashtray, resting in one of the grooves cut for that purpose.

"Very admirable, Glenn. Isn't that an example of why your late father called you a *mensch*? Did I say it right? Hebrew, isn't it?"

"Yiddish," Glenn replied. "But good thinking, and what a memory." Glenn realized he hadn't touched his Romeo y Julieta for several minutes. He saw that it was still burning, and took two small puffs, which he exhaled in small circles of smoke. The General began to speak as the smoke dissolved into the early morning air. The scent of the fine mild cigars blended with the stronger, constant scents of the jasmine, hibiscus, and frangipani in the General's garden. Glenn loved the smell of well-tended Thai gardens. The frangipani reminded him of pineapples and citrus drinks, the hibiscus brought to mind the taste of pomegranate juice and the pretty woman who sold it to him each day on the corner of his soi and Sukhumvit Boulevard. The jasmine was the most powerful scent: intense, almost intoxicating. One of Glenn's Thai girlfriends told him jasmine was an aphrodisiac. *Was she telling me something else?*

"If you'll listen to what I have to say, and do as I suggest, you will be able to leave Phil Funston in good hands, and live out your life as it pleases you, with no risk and no danger. I promise you this."

Glenn saw his cigar was still less than a third smoked. He took a draw and slowly exhaled smoke as he pondered whether he wanted to pursue this conversation, which was clearly the General's intent, or cut off his friend, which Glenn knew would be greeted as a serious sign of disrespect.

"Let's hear it," he told the General.

∽

"I don't know what you think my businesses are all about, or what I do when I'm not at the NJA Club," the General began. "Let me assure you, I do nothing illegal, aside from payment of necessary bribes, which is unwritten law that takes priority over the actual laws."

"Nothing illegal?" Glenn asked. "You had Sleepy Joe busted for dealing with someone else, but you're not involved in dealing weed?

"Not that I mind, of course," Glenn continued. "But it really makes it hard for you to say your businesses are all legal."

The General's phone rang. He looked at the screen and ignored the call.

"Deputy Foreign Minister. He knows better than to call me before eight thirty, because the early morning is my time. So let me take some of that time to explain a few things."

The General explained to Glenn that he had three sources of wealth: his security business, his real estate holdings, and his American stock market investments. Aside from that, he had his military pension and money from his wife's family. "I don't have to touch that," he explained about his wife's money. "It's all for my wife and our daughter."

His security business had many reputable clients, including celebrities, foreign executives, rich Thais, even a few foreign embassies and consulates.

"This is completely under the radar, Glenn, but from time to time, I am called upon to assist my government or yours with some problem they can't solve on their own. That's how I came to know Oliver so well. I use him for information all the time.

"Any involvement I have with the ganja trade is simply because it allows me to tap the dealers and the cops who protect them for information any time I want. My only role is to make sure that there are no competitors outside their orbit. We Thais are never going to end the farang obsession with this plant, but we can make certain the dealers are Thai, answerable only to themselves and their cop allies. Didn't we almost lose our lives fighting North Koreans who wanted to flood the streets of your country with heroin? If someone like me didn't control things here, we'd have the North Koreans, plus Chinese triads, Burmese generals, and criminal Thais we can't control."

Glenn saw that the General's cigar had burned to the halfway point, cradled in an ashtray groove, the burning foot slowly going out.

"A gentleman never smokes a good cigar more than halfway," he said, pointing to Glenn's Romeo y Julieta, which was a hair short of the General's line of demarcation.

"That's quite debatable," Glenn replied. "Many people say a good cigar changes taste as you smoke it down, and one could just keep smoking until it no longer feels right."

The General glanced at the ashtray.

"I'm a traditionalist," he said. "And I didn't bring you here to talk about cigars. Smoke them, yes, but then to talk about your new job working for me."

Glenn nearly spit out a mouthful of coffee, catching himself just in time.

"Working for you? I'm not working for anybody. I'm retired."

"Tell that to your friend Phil Funston," the General replied. "Looks to me like you're working and hating it. I already told you how sorry I was for pushing you into it, and now I'm trying to make amends and help you out. I can make it happen. Even Funston is not crazy enough to try and interfere with what I want."

"What is it you want from me?" Glenn asked.

"I want you to be my lawyer," the General said.

Six

GLENN TOOK a longer-than-usual draw on his cigar, slowly exhaling smoke rings.

"First of all, I'm retired," he said when all the smoke was expelled. "Even if I were still in practice, it would be limited to American law. We are in Thailand, remember."

The General examined the ash on his cigar. Satisfied it was cold, he placed it back in the ashtray.

"I have no need for a Thai lawyer. It's an American lawyer I need. You are still a member in good standing of the California State Bar, as well as several federal courts. It just so happens we're dealing with an American company based in Florida."

Glenn saw his cigar was a little past the halfway point. *Time to say goodbye.* He placed it in the ashtray opposite the General's.

"Why are you dealing with an American company, and why must a lawyer be involved? If it is contracts or joint ventures we're talking about, you've got the wrong guy. I was a criminal lawyer, and that was all I ever knew."

The pretty maid suddenly appeared and removed the ashtray and refilled the coffee cups. The General caught Glenn's eyes following her as she returned to the house.

"Any time you want, Glenn. I'm sure of it."

"Let's stay on track," Glenn said. "What's the need for a lawyer, especially one who knows nothing about contracts or business law?"

The General sipped his black coffee. "You picked up immigration law very quickly when you represented that North Korean defector on her asylum application."

Glenn nodded. He was proud of how sharp his professional skills had been, even after years of retirement, and in a field he learned by reading law books online the night before the interview.

"I believe you slept with her after your representation ended," the General added. "If you can stomach sex with a North Korean communist, it surely isn't asking much for you to give my maid or my mia noi's best friend a chance to find out what mysterious attraction you hold."

"Back to why you need a lawyer," Glenn said.

"Exactly. I need someone whose insight and judgment I trust without question. The way I trust Wang. The way you trust Sleepy Joe. That person is you. You are smart and you are tough and loyal to the end. Principled as well, though to be perfectly frank, that isn't all that important to me if you possess the other qualities."

Glenn leaned back as far as he could without tipping his chair. *He's trying to trip me up, confuse me, get off track, and then sucker me into doing something I should not even think about.*

"General," Glenn said, "I could have been on a run with my group this morning, but of course, an invitation from you comes first. Can't you at least tell me what it is you think I can do for you? That way I can decline politely and finish a cup of excellent coffee."

"Fair enough," the General replied. "I am deeply honored that you gave up a run to have coffee and cigars with an old man. I know how the running rids you of some of the guilt you feel for enjoying an occasional cigar.

"An American company, in the security business to be precise, has proposed investing in my company. They say they have a conduit for lucrative Southeast Asian security and investigation work, and they realize they need someone with my contacts and experience. That means my company, of course, with Oliver and Sleepy Joe, though I doubt they know of Joe. Who can blame them for wanting the best? And who could blame me for wanting to be certain I'm not getting myself and my friends into something we ought to avoid? Oliver checked out the American business. They have the money to turn my operation into the biggest in Southeast Asia, and they are legit and able to pay me a rather handsome amount of U.S. dollars for a buy-in."

Glenn remained unmoved.

"Sounds like something you can handle on your own. You might need a local lawyer to make sure all contracts comply with Thai law. I'll be glad to read any English translations and give you my opinion, though it probably isn't worth a whole lot."

The General interlaced his fingers, stretched his arms over his head, and stretched backward in his chair. Then he straightened out and dropped his arms.

"I'm not growing younger, despite spending a fortune on stem cell injections, hyperbaric oxygen, skin treatments, and of course, Thai aphrodisiacs," the General said. "My son can't take over the business, because even as my son, he never rose above lieutenant during his brief military career, and that took all of my influence. No, he's my son, but he's not meant for this kind of work. I'd rather have the money to leave him. This case could pay enough to force me to retire not too far down the road. It's been made clear that money is no object. All they want is the right people. The strange part is they refuse to tell me anything more. Everything is done by email. They say they'll talk more in person when we meet."

The General explained that the Americans were flying to Bangkok in a few days, and wanted a meeting. Presumably, they would bring legal counsel as well. Glenn saw no reason why he himself was needed, and in fact, thought it counterproductive. The General explained that in Southeast Asia, it was typical that a trusted agent begin the negotiations, and the Big Man comes in when the details are agreed upon. However, the Americans would not be told this until right before Glenn walked into the meeting in lieu of the General.

"You want me to make sure they are on the up-and-up, and check all the contracts to make sure everything is in order?" Glenn asked.

"Actually, more than just that," the General said. "Oliver has already vetted the company and its officers and directors, and they all seem to be legitimate. There's something that doesn't seem quite right. They seem too eager to make the deal. They must know my services do not come cheap, and when they tell a man like me money is no object, they accept that the sky is the limit. The fact that they also insist on such secrecy suggests something very important or something very wrong. We can't have that in Thailand right now."

Glenn sniffed the collar of his shirt, determining the cigar smoke had not worked its way into the fabric. Glenn hated smelling like a Corona or a Churchill, and he made certain to blow the smoke directly in front of him so as to avoid contact with body or clothing. It wasn't a hundred percent perfect, and after each cigar was smoked, Glenn carefully washed his hands and face and rinsed his mouth.

"General, it does sound suspicious to me. I find it difficult to believe that a successful American security company, savvy enough to find you, would be so foolish as to offer a blank check before they have even met you or seen your operation firsthand. Even if there is a need for a security or investigative company to protect American business interests against counterfeiting, kidnappings, or extortion and they recognize they need local help, I would expect a more professional business approach."

"Go on, I'm interested in hearing more of what you think," the General said. "You're getting it right away. That's why I want to retain you as my lawyer."

He said retain, Glenn thought. He continued with his initial assessment.

"Here's one reason why they might be so tight-lipped. Just as you do work for governments, it would not surprise me if these people did the same. If they are gathering information for Western government clients, it's understandable why they would want to be partners with someone who can open doors for them."

"And just why is it you think anyone needs to gather information here in Bangkok?" the General asked.

Glenn moved around in his chair, as if he were uncomfortable with it. He was uncomfortable, but not with the chair

"General, this is also a place that is crawling with spies and intelligence experts from every corner of the globe. It's no secret that your government has been growing closer to the People's Republic of China, and gradually drifting away from the West. China and my country are, at best, rivals; at worst, adversaries."

"Do you think your country is hiring people to spy on us through an

American security agency, and they think I'd help them?" the General asked.

Glenn took no time to answer. "I doubt that's necessary when it comes to spying on Thailand. We've been doing it for a long time. I believe it was you who told me this." During the fight with the North Koreans, the General confided in Glenn that his son was the product of a relationship with a Thai woman who had been stealing information from the Thai military and giving it to her CIA husband. Exposing this was the first step in advancing the young officer's career, and it required a sexual relationship, which produced his son. The General fell in love with the woman, but they were forced to separate forever. The General finally met his only son when he reached the age of twenty-one. As for the woman, the General never revealed a word of what became of her.

If the General felt anything upon hearing Glenn speak of this history, he did not show any, and Glenn continued.

"No offense, General, but it's probably quite easy to spy on you guys and find out what we need to know. It's different with China. They're good at keeping secrets, and they play rough when they think it's helpful. They are the ones we most likely want to spy on. They're all over this Kingdom, like it or not. They're taking over Laos next door, threatening Taiwan, grabbing islands from the Philippines. The CIA would want to compromise any of them they can. Easier with locals on the Chinese payroll, but I have a sneaky suspicion that almost every Chinese agent can be bought for the right price, especially if a green card gets thrown in with the deal. There's no easier place to pick up good intelligence and recruit assets than here in Bangkok, and no one better than you to help. You hate the commies, so getting paid to screw them makes it even better."

The General was impressed.

I didn't remember Glenn was so aware of all of this. He knows everything, it seems, except how to find a good Thai woman. He's definitely the right man.

"Glenn, you passed the audition. You're hired. I'll have Oliver prepare a background packet for you and send it to your condo with a decent retainer."

Glenn knew better than to ask the amount. *If he gets me out of managing Phil without making me look bad, that's worth it to me.*

"Sleepy Joe will be available in a ew hours. He's going to be around for a while, and he'll be with you at all times on this job. You two will be together most of the time, like in the old days. I'm sure this makes you very happy."

"It does," Glenn replied. "But if there's no danger, why send Sleepy Joe along with me?"

The General did not answer. He stood and arched his back again. "Too much sitting around for this old warrior," he said. "I must be going, Glenn. Time to start making my rounds. You're free to stay as long as you like. Call my maid for anything you want." The General started towards the door to the house. Glenn left his chair and followed.

"You never answered the question," Glenn said. "If this is just a garden variety legal check, why Sleepy Joe?"

"Well, with you, Glenn, we never know."

I wonder what he does on his rounds, Glenn thought. He followed the General through the house and out into the driveway.

"Would you like a lift home?" the General asked. "My driver can take you there ater he drops me off along Thong Lor."

Glenn told the General he could use the walk home. He stopped at

Benjasiri Park and commandeered a bench beneath the canopy of a large tree, not far from the lake. A young Thai mother with two toddlers sang them a song. It must have contained funny lyrics, as the little children laughed. Glenn wished he understood enough Thai to be on the level of a three- or four-year-old.

He looked forward to reading whatever Oliver sent him, and of course, he would speak with him privately, outside the General's presence. Most of all, Glenn looked forward to having Sleepy Joe in town for an extended stay.

The General didn't bring his best field agent home just to keep me company. There's a reason the General wants Sleepy Joe with me when I meet with this supposedly harmless bunch of American lawyers and business executives.

The skies had taken on the blue of daytime, and the sun was hidden behind clouds and pollution. A mild but steady breeze over the water kept the temperature at a tolerable eighty degrees Fahrenheit, a bit less than twenty-six Celsius. A fine time to smoke a cigar, except he had just smoked one, and Glenn's strict limit was two a week, not two a day. He wondered if cigar smoking was allowed in a public park these days. The government was instituting laws and regulations at every turn, governing every aspect of human behavior, generally by a flick of the Prime Minister's wrist. Freedom of expression was being choked to death. The coup-leading Prime Minister even wrote a history book which was mandatory in public schools, and which every notable Asian historian denounced as sheer bunk. Glenn believed the Thai people wanted more liberty, especially young and educated Thais who demonstrated for pre-Trump American-style democracy. Glenn sensed a growing despair and darkness brewing among the Thai people, based upon what he read in publications he trusted, and what he was able to glean and interpret from the Thais he knew: NJA Club regulars, Lek, his regular motorcycle taxi drivers, and more than anyone else, the General.

The General was terse but to the point on the current government. He made this clear one day over martinis at the Club.

"I'm a retired military officer, and as such, protocol and tradition require that I refrain from any comments on a government dominated by my fellow officers."

Glenn understood this as a thinly concealed criticism. There were no traditions or protocols stopping the General from praising the government, only against criticizing it.

Smoking a joint in the park would have been a delight, but Glenn knew for certain that it was illegal. A street-savvy brown uniform would spot Glenn as an affluent expat, and the fee to avoid arrest would be several times more than for the average farang. The smoke option ruled out, Glenn chose another, and called Oliver.

Seven

WHEN OLIVER finished speaking with Glenn, he poured a shot of Irish Whiskey—Jameson—and walked onto his balcony. He chugged the shot as he watched the white clouds above Bangkok lounge lazily in the skies, which that day were unusually blue for the generally polluted city.

Had the General told me he was bringing Glenn into this, I would never have agreed. Why isn't the old pirate going himself? If there's any chance of danger, he shouldn't't risk Glenn's life. I'm almost of a mind to return the payment, but the old pirate already has my reports. The big Australian mulled the situation for almost a full minute.

The money's always good. Helps support a house on Koh Phangan and a condo here. I'll just have to see that Glenn gets through this alive. Maybe it's time to tip off Sleepy Joe. I'm even a little worried about him. He thinks the General is just being a nice guy, coming up with an excuse for him and Glenn to hang out together again. The General smells a rat but wants to make sure before he walks away from a potential fortune. I know he loves Glenn, and Joe as well, but money can do strange things to people. Look at what it's done to me. I'm not telling Glenn about my fears because I'm well-paid by the General.

You'd think by now Sleepy Joe would realize the General never does something just to be a nice guy. There's always something in it for him.

What do I tell Glenn when we meet for lunch to celebrate his birthday today?

∽

Glenn thought Margarita Storm was the best Mexican restaurant in Bangkok, maybe the best in Asia. Sunrise Tacos was more than adequate, though the original place in the mall near the Nana BTS stop was the best of all their branches. Margarita Storm offered diners a choice of the Sunrise menu alongside their own more expensive version, which Glenn always chose. The restaurant offered a free meal and desserts on one's birth-day, and Glenn and Sleepy Joe had spent each other's birthdays at Mar-garita Storm right up until two years ago, after Joe began working for the General.

Oliver came up from Koh Phangan on Glenn's birthday last year and again this year. Glenn appreciated the free dinner and desserts, and it was his tradition to take advantage each year. If he couldn't have Sleepy Joe in the role of Best Friend at Birthday Time, Oliver was a fine substitute.

Hard to believe this is the thirteenth birthday I am celebrating here. Hope thirteen is not really an unlucky number. Speaking of numbers, I am officially fifty-two years old. I don't feel it. How is someone supposed to feel at fifty-two? How was I supposed to feel at forty-two? Thirty-two?

Glenn was seated and studying the menu when Oliver tapped him on the shoulder.

"It never changes, mate. That makes it easy."

Glenn looked up at the six-foot, well-built Australian with a shaved head. Unlike Phil Funston's lumpy and misshapen skull, Oliver's resem-bled a perfect billiard ball. He lowered himself into a chair just a bit too small for him. Glenn spoke first.

"Before I read any of whatever you send me, I want to hear it from your mouth. The whole story, not just the parts the General tells me. Birthday or no birthday, I need to hear it from you."

Oliver leaned forward and spoke softly.

"May I intuit my American lawyer friend does not have full faith in what our General tells him?"

"You may," Glenn replied. "What he says makes no sense. First, I don't believe he would pass up the opportunity to meet these Americans face-to-face and deal directly with them. He could have me and Joe at his side if it made him feel better.

"Second, no way a successful and wealthy American security company with a client needing work in Southeast Asia emails the General and says they want to become his partner but won't talk about anything right now, even though the General can name his price and they'll pay it. What business operates like that?"

"Regarding foreigners, the General does have Sleepy Joe and me, not to mention the times you have been of service," Oliver interjected. "Presumably, these fellows have assets in America who know this part of the world who are telling them they need someone local to operate here. They are in the business, you realize. They made this unorthodox offer knowingly and intentionally, and the General responded just as they'd hoped by agreeing to discuss it. Any more arrows in your quiver?"

"Yes," Glenn said. "Reason number three. The General would never send Sleepy Joe out unless he thought my life was in danger. Sleepy Joe is one of his most valuable assets." Glenn hated calling a human being an asset, but had learned to accept the term when dealing with professionals like Oliver or Rodney Snapp, his friendly CIA nemesis from the past. "The General would not risk Sleepy Joe just to keep me company. He could be exposed, whereabouts made known, made vulnerable to someone with a grudge. Come on, Oliver, if I'm only acting as his lawyer, there should be no need for either a fun-loving sidekick or a bodyguard."

Smart as ever, Oliver thought. *Why else would the General insist on him?*

"You're on a roll, so keep going," Oliver said, and Glenn went on.

"With all due respect to our General, we can rule out the possibility that he's telling the truth about why he doesn't want to attend the meeting. We must also accept that he is a Thai patriot wanting to know why these Americans are poking around his country. His rather impressive career started on that note, and it may be fitting that he finally retires from intrigue and danger on the same. On the other hand, we must accept as established fact the General's belief that my investigative abilities and Sleepy Joe's Special Forces skills are required. Without questioning the purity of the General's motives, there's still the question of whether he's placing Joe and me at risk."

"Keep going," Oliver counseled.

"Like I said, one would expect to meet with the foreign buyers. One would think he needs to be there as much as me or Sleepy Joe. He's at least as good a judge of character and situations as I am, and he knows the security business better than anyone on earth. If he's not going, he's concerned about something. We're talking about a man who killed people for a living," Glenn said.

"Sleepy Joe, or the General?" Oliver asked.

"Both, at various times," Glenn replied. "Which is what makes little sense. I find it hard to believe there is a meeting so potentially dangerous that the General won't go but would send me. If Joe is a guarantee, why wouldn't the General feel comfortable with him at his side? I don't buy the cultural excuse, and I don't buy that there is zero danger."

They stopped talking when the Filipino waiter came and took their orders. Glenn showed him his passport, and the waiter smiled.

"Happy birthday," he said. Glenn and Oliver ordered their meals, and the big Australian ordered two margaritas for the birthday toast. When the waiter left, Oliver answered Glenn's query.

"I don't think the General fears for his personal safety any more than he does when he leaves his house every day. On one hand, the man is a total paranoid, on the other hand, he is absolutely fearless and about as cool as they come. I think he doesn't want to meet face to face with these Americans, if for no reason other than he just doesn't trust many people. There's you and me, Sleepy Joe, Wang, some of those old retired Thai military guys that sometimes drop by the Club for a drink with the General. One can be concerned but not afraid."

Glenn slowly twisted a napkin in his hand, rolling it as if it were a cigarette or joint in progress.

"That makes no sense," he told Oliver.

The big Australian nodded and smiled.

"Maybe it makes no sense to you, probably not to me either, but you can bet your bottom dollar, and make it a U.S. dollar, it makes sense to the General."

The Filipino waiter brought the drinks. Glenn tasted his margarita.

"The best part is the salt," he said. "Though I must admit the buzz is better than a martini, it can't hold a candle to good weed."

Oliver raised his glass in a toast. Glenn clinked his glass against his friend's.

"Here's saluting another trip around the sun," Oliver said. "And here's to good weed, good friends, and good luck, though not necessarily in that order."

And here's to Sleepy Joe, Oliver thought. *He's the reason we're not worried about you.*

There was nothing more to be said on the subject. The food came, and they chatted between mouthfuls. Oliver shifted to his favorite topic, the benefits of life on Koh Phangan versus life in Bangkok.

"We've got the beaches, the food, the beauty, the laid-back pace. Even great smoke. You need to come down more often. This once or twice a year business has got to cease. If you're not coming down permanently, I'll take nothing less than once a month."

Glenn had the drill down pat.

How many times must we go through this?

"I love Bangkok. It's the home I never really had, the one I was looking for my whole life. I lived in New York and San Francisco before this, and I can swear that Bangkok is the best city on earth, and it's the best place for me."

"You're nuts," Oliver replied. "The air is unbreathable most of the time. If you need to go somewhere off the BTS or MRT lines, it means sitting in traffic for hours. The place is getting dirtier, more crowded, and even a little more dangerous, but hardly anything to alarm you Yanks."

"What can I say?" Glenn replied, throwing up his hands in mock surrender. "It may not be much, but it's home."

"That's what I don't get," Oliver said. "I don't see what you're doing here that's so great. You love the blues but can't stand being near that jackass Phil Funston. You're not using any of your many talents, except when you are forced to, and then it's dangerous and you don't enjoy it. You made money, but that doesn't seem to do much for you. Aside from cheap weed and good food, what are you getting here that you can't find elsewhere? On Koh Phangan, you'll have beauty and a mellow pace of life."

"Sounds good," Glenn said as he examined his spicy Mexican tortilla soup, the sour limes and the red-hot chili he added combining in a way that was unbearable when he first arrived in Thailand and tried their spicy food, but thirteen years later he savored every spoonful. "But I've got friends here. You were one until you moved away."

"Hey, we'll always be mates," the Australian said. "But I'm sure you had friends back in America."

Glenn stared at Oliver.

"Oliver, have you forgotten? You met one old friend in person, and dealt with the other by phone. Surely you understand why I prefer the friends I have here."

Oliver couldn't disagree. He pictured that unexpected visitor and weasel, Gordon Planter, who helped North Korea sell heroin in America, and almost caused the deaths of Glenn, Oliver, the General, and Sleepy Joe. Oliver knew Glenn was nonetheless still furious at Rodney Snapp, their CIA contact, for killing Gordon and dropping his body into a filthy canal. Whatever Gordon may have done, Glenn could not abide what was in his mind a vigilante killing. Oliver strongly approved of the action, and wished he could have helped.

Charlie was a different story. Glenn was unaware that since being introduced by phone to Charlie during the North Korea caper, Oliver and Charlie had worked together on a number of ventures, several in the gray area between legal and criminal, often involving the transfer of money. Both men were willing to take assignments that most would not, and each appreciated the other's unique talents. Oliver couldn't understand why Glenn feared another call from his old lawyer friend. Every time Charlie called, it brought money and excitement, always for the right side.

Being on the right side was as important as the money for Oliver. If they were not fighting for the right side, none of them would have joined the battle. Whatever one might have been told, America and her allies were the right side. *A liberal Democrat from America like Glenn could never understand this and was in the battle for personal reasons.* A good, solid Australian conservative like Oliver knew better than to think the world revolved around him and his values, as could a Bangkok elitist and monarchist like the General. A trained killer like Sleepy Joe understood this; even a grubby little crook like Edward knew that getting around the official rules could sometimes be more moral than following them. Edward told Oliver he preferred being paid by the CIA as opposed to his bread-and-butter criminal trade, since the CIA were actually the good guys. Glenn didn't see it this way and thought that because both broke laws they were the same. *Love him anyway*, Oliver thought.

"In case I forgot to say it, Happy Birthday, Glenn."

Glenn looked at their empty plates and then at Oliver.

"You already have, my friend, and spending the time with me on my special day says it all. I miss having Sleepy Joe around all the time, but when we get together, I know I'm with someone who's just as good a friend as Joe."

May you always feel that way, Oliver thought.

Eight

THERE'S NO *way the General is being straight with me*, Sleepy Joe thought as he struggled to make sense of the General's new assignment to accompany Glenn to a boring business meeting. *If anyone can determine the good faith and legality of the American company's offer, it's Glenn the lawyer, not me an ex–Australian Special Forces guy. You'd think the General would want to be there to meet these Yanks.*

Sleepy Joe knew the General sensed the possibility of danger. The General could be hard-hearted and callous in business or defense of Thailand but had the softest of soft spots for Glenn. The General told Sleepy Joe why he felt this way about their American friend, and Joe remembered every word.

"He lives by a code, just like I do as a military man," the General said. "In that way, Glenn and I are the same. My code is designed to enable me to protect my King and my country, while Glenn's code is an end in and of itself. In his mind, so long as he follows the rules, all is well. It's different for me, because the end goals are different. In other words, I can bend my rules to protect King and country. I don't know if Glenn allows for this sort of thing. That's what makes him special. I don't know anyone else who so stubbornly refuses to bend their own rules. I definitely do not know anyone else other than a Buddhist monk who is less motivated by money. For a rich guy, he doesn't place much value on wealth."

Sleepy Joe wanted to remind the General that Glenn spared himself few of the luxuries available to an expat with dollars. He lived in a fancy condo, dressed like a movie star, and each month spent on coffee and weed what a Thai worker might earn over those four weeks. Joe said nothing of the sort because expressing those thoughts violated his own personal code developed as a member of the Aussie Special Forces. One's mates were the most precious treasures in the world, and loyalty was unyielding. Never speak ill of your mates and they will never speak ill of you. Were Joe to remind the General of Glenn's refined tastes, he would be implying either that Glenn was a hypocrite, or the General didn't know what he was talking about. Either would be speaking ill of a mate.

In the privacy of his own personal safe house, known to him alone, Sleepy Joe lay on his bed and allowed all thoughts to wither away as quickly as they'd arose. He was grateful to the General for insisting he study meditation. It definitely sharpened his powers of concentration, even better than what he was taught in the Special Forces. Some Westerners thought meditation required sitting cross-legged, but the Buddha said it could be done sitting, walking, or lying down. Sleepy Joe preferred the supine position. He closed his eyes, relaxed every muscle in his body, starting from his head and working his way down to his toes. Thoughts fled his mind like Iraqi troops fleeing the battlefield in 1991. Joe had been one of almost two thousand members of the Australian Defence Force to fight alongside the Americans that year. He was a twenty-year-old enlistee, and his bravery under fire won him a coveted place in the Special Forces.

The first thought to go was of Namwahn, who always lingered somewhere in the back recesses of Joe's mind. *She was right.* Sleepy Joe was a man unable to commit to a relationship. She was right: he'd rather be hanging around with Glenn or risking his life for the thrill of it all, than settle down and raise a family.

The General was next. *Maybe he thought he had a hold on me, but I have the hold on him. He lets me slide on things that would get anyone else purged.* The General never showed emotion when explaining an assignment, and even when Joe returned to report success, it was impossible to tell if his lips curled upward enough to be called a smile. *Took me a while to realize those are good signs.*

Oliver came into view. The image of his countryman brought a warm feeling. *He's a good man. Born into a rich and connected family but acts like an ordinary bloke. He's got all this education and knowledge, treated with respect everywhere. Me? Jewish mother, never knew my father, joined the military only to get out from under a drug possession charge. Who figured I'd like it and be really good? Oliver, like Glenn, is good with his head. Me, it's more the hands. But Oliver is like Glenn in other ways. He isn't bothered if someone is different from him. He connects with whatever is the same between them. And education and breeding aside, Oliver is one tough son of a bitch.*

But not tough enough for the General to send to this meeting to make sure nothing happens to Glenn. That's my job, whether he admits it or not.

Nine

End of the Second Week in December 2019

OLIVER DISLIKED Patpong and went there only when required. Patpong was the oldest of Bangkok's three celebrated red-light districts for foreigners, servicing deluded farang men since the Vietnam War. It was much older than its rivals, Soi Nana and Soi Cowboy, allowing more time to degenerate into greater seediness and sleaze.

Patpong was just off of busy Silom Road, one of Bangkok's commercial centers. During the day, Silom's sidewalks were filled with shop-pers, tourists, corporate executives, working people, touts, and expats. Overweight foreigners in shorts sat at outdoor cafes next to tables of Asian and Western men in suits despite the heat and humidity. The streets were clogged with cars, buses, motorcycles, trucks, *tuk-tuks*, and the rare foolish bicyclist.

Patpong was home to many Japanese businesses, including several in the sex trade. Oliver's client owned one such establishment, an expensive soapy bath and massage parlor. He retained Oliver to investigate a Japanese-New Zealander he was considering as manager. The man checked out perfectly, and Oliver dropped off his report and collected the balance of his fee in cash, which took some sting out of being in Patpong. The client offered Oliver the option to take the balance of his fee in trade, which the

Aussie politely declined. *No way I take off my clothes in Patpong.* He took his money and left.

Oliver navigated the narrow side soi, walking in the street because the sidewalks were too narrow and crowded. With the practiced skill of a long-term expat, he artfully weaved between pedestrians, stooped old men and women pushing carts laden with produce, clothing, and cooked food, motorcycles, and one passed-out farang, snoozing away against a curb as people gingerly stepped around him. Oliver could scarcely breathe between the crowds, the fumes, the heat, and the pungent odor of durian fruit when he passed a fruit stand. Twenty meters from where the side soi emptied into Silom, Oliver heard a man cry out for help in American-accented English. He turned to the doorway where the noise came from. A small farang man dressed in khaki cargo pants and a white polo shirt stood on the sidewalk, surrounded by three unsmiling Thai men, each half a head taller than the diminutive American. They shouted at him in a mixture of Thai and English, demanding that he pay. The little American protested that there must be some mistake. One of the Thai men kicked him hard in the shin, and the American fell to the ground face first. Oliver winced when he saw the little man's cheek strike the pavement. He moved towards the disturbance. The fallen man shouted at him.

"Help me, please! They're trying to get me to pay five thousand baht for two beers."

"What's the problem here?" Oliver called out in Thai. The man who had delivered the kick turned and faced him.

"You speak pretty good Thai for a farang," the Thai man told Oliver. "You must have lived here long enough to know to mind your own business."

Oliver stared hard at the man.

"It is my business." He pointed to the sign above the doorway. "Go tell the owner that Oliver asks that he let this fellow slide as a favor."

The kicker spoke with one of his companions. They conversed in the Isan dialect of the Northeast. *Think I won't understand,* Oliver thought.

"I assure you your boss knows who I am, and will be happy to honor my request," Oliver interjected in near-perfect Isan. The three Thais looked at him, their stares blazing with intensity.

"I'm impressed," the leader said in Isan. "Wait here for a minute." He walked through the door and up a flight of stairs. Oliver, the short farang, and the two Thais waited quietly. A minute later, the leader appeared in the doorway.

"Go," he said in English. Oliver nodded, and with his big hand on the small American's shoulder, guided him around and they walked away. They hurried around the corner, walking on Silom towards the BTS escalator. Oliver sized him up as they walked. Well-dressed in what Glenn called "smart casual." Decent haircut, clean-shaven. The American reminded him of Glenn. Smaller and thinner, but healthy and fit. A decade or so younger as well. Not the typical sexpat who falls for the oldest trick in the tourist trap book, and one of the most dangerous.

"It wasn't two drinks you bought," Oliver explained as they rode the escalator to the Skytrain. "You bought at least a dozen for the girls, and the boss, whether you knew it or not. You ran up against their collection team."

"Well, thank you for saving me," the smaller man replied. "What do you think they would have done if I didn't pay?"

"More of what you got, just a lot more painful," Oliver said. "They would have taken everything you had and left you lying there in the street. Good chance a cop would come by and shake you down for more."

"For what?" the American asked.

"For being stupid enough to wander into a bar in Patpong, and even stupider to argue about the bill," Oliver said.

They followed the walkway running above Silom, heading to the stairs leading to the Skytrain lines. Oliver stopped and held up a hand at chest height, and the American ceased walking.

"Before we proceed, there are two items of information I must have," he said. "First, what is your name?"

"Boston," the American said. "Tom Boston. Just like the city."

"There's a city named Tom?" Oliver asked in mock surprise. "Second question is: which direction are you going?"

Tom Boston gave Oliver the name of his hotel. It was on the Siam line Oliver needed, two stops before his. He suggested that they get off at Phrom Phong and grab a beer or coffee.

"I'll pay," Tom Boston said.

∾

TOM FOLLOWED the big man across the BTS platform at Phrom Phong, through a large plaza filled with shoppers and workers on a late lunch break. They entered a large glass building which Tom immediately recognized as a high-end shopping mall, the kind his wife would occasionally visit back home and run up credit card bills larger than the budget of their local police force. While Boston studied the crowd, Oliver studied Boston.

I don't think it's possible he's part of a setup. No way these goons could have known I just happened to be passing by. And if he were intending harm, he wouldn't bring me to such a public place. And I'm too smart to be easily fooled. Well, hopefully not. Oliver saw Tom Boston's shin was hurt where the Thai thug kicked it. The big Australian noticed his slight limp.

"Don't worry mate, we'll be seated momentarily." They walked through double glass doors into an ornate and expensive looking restaurant.

"A fine place to unwind after such a harrowing experience. You get to see the better side of Bangkok," Oliver explained. "Fine food, excellent selection of wine and beer. Some of the best desserts and coffees around. Owned and operated by my phone service, open to subscribers only and then only those above a certain subscription level." Glenn had recom-mended the place, and when Glenn says a place has good coffee, it had to be true.

"By the way, I'm Oliver," he said as they stood at a podium, waiting to be seated. "If you haven't guessed, I'm from Down Under." He extended a big hand, which Tom Boston grasped and shook vigorously.

Same firm handshake as Glenn. Must be an American thing.

"No last name?" Tom Boston asked.

"Oliver will do. Anyone who knows me understands. If they don't know me, you shouldn't be wasting your time talking to them." He smiled at the American and put an arm around his shoulder just long enough to steer him to a table. A waiter came over immediately. Oliver ordered a pint of Foster's. Boston asked for the same.

"Can I see your passport, please?" Oliver asked when the waiter left.

Boston hesitated for several seconds.

"Do you have some authority?" the American asked. "I'm just curious. Of course, I'm not going to deny something like that to the guy who saved me from a serious beating or a serious rip-off." He handed Oliver his passport.

"I have all the authority I need. I believe you witnessed that when the mention of my name saved your rear end," Oliver said. "I'm curious too." *When a guy chased out of a bar in Patpong says his name is Tom Boston, you ask for identification.* Oliver thumbed directly to the biographic and photo page. Tom Boston's face and name stared back at him. Forty-two years old, born in Cherry Hill, New Jersey. Passport was one of the newer ones issued by mail by the U.S. State Department. Oliver felt a hard object amidst the passport pages. The same thumb located it and pushed it upward until Oliver could see it was a California driver's license with a San Jose address. Same name, face, birthdate. Oliver flipped the pages until he found the thirty-day visa and the entry stamp dated three days before. He handed the passport back to Tom Boston.

"What is it that makes a man from San Jose with the name of Boston to come to Bangkok?"

Oliver thought Tom Boston hesitated just a hair too long before answering.

"I'm a scientist. More specifically, I'm an epidemiologist. PhD in the field. I work as a researcher for a private institution in California. Our specialty is a very contagious and often deadly strain of virus called the coronavirus. There are several instances where the virus was traced back to Asia. The most well-known variant was SARS, a major threat earlier this century, eradicated by antivirals and steroids even before a vaccine was available. SARS was deadly but not highly contagious, so there were less than a thousand deaths worldwide, zero in America. Knowing about it early saved lives. We've received unconfirmed reports of a new strain of coronavirus in China—Wuhan, to be precise. I'm here to find out what I can. Like I said, knowing early saves lives."

Oliver swirled his beer.

"Say, mate, if the bug's coming from Wuhan, China, may I ask why you're in Bangkok?"

Tom Boston nodded his head and smiled.

"It should come as no surprise that China is hardly cooperative in sharing information. That's in the best of times, and a new virus starting in China is hardly what they see as the best of times. The epidemiologists and infectious disease doctors of the world need to know how contagious and deadly this virus might be, if it exists. I have some good contacts among epidemiologists and public health experts throughout Southeast Asia, colleagues from conferences, and some I'm in touch with fairly regularly. They have contacts in China my colleagues and I back home lack and have a better understanding of Chinese science practices. As you might imagine, this part of the world is of great interest to anyone involved in infectious viral diseases, and there are indeed many outstanding experts in Southeast Asia."

Sounds exactly what Glenn or I would do in a similar circumstance. Get the truth. This fellow is no ordinary sex tourist. He knows what he's talking about. Not always the case with farangs in Bangkok.

"I would appreciate it if you would keep this to yourself," Tom Boston said. "I am really grateful to you for saving me from some really bad happenings, and I felt I had to be upfront with you. But please, understand that if word got out that I was here, and why, it might create panic. We don't have enough information to verify any problem at this point. China won't look fondly at my poking around. No government wants the world to think they might be unleashing an epidemic. The domestic and international rami ications would be enormous, political, economic, and social. China watches their scientists like hawks to make certain they keep their mouths shut."

A man after my own heart. Knows the value of contacts and how to work them. Understands discretion. Just one question. What the hell was an epidemiologist with a PhD doing in a sleazy tourist rip-off bar in Patpong?

Tom Boston turned slightly red and grinned when Oliver asked.

"I came across all this stuff about the red-light districts when I was doing my research," he explained. "Sadly, it was a source of AIDS transmission and is still a source of many other communicable diseases. Certainly could be a hot spot for this new virus if it is real. However viruses are spread, sex can do it in every case. But infections in the sex industry are not my particular expertise."

"Trying to make it so?" Oliver asked.

"No, just being stupid," Tom Boston replied.

Oliver ran the situation through his well-oiled machine of a mind. Tom Boston was not the first American visitor to walk into bar in Patpong and wind up on the wrong end of an extortion scheme. Nor would he be the last, as the endless customers demonstrated. Tom Boston was surely among the more fit, better-dressed, best educated, and most impressive customer any of those bars ever saw. This was no deluded Yank on a sex holiday, nor was he a naive waif roaming the Big Mango with eyes wide as saucers. He studied Southeast Asia, even the sex trade. Yet he fell for one of the oldest scams in the book. *Could anyone with his background be that stupid?*

He could picture Glenn saying, *"Yes indeed, people can be and are that stupid, or else I wouldn't have had a career as a criminal defense lawyer."*

Oliver's experience in the world pushed him to agree with Glenn. Any act of stupidity one can imagine is likely being acted out at every moment somewhere.

Tom Boston asked Oliver what he was doing in Bangkok.

"I live here," he said. He didn't explain that he kept his condo in Bangkok, but for the past several years spent most of his time in Koh Phangan. No reason Tom Boston needed to know such personal matters. "I have my fingers in a few businesses, a few investments, and Thailand isn't very expensive. Lovely place to live. Wonderful people, and we have everything anyone could ever want."

Tom Boston said he expected to be in Thailand for several weeks. Oliver offered to show him around town when he had time the following week. They exchanged cards. Tom scrawled his local cell phone number on the back of his.

When they finished their beers, Oliver paid the waiter and they walked out of the restaurant and kept going until they were back in the outdoor plaza that led to the BTS. Oliver told Tom to expect a call next week. Oliver walked towards the BTS turnstile and Tom, whose hotel was nearby, walked down the stairs to Sukhumvit Boulevard. Oliver watched the back of his head disappear as he descended.

Ten

THE GENERAL agreed to join Oliver for a drink, but not at the NJA Club. Both wanted to avoid anyone knowing they had something important to discuss. Isolating themselves at the Club would be a tip-off. Oliver suggested the well-known rooftop bar at Distel, a bar on the sixty-third floor of the Lebua at State Tower, a luxury hotel. The Sky Bar one floor above was more renowned, but at Distel, they could walk out on the outdoor terrace, and with the wind and altitude, be impervious to eavesdropping. A tail would be obvious.

The General was at the bar when Oliver arrived. The General's bodyguards stood a few feet behind him, attempts at blending in unnecessary, as bodyguards were increasingly more common and didn't imply one was a government official or billionaire. The General wore a navy blue blazer with shiny brass buttons over a black silk shirt. He motioned to Oliver to head out on the terrace, and the General followed with his bodyguards.

"A waiter will bring you a whiskey," the General said when he was seated in a wrought iron chair next to Oliver in the cool air outside. "You'll need it up here. This is as cold as it can get in Bangkok." Oliver wore only a long-sleeved shirt. When the waiter brought his whiskey, he took a deep swig.

"Should keep me warm for a while," he said. Then he explained why he wanted the meeting.

"I've got to hear your thoughts on what these Americans are really up to," he told the General. "And why you won't meet with them yourself."

"The second question is easier to answer," the General said. "In Asia, it is customary for representatives to work out the arrangements before the real signatories come forward. If Glenn feels confident after he checks them out, they will meet me.

"As for the first question, I don't believe their claim that they are coming here on behalf of clients who need investigations or security. There's no way a dollar-based corporation finds it worthwhile to come all the way here for a preliminary meeting when they could conduct all business by Skype. It's unheard of for an investigative and security agency to buy ownership in an overseas firm, at least in Thailand. They could hire us as needed. There's another reason, maybe not anything to be concerned about, but I need to know. My thoughts are they are looking for a cover to do something else. Something very sensitive, something requiring people with reputation and connections and the skills and experience we can provide. I just can't figure out their real needs or purpose. I hope Glenn can. In fact, I'm sure he will."

Oliver's large frame moved uneasily in his chair. Seemed like most chairs in Thailand were too small for his frame.

"But why Sleepy Joe? You usually don't send a trained combatant and stealth killer into a routine business meeting. Ninja warriors aren't really good in these matters."

The General looked into his glass.

"Here's the story, Oliver, and it is the only story. If these Americans pick up on who and what Sleepy Joe really is, my assumption would be they really are security people, and they wouldn't dare try anything out of the ordinary against us unless they want to die. If they don't recognize Sleepy Joe, that's a different story. Maybe they are not who they claim, or maybe they just aren't very good. If they don't make Joe, we can figure out later if it was ignorance or caution. We'll be a lot closer to figuring out who these people really are and what they really want from us once Glenn gets a close look."

Oliver felt the chill but had a few more questions.

"How are we to know if they make Sleepy Joe?"

"We'll rely on Sleepy Joe to tell us," the General replied. "He knows these things."

"One more question before I turn into an icicle," Oliver said. "What happens if they figure out what Sleepy Joe is, but he and Glenn aren't so sure of their intentions, and think they're in trouble?"

The General looked into Oliver's eyes, his face a blank slate with sharp eyes the only sign of feeling.

"Then I leave it to Sleepy Joe to decide if they live or die."

"Does he ever decide to let them live?" Oliver asked.

"I don't know of any such cases," the General replied. "I'll let you know if I ever do."

Oliver hugged himself and shook slightly, initiating a shiver. The General understood, and they stood and walked off the terrace into the bar.

Oliver intended to eventually tell the General of his strange meeting with Tom Boston, PhD, and his concerns of an epidemic. It was too cold on the terrace for such a complex discussion.

"There's something else I wanted to tell you about," Oliver explained as they headed to the elevator. "We're supposed to get together over at Glenn's place tomorrow night, to help him begin finishing off his cigar collection. He's moving on. Don't worry, I'm sure our brilliant American friend will find another obsession to occupy time not consumed by coffee or ganja. Maybe we can talk about it then." Glenn had become enamored—Oliver thought perhaps even obsessed—with expensive hand-rolled cigars, with the same intensity he approached his beloved coffee and weed. His lawyer friend's analytical mind determined the health risks outweighed any benefits, and the practice had to be abandoned, but not until he emptied out his humidor. Oliver and the General, both occasional cigar smokers, were pleased to assist him.

"I think he's down to his last two dozen," the General said. "All of them Romeo y Julietas, Montecristos, Cohibas, Ashtons, Davidoffs. "

"I'd expect nothing less from Mr. Glenn Murray Cohen, Esquire," Oliver said.

~

THEY SMOKED their cigars outside on Glenn's balcony, all but Sleepy Joe, who stood to one side smoking a joint. Glenn permitted weed smoking indoors, as he did so himself, but tobacco could not be burned inside the Cohen condo. None of his friends smoked cigarettes anyway, and a cigar smoker comes to understand they can't just light up anywhere. Getting together at his condo to smoke premium hand-rolled cigars had become a monthly tradition sometime the year before. None of them smoked all that often, once a week on the average, but Glenn took it seriously. He could explain why the dark Sumatra wrapper on his beloved 1875 was actually superior to the Connecticut shade-grown leaves found on most of the better cigars.

Darkness swallowed the sun a half-hour before, and the lights of thousands of apartments, offices and hotel rooms twinkled like stars set low on the horizon. The dining table inside was covered with the carcass of a barbecued chicken, plates of spicy papaya salad known as *som tam*, and the empty six-pack of San Miguel beer Oliver and the General finished off over dinner. The two could never agree on Australian Foster's versus Thai Singha, so they settled for Filipino San Miguel. Glenn had consumed his daily alcohol intake with a martini during a late lunch with the General, so he swigged Coke Zero the whole night.

Oliver told the other three everything that had transpired between him and Tom Boston. When he was done the four men sat in quiet to consider the unusual encounter.

Glenn smoked one of his last Romeo y Julieta 1875s, the lightest cigar he'd discovered. The General puffed on a Davidoff, not quite as light as the 1875, but significantly more expensive. They were even better than the Montecristo Robusto Largo the General usually favored. Oliver puffed on the largest cigar in Glenn's humidor, a seven-inch Cohiba Churchill. They sat and looked out upon the city, their small table cluttered with ashtrays, a bottle of Jim Beam and two shot glasses filled with amber bourbon. Glenn's two friends chugged their shots simultaneously. The General poured himself a second shot just before Oliver did the same. Glenn was tempted to join them, but he decided the fat joint in his pocket would serve him better.

"Was this Tom Boston fellow on the level?" Glenn asked Oliver. "Is he even who he claims?"

Oliver put down the shot glass he had just drained.

"Glenn, I wouldn't be telling you any of this if I hadn't verified it all myself. He is a respected epidemiologist for that institution. No question about it. I spoke with my contact in the Thai government forensics lab, as well as a good friend who works for your American CDC. While it's damn near impossible to get any information out of the Chinese, any reliable information at least, all my people agree something started in China, and it is absolutely going to spread, as all viruses spread to some degree. The fact that Boston's outfit sent him here confirms these suspicions. The big questions are: how contagious and how deadly?"

The three men sat quietly again, the tips of their cigars glowing red in the dark night as they took puffs in near unison. An onlooker might have believed they were choreographed. The General broke the silence.

"Did anyone give a timetable, even a rough one?"

"That's the thing," Oliver said. "Right now there just isn't enough data to make a prediction about anything. It's not completely certain ours is reli-able. No one knows for sure exactly what kind of coronavirus we're talking about, how contagious it is, what symptoms indicate infection. My experts tell me that unfortunate as it may be, we're not going to know very much until those things start happening and they get accurately compiled. Don't expect any cooperation from China. Anything this Boston fellow can learn is of immense value."

The General rose from his chair and walked to the balcony railing, staring at the city. He turned and faced his friends.

"Oliver, seems what we've got here is a threat we know nothing about, won't know much unless it attacks us, and the only people who know anything are the Chinese. Is that pretty much the situation?"

"Indeed, it is," Oliver replied. "The whole world as well."

The General poured another shot of whiskey. Glenn knew a shot of Jim

Beam would calm him down, but the one-drink-a-day rule was meant to be tested in crisis. *Time for the joint*, he thought. He really didn't want any more cigar. Without saying a word, he picked a lighter off the table and fired up his joint.

"Any suggestions?" Glenn asked the other two, after he released his first blast of white marijuana smoke.

"None I can think of right now," the General said. "Maybe Oliver has some."

"Sure," the big Australian said, turning to Glenn. "Compared to some virus that could wipe us all out, the health risks from cigars seem rather inconsequential. Especially for someone who started after the age of fifty. Perhaps you'll rethink your decision to quit. I'm starting to enjoy these cigar get-togethers, particularly under happier circumstances of course."

The General was back in his chair. He held his Montecristo between thumb and index and ring fingers, pointing it towards Oliver.

"I have no intention of quitting, especially after this news," he said. "Since we don't know much, and can do even less, let's put thoughts of viruses and epidemics aside and focus on pressing matters like Glenn's meeting with the prospective Americans. I assure everyone the meeting is safe, so don't read Sleepy Joe's presence as otherwise. I have a reason for everything I do. They will be here in less than a week. I think they want to take care of this before their Christian holidays and the New Year. We'll know soon whether there is going to be a deal. As for this virus, we just need to find a way to relax and see what happens."

"Any ideas?" Glenn asked.

"Not a one," the General said. "Aside from spending time with you at the NJA Club and smoking the occasional fine cigar."

"No time with the mia noi?" Oliver asked, in feigned shock.

"I was talking about relaxing, not exertion," the General said. "There's always time for her. And her friend is always waiting for Glenn."

Eleven

Beginning of Third Week in December 2019

THE NJA Club was as crowded as Oliver had ever seen. Every table and bar-stool was filled, and throngs of people stood with drinks in their hands. It was Friday evening, and in addition to the regulars, the place was filled with professionals and workers who lived in the neighborhood or stopped off on their way home to apartments in other neighborhoods, especially On Nut. The latter was the newest favored expat address, as it was less expensive than other neighborhoods in or near the Green Belt. The crowd this night was mostly farang, but with many more Thais than expected in a Western-style bar and grill located in the middle of the farang-centric Green Belt.

Oliver knew many of the Thais were drawn to the NJA Club through military connection with the General or Wang, who was the NJA's owner and cook, courtesy of the General's generosity. Wang was his adjutant during the war with the communists in Isan, and the General credited him with saving his life more than once.

"Looks like Phil finally found some friends," Kit the waitress told Oliver in Thai as she brought him his pint of Foster's. She spotted his bald head bobbing up and down across the room. He was an obnoxious customer and a poor tipper, the kind Thais derisively call a "Cheap Charlie." Kit liked the big Australian Oliver, who spoke Thai, understood Thai people, was a generous tipper, and was never rude. She saw him as a father, although never having known her own, she was unsure exactly what that meant. Her heart belonged to Glenn, except he refused to acknowledge this. Glenn spoke almost no Thai, and didn't seem to know as much about the people as Oliver, but his calm, reserved nature made him seem almost like a Thai. *Perhaps that's why the General likes him so much, and why the lady who had this job before me is in love with him*, she thought as she pictured Glenn with his perfect hair and teeth, the athletic body, the clothing that always fit perfectly, and the soft look in his eyes.

Edward often told her about Mai, and the torch she carried for Glenn.

"She's had it burning for many years, and I think her going to Israel was somehow to reach Glenn as a Jew."

Kit told Edward she disagreed.

"Khun Edward, you have to know that some Thai people will go far away to make money for the family." Her English had improved exponentially since starting her job at the Club. She read books in English and watched American movies on her phone. *Easier to talk to Glenn*, she reasoned.

She learned much more English, though it did not yield the results she wanted. Glenn was always polite, even kind in his dealings with her, but there was no sign he was interested in her as anything other than his waitress.

"Don't give up," Edward counseled. "He won't be able to resist your charms forever. Deep down inside, he's very lonely but just too afraid to do anything about it.

Edward, a Welshman, had been a regular at the NJA Club for over fifteen years. He was previously a tax auditor for the Crown back in the U.K. and had taken a well-deserved Thailand vacation to avoid burnout. It was in the Kingdom that Edward felt secure enough to come out as gay. He resigned his position upon return, moved to Bangkok, and found a niche as an adviser to foreigners looking to avoid financial reporting requirements. His best clients were Americans seeking to avoid the legal requirement to list all foreign bank accounts with the IRS. Glenn called it money laundering, but Edward insisted he was merely informing businessmen that Laos did not cooperate with America, and explained how to move their money to some very special banks in Vientiane. He even had a nice side gig going with Noi, the past object of Glenn's unrequited love, who carried money across the border. The profitable venture ended when the CIA ordered Edward to cease all operations unless they ordered him to do something. Edward was intimidated into telling the CIA agents everything he knew about Glenn and his friends. The CIA paid Edward fifty-thousand dollars for his troubles. *Or was it for giving up all that information on me and my friends?* Glenn sometimes wondered, and Edward knew this.

Edward was aware Glenn did not like him and held him in low esteem. He knew it was not based on his sexual orientation, but because Glenn believed him to be weak and untrustworthy. Glenn was a good man, and both he and Kit would benefit from a relationship. Edward sensed Glenn was damaged inside, just as he was. Edward understood the secret behind the illusion of paradise.

Every farang expat is damaged somewhere inside. Otherwise they wouldn't be in Thailand. He told this to Kit.

Everyone has some hurt somewhere inside, Kit thought but did not say.

"Do you think I still have a chance?" she asked.

"Absolutely!" Edward exclaimed. "As long as you always remember Glenn is coming from a place of hurt, not arrogance." Kit asked Edward to type the word "arrogance" into her translation app. When she saw the Thai word, she nodded.

"Do you mean I have to be the one to start?" she asked.

"Exactly," Edward replied.

"What if Khun Glenn doesn't like it?" Kit said.

"Keep trying," Edward advised. "Sometimes it takes a man a while to know what he likes."

∼

ACROSS THE room, Phil Funston held court over Rong and his friends. Two friends were musicians, and the other three were dedicated blues and rock fans like Glenn. In Bangkok, Phil Funston's talent made him the closest substitute for a resident Western rock star. Anyone else with his talent actually would be earning millions in the West. At first, Rong could not understand why success escaped Phil, more talented than most big-name stars he had seen live. Rong scraped together the money it took to attend every major concert that came to town. A year ago he'd paid five thousand baht to see the Foo Fighters. It took him months to pay back the money he borrowed from the neighborhood lender, which he believed in America would be called a loan shark. He hadn't seen a guitarist as good as Phil, which made his lack of fame even more frustrating to Rong. Then again, how many big-name rock stars got into fistfights with hookers on Soi Nana, or got punched out by a motorcycle taxi driver in front of Terminal 21? Whenever Phil screamed at him during a practice, Rong understood what drove the hooker and the driver to violence. Rong understood Phil Funston's talent could free him from the difficult life of being a working person in Bangkok, and lift him above the dead end music store job. His problem was that Funston either did not understand or did not care about greater success if it meant acting like a normal person.

Glenn hinted he wanted to stop managing Phil and began paying Rong to handle the details he usually undertook: confirming dates, setting up auditions, waking Phil in time to get him to places on schedule. Glenn grew to entrust him with more delicate assignments: soothing the ruffled feathers of Thais with whom Phil had crossed the line. Rong did a better job than Glenn, being Thai, and got Phil out of the problems for less than Glenn would expect to pay. Everything Rong did in his place afforded Glenn great relief and pleasure, making the young Thai a favored person in his life.

All of this pleased Rong to no end.

I think he's grooming me for the job. It's a start.

Rong liked Khun Glenn more than any other farang he'd ever met. He came across quite a few at the University, working in the music store, or playing music throughout Bangkok, jamming with any foreigner he could find. Many farangs who came to Bangkok were clueless, often repulsive, the kind he saw ogling counterfeit goods in the sidewalk stalls along Lower Sukhumvit, or worse, the obese old white men parading around the vicinities of Soi Nana and Soi Cowboy, the farangs' favorite red-light districts, with women a third or less their age walking beside them, ignoring them as they scrolled their phones for messages from overseas "sponsors." They carried the look all working people understand: *the things you have to do to make a living.*

Rong knew Khun Glenn could never be one of those men, not now or ever, and Rong respected him. A real Thai could never be pleased to see farang men judge the entire nation through the cracked lens of the sex trade. Rong and his friends rarely discussed the impact of sex-crazed farangs running amok in their city, but their mutual thoughts were intuitively understood. Many of the foreign students at the University told Rong how interesting they found the Thai attitudes towards sex and prostitution, believing the silence of most Thais to be acceptance or even approval.

They don't understand it's just our nature to be silent, even when angry. A man like Glenn Murray Cohen did and was the kind of farang Thailand could use. The fact that Glenn loathed the same farangs as the Thais created an instant bond that deepened as he got to know Glenn better.

Rong knew Khun Glenn was unhappy being Phil's manager. While this was obvious, the American also told Rong as much.

"My friends the General and Sleepy Joe persuaded me to take the job," Glenn explained to Rong one day after the young Thai finished practicing with Phil. Glenn told Rong how Funston had made it a point to say what a fine bassist Rong was and how working with him made Phil himself a sharper musician.

"One day maybe I'll find a band that needs a bass and guitar, and package you two with them," Glenn explained. "I do think you're ready to take the stage. I will keep my ears open for any openings for the both of you. But really, Rong, I'm hoping you'll like the business end and take over for me as well."

Rong's thoughts of Glenn were jarred by Phil Funston's barking.

"What's the matter, Rong, you didn't hear my question?"

Rong apologized, and Phil repeated himself.

"The General's son is a piece of work, isn't he? Little prick never had to do an honest day's work in his life, and he spends his life ripping off people like us."

Rong and his friends looked at each other before Rong spoke to Phil.

"Better we drop the subject. Especially here. Maybe forever." Rong tilted his head in the direction where the General and his son sat a few tables away, drinking and laughing with two Thai men. One was the General's age, the other looked to be no more than thirty. The General's son looked at Rong and his friends, and while his mouth was laughing, his eyes were not.

~

GLENN HAD not seen the Club this crowded in a long time. He had to choose between Oliver, who was enjoying a beer by himself, Rong and Phil's table, or the General and his friends. The General, of course, demanded the respect of Glenn joining him first, even if it meant suffering through the presence of the General's son.

The son inherited no visible signs of his father's best character. The General was remarkably fit for his age, still fitting into his military camouflage from the war against the communists back in the late seventies. The son was overweight, his belly spilling over his belt line, his face fleshy and fatty. In contrast to the General's finely tailored clothing, the son dressed as if his designer were Omar the Tentmaker, the mythical maker of clothing for the grossly obese often cited by Glenn's late father. The General was reserved with words and demeanor, the very model of calm in the eye of the storm, speaking perfect English with the slightest trace of an accent, and soft, almost melodious Thai, much different from the sharp, choppy, slang-ridden Thai of the motorcycle taxi drivers and laborers from the remote provinces who flooded Bangkok, taking jobs the urban middle class declined. The son's Thai was of the uneducated working class. Even Glenn could tell the difference, not that he thought accent made one a better or worse person. The son spoke English with a grammar that would have him held back in the third grade in America, delivered in an accent cultivated listening to *Goodfellas* and *The Sopranos*. Glenn cringed when he realized his Thai was far more deficient than the son's English.

Rong took surreptitious glances at the son, a poor imitation of second-tier Brooklyn mobsters Rong saw in American gangster movies. *Ridiculous, considering he's already a legitimate Thai mobster,* Rong thought. *It's just that without his father, no one would be afraid of him, and he knows it.* Rong once told Glenn the General's son had all the arrogance and cruelty of the rich Bangkok elites, called "Hi-Sos" for High Society, but lacked any of their style and finesse. The General's son was uncharacteristically loud and obnoxious for a Thai. He treated anyone of a lesser station with disrespect and disdain, even worse than Phil Funston. Considering most Thais lacked his power and money, it meant he treated almost everyone except his father that way. Glenn knew he had to accept rudeness and hostility from the son, but it was a small price to pay for the General's friendship.

Glenn understood the General doted over his son because the two had been separated from the son's birth until his twenty-first birthday, and the General felt obligated to make up for lost time. Glenn did not know anything of the young man's upbringing, other than he was the product of a relationship with a woman the military determined the General could not be with, and thus, the twenty-one year separation from his offspring. Glenn recognized by the time the two connected, the damage to the son was done, but the General apparently did not.

The son ignored Glenn as he sat down next to the General. Glenn greeted the General and his two military friends while the son attacked his plate with the same bravado his father displayed fighting communist rebels in the forests of Isan. Glenn did not mind that the son ignored him, even if it were meant as a slight. He suspected the son feared a smart farang who had his father's ear. *The less I have to do with him, the better. So long as he remains the General's son, I have to take it all in stride. The son of a bitch isn't worth ruining a friendship.* Sometimes when Glenn was working out with a sandbag, he imagined he was punching the son's face. The son had two mean-looking bodyguards seated a few feet behind him, so today the bag would not be replaced with the real thing.

Glenn recognized one of the General's friends as Colonel Somchai, who dropped by the NJA Club a few times a month. It seemed one out of every three Thai men were named Somchai. This particular Somchai was a pleasant fellow, as fluent in English as the General, except with an Australian accent. This was never explained to Glenn, who decided Somchai was once a military attaché to Australia, just as the General was in America. *Makes sense all these guys with the Western military connections would know each other,* Glenn reasoned. *Now I'm even starting to think like them. Have I been here too long?*

"Let me introduce Khun Glenn and Major Parhat," Colonel Somchai said.

Glenn looked toward the younger man with Somchai. His ramrod stiff spine, observable even in a chair, and his short hair shouted "military," unsurprising for an officer out of uniform. Glenn nodded to him, and the young man nodded back.

Colonel Somchai said he had a joke he wanted Glenn to hear, and without asking if Glenn wanted to hear it, began his narration.

"This farang I know, American like Khun Glenn, tells me how great his country is. He tells me in America, everybody has free speech. Anyone who wants can stand up on a soapbox in front of the White House and yell 'down with Trump' and nothing will happen to them.

"I tell my farang friend that it is the same here, but he does not believe me. He asks if I mean in Thailand, anyone can go stand on a soapbox in front of Government House and do the same.

"Of course, I tell this farang. Anyone can stand up on a soapbox in front of Government House and shout 'down with Trump,' just like in America."

Glenn forced a laugh, which he hoped sounded sincere. He'd heard the joke many times, with different countries, but appreciated that the old officer had tried to make him laugh.

Kit the waitress passed within a few feet of the General's son. He yelled something out to her, but she kept walking. The son rose out of his chair, and stood in front of Kit. He wasn't much taller than her, but he was twice as wide. He was angry and pointed a finger at her as he yelled in Thai.

"He's angry because she didn't stop what she was doing and run over here when he called her," Colonel Somchai explained. The General said nothing and wore his standard poker face. The son's bodyguards continued looking sullen.

"Maybe she didn't hear him," Glenn said. "It is kind of noisy in here."

"That won't do with this young man," Somchai said. "When he says something, he expects people to listen." The General remained expressionless.

Kit yelled something in Thai.

"She asked him who he thinks he's talking to," Colonel Somchai told Glenn. "Not a good thing to say to him when he's this angry."

The son lifted his right arm, and swung it, his palm landing on the side of Kit's face with a smacking sound. She cried out in pain. The sound was loud enough to be heard at the table where Rong and Phil sat with their entourage. All of their eyes were on the son and Kit, as were Edward's.

Glenn stood and stormed over to where the General's son stood screaming at Kit, who was touching the side of her face. Glenn squeezed between the two and faced the son, his nose hovering just above the younger man's scalp.

"You are a coward and a punk. You want to hit someone? Try me," Glenn said. "Unlike this woman, I will hit back. Very hard.

"If you ever touch this woman again, I'll break both your arms," he said. He glanced over the son's shoulder and saw the General look down for a moment and then raising his eyes to take in the scene. He also saw the two bodyguards begin to leave their chairs. The General raised a hand and they sat down. Colonel Somchai could not take his gaze away from Glenn.

When the son realized his bodyguards were not coming to his rescue, he muttered something and returned to his seat.

"Are you okay?" Glenn asked Kit. He saw discoloration where the son had hit her face. He thought it must hurt, yet she was smiling.

"Thank you, Khun Glenn. That was very brave of you. But maybe you should not have done it. Embarrass him in front of so many people. Call him names. Not a good idea for a farang to make an enemy of the General's son."

"Don't worry about that," Glenn replied. "The General and I have been very good friends for over a dozen years."

"But we are talking about family," Kit said. "Plus, you are a farang."

"And a very good friend," Glenn said. "And without bragging, I'm sure the General knows I'm a better person." *Even I meet that standard.*

"Doesn't matter," Kit said. "It's his son and you are farang. No question who the General has to side with. Sorry to tell you this, Khun Glenn, and sorry to cause you this problem."

"No problem at all," Glenn said. "I better get back to the table and act like it's no big deal."

"But it is a big deal," Kit replied. "Call me, and I explain it all," she said, handing Glenn a piece of paper with her phone number.

⁓

IT WAS only when Glenn was seated again that he realized what so alarmed Kit. He'd publicly threatened and humiliated the son of one of Bangkok's most important figures in front of Thais and foreigners, as well as the General himself. In Thailand, to lose face was a disgrace, and the son had lost a great deal of face in front of some very important people. The fact that Glenn was entirely justified was of no great consequence in Thailand. Seated to each side of Glenn were the General and his son. The General sat as stone-faced as usual, not revealing any more feeling than on any other day at the Club. The son's eyes bored in on Glenn, his lips struggling to remain closed. Glenn saw this and hoped they remained shut, as the last thing he wanted was escalation of an already dangerous situation. Somchai, the retired officer, and the younger military man sat in silence with Glenn and the General's son and his bodyguards. The General's own bodyguard smiled slightly at Glenn. Colonel Somchai broke the quiet, speaking softly in English.

"You have a wise son, my General. He knows not to challenge Khun Glenn when he is right." Major Parhat, who had not uttered a word, looked at the Colonel and nodded his head. "Also when he cannot win. Loss of face is better than a beating in some cases, and this was one." Parhat nodded again.

The General's son rose and walked away, his bodyguards trailing like lapdogs, except these lapdogs were armed with semiautomatic rifles. As the son headed towards the door, Colonel Somchai spoke in English.

"You need to get him on a diet, my General. He's got quite a fat ass." No doubt the Colonel used Glenn's language to make certain he understood.

Who are these guys? I've never seen anyone talk to the General this way, especially not when it comes to his son. There's a story here. Glenn was determined to learn that story but knew he never would.

◦

THE REST of the evening proceeded as if the son had never been there. Glenn glanced at the table where Phil and Rong had sat, now filled with actors from the improvisational comedy club a half mile down Sukhumvit. Glenn recognized them from the many Friday night shows he had enjoyed. They were quite talented, an opinion shared by Sleepy Joe, who dropped by Glenn's condo many a Friday evening with an oversized joint. After smoking it, Glenn and Joe were ready for the laughs that flowed from the stage as long as those actors stood upon it. Both Phil Funston and the General's son, his nemesis, were gone, and Edward had departed, leaving only people Glenn liked.

"Excuse me," he told his table mates, and walked over to Kit, who was leaving another table with the order in her head. She never wrote them down, and never got an order wrong. As soon as she saw Glenn, her eyes brightened and a smile spread across her face.

"My hero. Is that good English?" she asked.

"Your English is fine, but I'm no hero. Besides, a few minutes ago you told me I was a fool who got myself into a very bad situation for a farang."

"I did say that," Kit replied. "But that was before I saw how the Colonel and his friend felt."

"How did they feel?" Glenn asked.

Kit gently touched Glenn's hand.

"They made it clear by their faces and words they think someone should have done this a long time ago. They want you to know this also, so the Colonel spoke English. If they only wanted the General to know how they feel, it would be in Thai."

"You mean they wanted to embarrass the General by letting him know how they feel?" *Very un-Thai*, Glenn thought.

Kit stared at Glenn before explaining.

"Not embarrass, let him know you were right. General knows this, but important he understand his friends don't like how his son acts, but like Khun Glenn. Letting you know everything is ok, General will not be angry."

"What about the son? He doesn't seem like the kind to forget and forgive. And I have to deal with him on the music side of my life."

"What son thinks don't matter," Kit said in a reassuring voice. "Son is too scared of the General. Everybody is scared of General, except Khun Glenn." She lifted her hand from his.

That's what you think. Every time I think I know the General, I find out I am wrong. Then he remembered why he had approached Kit.

"Buy that table drinks," he said, pointing to the actors. "Tell them it's from me, a way of saying thanks for all the laughs." Kit nodded and went off to take the drink orders.

Twelve

THE GENERAL'S son fumed in the passenger seat of the black Hummer his father had given him as a birthday gift. The bodyguard who drove listened in silence, but the one seated in the backseat spoke up.

"You cannot hurt the farang, even if he had deserved it. Your father made it very clear to all of us many times. No violence. We are paid to protect you. We can only use force when you are in danger. You notice your father told us to sit down when the farang confronted you. Being embarrassed is not the same as being in danger."

"Yes, but what about losing face?" the son said loudly. "I don't give a shit what farangs think of me, but he made me look bad in front of many Thais. Army officers and businessmen. That little bitch waitress is probably laughing at me."

The bodyguard in the rear answered.

"Your father made it clear that nothing is to be done. If the General had any doubts, Colonel Somchai ended them. Sounds like he would have been happy to act in Glenn's place. Remember, this just isn't any farang. Your father loves this guy."

"More than he loves me?" the son asked. This time, the driver spoke.

"That's not something we ever want to have to decide. If you are so concerned with face, why did you treat that girl the way you did?"

They saw how my father sat there and did nothing, not even when his friends made sure the farang *knew they don't think much of me. Now even the hired help feels free to say whatever they want to me without any fear. Since my father pays them, I can't even fire them. But I can't forget this either.*

∽

GLENN RETURNED to the General's table after speaking with Kit. The old officers switched from Thai to English when they saw Glenn.

Glenn was supposed to meet Sleepy Joe at his condo in a short while. They planned to watch a few movies, smoke up a storm, and perhaps order a pizza at midnight.

Glenn explained to the General and his two military friends that he had to leave. Colonel Somchai said he hoped to see Glenn again. The young officer nodded. The General told Glenn to meet him for breakfast the following morning at the Au Bon Pain on Ekamai, not far from where Glenn lived.

"We'll talk about your meeting," he said. "It's coming up soon."

"Whoever gets there first grabs a table," Glenn replied. *Seems like he doesn't care if these guys know. Probably told them everything already.*

"Not necessary," the young officer interjected. "When my General wants a table, he gets one." Glenn left the three military men, thinking about the joint he would roll the minute he was home.

∽

"YOUR FARANG friend should be quite convinced of your loyalty and concern for him," Colonel Somchai said in Thai when Glenn was through the door. "Letting him make your own son look like a coward and a bully. Allow us to talk that way about him as well."

"Khun Glenn acted honorably," the young officer said. "How can we condemn farangs who disrespect Thai women if we allow our own people to do the same? In front of a national hero like our General, in a nice restaurant owned by Khun Wang. It should have been a Thai who stood up for her. Your farang friend was right. He acted honorably. I am sorry if it hurt the General."

A hint of a smile struggled at the corners of the General's mouth.

"Major, I'm pleased to hear that they are still teaching about Wang in the Academy. Best adjutant the Army ever saw. Neither Somchai nor I would be here to tell our stories if Wang didn't save us all those times we didn't see Reds sneaking up. He hears and feels everything, has eyes in the back of his head."

"Major Parhat was not yet born when Wang was saving our lives," Somchai said. "Someday he will be telling stories about his own Wang. Is it true you're being sent to the South next month?"

The major stared into the empty whiskey glass in his hands.

"Yes, this is my chance to do in the South what you men did in the North," he said.

"Maybe that was even before your parents were born," the General said.

"Sorry, but I'm not that young," the Major replied. "But as far as I know, I am the youngest major in His Majesty's army."

The General turned to Colonel Somchai. "If I don't watch out, he'll beat my record for becoming the youngest General to serve His Majesty."

"He's definitely going to top me," Somchai replied. "I didn't make full colonel until I was thirty-nine. I was not meant to be a general. Intelligence is not the easiest path to general. They never let go of someone who knows what they are doing. I guess I was just too good to be wasted as a general.

Oh well, I was always happy and still am. But this boy is going to pass me very soon."

The General held his thought to himself.

When an officer is sent South, they come back either with a promotion or in a body bag.

~

SLEEPY JOE wouldn't arrive for another half hour. Glenn rolled a good-sized joint, adding at the smoking end a "crutch" made from a strip of cardboard torn from a business card. The crutch prevented the tip from becoming too moist or collapsing and making the draw difficult. Glenn usually didn't take the time to do this, and relied on Sleepy Joe when he was around. *Since he's gone so often, I learned to do it myself.*

Glenn wondered why the General insisted on again discussing the meeting, since he'd already assured Glenn there was nothing to worry about. Glenn was entering a situation where the General himself would not venture, and Sleepy Joe was being sent with him. Since Sleepy Joe possessed no legal, business, or diplomatic skills, his presence could only be to avoid harm befalling Glenn. Much as Glenn loved the General, he still would not put it past him to risk Glenn's life if he believed the stakes were worth it.

Then again, he just allowed me to bully and humiliate his one son, in front of men he admires. He wouldn't do that for someone he might risk having killed in a short time.

"White Bird" by It's a Beautiful Day poured from Glenn's speakers. The song was from the San Francisco band's first album, released in 1969, and titled with their name. Band leader David LaFlamme and his wife Linda wrote the song sometime during the Summer of Love, and fifty years later, its elegiac beauty still stirred Glenn's heart. Maybe it was La-

Flamme's violin, or maybe the beautiful soaring harmonies of David and Pattie Santos. Pattie died many years ago, and her husband, the band's former bassist, Bud Cockerel, died a few years ago. The couple left the group in the seventies and went their own way, but they were destined to be immortalized by this one song, which Glenn—and Sleepy Joe—placed in the ten most important rock songs ever. They had not yet established the guidelines for such an honor, other than what they liked.

When the song ended, Glenn turned off the music and switched to television. CNN reported former Vice President Joe Biden was struggling in his quest for the Democratic nomination for President, and it looked like Bernie Sanders, the septuagenarian Socialist from Vermont, was the clear frontrunner. Glenn was a registered Democrat who religiously voted by California absentee ballot. He was torn. Personally, he liked Bernie Sanders, with his strong opposition to war and his concern for people in need. On the other hand, he thought a more moderate fellow like Joe Biden had a better chance of beating Donald Trump, whom Glenn saw as nothing more than a criminal, a traitor, and a racist. Getting that bastard out of office was more important than which particular Democrat took the honors.

Glenn was a firm believer in one of his late father's favorite maxims: *The worst Democrat is better than the best Republican.* This wasn't the most prevalent view among American expats in Thailand; the high concentration of ex-military, CIA, and DEA people guaranteed that Trump had a following. The only American Glenn regularly interacted with was Phil Funston, who'd never expressed a political thought in the entire time Glenn knew him. All Glenn's closest friends were from other countries. Oliver was a staunch Australian conservative, and the General a strong monarchist and elitist. They never raised any objections on those occasions where Glenn railed against the man he felt unfit to hold the office of President of the United States. Glenn heard on CNN that in America, families and friendships were being ripped asunder by these political differences, and Glenn appreciated that that was not the case in Bangkok. He didn't know if his friends shared his opinions, but no matter what, these political views would never harm their friendships.

I'll wait and see who looks like the best person to beat that son of a bitch, he thought. *First let me get through this meeting.*

There was a very brief mention of "an unconfirmed viral outbreak in Wuhan, China." No further details were forthcoming, and the World Health Organization had not issued any warnings. Glenn recalled Oliver's account of meeting the epidemiologist, with the dire warning he implied. *Then again, this was an epidemiologist who did his research in a sleazy Patpong bar. Maybe not the most reliable source.*

Despite this self-assurance, a chill ran up Glenn's spine and a knot formed in his stomach. He felt the same sensation when he faced death during the kidnapping of the Russian, and when he was attacked by North Korean hitmen. It was his body telling him to be afraid, because sometimes fear is the motivator for survival.

It was the feeling he'd had that day when he killed three North Koreans as they broke into the General's safe house. The feeling of fear and hopelessness faded after he survived. The feeling from killing the three men lingered on deep inside Glenn, and he knew it would always be there.

They tried to kill me, and I'm the one who carries the guilt.

How can I even think of doing anything that might bring me right back there?

Then he realized the choice was always his to make. He could just say "no."

But of course, he would not.

He did not say "no" after Panchen, the lawyer he so admired, was murdered by the CIA. He'd brought the lawyer into the intrigue to help Noi, the object of Glenn's unrequited love, the reason he joined the CIA kidnapping plot. Noi was alive and well in America, Panchen was dead, and Glenn was in Thailand bearing the guilt that really belonged to her.

Glenn did not say "no" when Charlie sent Gordon Planter, an old friend, over to Thailand to be protected. Gordon wound up being killed by the CIA too. True, Gordon was a sleazebag and a traitor who peddled drugs for North Korea, but still and all, it was Glenn's task to keep him alive, and he failed. *More guilt to carry.*

Glenn had watched Sleepy Joe and Wang the Cook kill several men. True, all the men were trying to kill Glenn, but watching death take over is the same no matter who it grabs. And of course, there were the three North Korean hitmen Glenn had personally killed, the first and only time he'd ever used a gun against human beings.

For a man who reviles violence and wants only peace and pleasure, I sure wind up in some situations I'm supposed to avoid.

Let's hope I'm not being dragged into another one.

Thirteen

THE GREEN Belt was dotted with Au Bon Pain franchises. This was unsurprising, as the Green Belt that stretched along Sukhumvit was the most farang-centric part of Bangkok. Glenn grew up in New York City and knew the Au Bon Pain bagel could not match the real deal, but he believed it was the best in the Kingdom.

Glenn liked the Ekamai location most of all. It sat right along Ekamai Road, an upscale street which gave the neighborhood its name, with a convenient BTS stop and two malls kitty-corner from each other. The wide street was filled with good restaurants and coffee shops, some of the better spas, nightclubs for the young Hi-So crowd, and some fine condos along the street and its many side sois. The place was only a short walk from Glenn's own condo.

Glenn sipped coffee and looked out the big window while waiting for the General. He saw the General's black Hummer pull up and park illegally in front. The General emerged, followed by his ever-present security guard. The General sat down at Glenn's table and the guard pulled up a chair a few feet behind his boss. Normally, customers ordered at the counter and had the order brought to them, but this time, a waitress came to the table and took their orders.

Everyone knows the General, Glenn thought.

The General gave Glenn's order as well as his own, and a coffee or his guard. Glenn and the General had met many times at one Au Bon Pain or another. Glenn always ordered an everything bagel with smoked salmon and cream cheese. Not exactly Zabar's in New York or David's in San Francisco, but more than good enough. The coffee was better than Starbucks, a low bar, but nevertheless appreciated. Glenn nevertheless added one packet o ake sugar as soon as the waitress brought their coffees. Their coffee may be better than Starbucks, but not good enough to drink black. He took his first sip as the General spoke.

"Are you afraid that perhaps your General is getting you into something dangerous, and you don't like it at all?"

"With all due respect," Glenn replied, "even if unintentional, that is a result I'm concerned about. I still have not gotten answers to the most basic questions and I'm still not convinced this is something that requires my legal services, rusty as they are."

"I can't understand why you have any concerns," the General retorted. "If my memory serves me well, twice in the past few years you've managed to get yourself dragged into some very dangerous situations, and it was me who got you out alive."

Glenn thought before responding.

"That might be true regarding the time I got sucked into kidnapping a Russian gangster," he said. "Wang saved me from a thug with a knife on Walking Street, and then from a CIA agent with a machine pistol at the pier where we dumped the Russian."

The General nodded.

"But the second time I had problems, when Gordon Planter's North Korean pursuers tried to kill me, it was to a large extent your fault. You sent me to Chiang Mai, where we were ambushed on the road, then you told me to try and work out a deal at the North Korean restaurant, and that almost got me and Sleepy Joe killed. Next you shuffled me off to your Bangkok safe house, which was promptly invaded by a North Korean hit squad. You've been a mixed bag, my General."

"No, Glenn, you have it wrong. Backwards, in fact." The General leaned forward and spoke just loud enough to be understood by Glenn and no one else

"In all of the situations you listed," the General continued, "you had gotten yourself into a dangerous place and sought my advice and my assistance. Every piece of advice I gave you was the best option at the time. At every moment, you were well-protected. If I'm not mistaken, we even taught you how to defend yourself with a gun, and it saved your life. Thanks to all of that, you are still alive to criticize my methods."

Glenn did not dispute the General.

A minute of silence passed, which they used to work through their respective bagels.

"Don't feel bad," the General said. "It's common to blame others for situations of our own doing. When I was a young Lieutenant fighting the Reds up in Isan, I found myself trapped and surrounded by the enemy on more than one occasion. All my own fault. This was before I was a captain myself with Wang as my adjutant. Fortunately, my captain was far more experienced than me, and always found a way to find me and my men and lead us to safety. On the way out, we were usually fired upon, explosives often tossed at us, not to mention booby traps all along the jungle paths. I blamed my captain for leading us through all that danger. I never bothered to ask why he had to do it. Thus you are forgiven. And if you're looking to be excused for humiliating my only son in public, in front of my military colleagues, don't waste your time."

Glenn's stomach started to churn like a cement mixer.

The General continued, "There's nothing to forgive. He deserved what you did to him, and more. He's my son, and always will be, but I wish he were the man you are."

Glenn smiled and called the waitress. He asked her to bring two almond croissants, heated.

"Celebrate the end of stress with something sweet," Glenn said.

"How did you remember this is my favorite?" the General asked.

"I'm becoming another Oliver," Glenn replied.

Fourteen

Middle of Third Week in December 2019

GLENN THOUGHT Sleepy Joe looked hopelessly out of place in a suit and tie, but perhaps it was because he knew his friend so well. The hair stylist did a remarkable job, allowing Joe to keep his ponytail while still passing for a corporate type. *The world has changed, and there are professionals and executives who have them,* Glenn reasoned. *It'll have to do.*

The Americans were staying at the Holiday Inn, a sensible choice for its location on the corner of Soi 22 and Sukhumvit. The meeting was to take place in one of the hotel's conference rooms.

"You look quite spiffy," Glenn said to Joe on the way up in the elevator. "You ought to do this more often."

"I promise to put on a suit for Phil Funston's funeral," Sleepy Joe replied.

The conference room was windowless but large Impressionist paintings hung on the walls. A side table was laden with urns of coffee and tea, pails of bottled water and soft drinks, and plates of sandwiches and pastries. A Thai man who looked to Glenn to be in his mid-thirties sat at the large conference table. A yellow pad and pen sat before him.

"Help yourself while we're waiting for the others," he said without looking at Glenn or Sleepy Joe.

Glenn poured a cup of black coffee, and Sleepy Joe piled a plate high with pastries. When they were seated, Glen asked the Thai man who he was and why he was there. He said he was the Thai interpreter.

"But everyone involved today speaks English as their native language," Glenn said.

"Goes to show what these farangs know," the young man replied. "Should be easy money."

A security company that doesn't know what languages will be spoken at the meeting they called? The trial lawyer's sixth sense kicked in again.

Sleepy Joe was halfway through his plate of pastries when the conference room door opened and three large men entered the room. They all appeared early middle-aged, in good shape, and all wore dark suits and blue ties. Glenn recognized the three men from the photos of the corporate officers provided by Oliver. They entered without saying a word and sat down at the same time. They made the Thai man appear small, and Glenn could see even while the man was seated that he was noticeably shorter than he or Joe. All three suited men simultaneously offered their business cards to Glenn.

Is this a corporation or a cult?

One of the three men stood a head taller and a half a foot broader in the shoulders than the other two. He sat at the head of the table. The other men sat at each side.

The six men sat in silence for a half minute. The big man at the head of the table broke the silence.

"It's a pleasure to meet you, Mr. Cohen. We fully expected you to appear on behalf of the General. But we were expecting you alone."

Glenn smiled at the man.

"This is my associate, Mr. Joseph Slippy. He's one of the General's chief advisers. Knows the business inside and out. If any details are needed today, Mr. Slippy will have them on the tip of his tongue."

"The first thing Mr. Slippy wants to see is some ID," Joe said.

The big man bristled.

"By this point, we'd assume the General and his people know all about us and who we are."

Sleepy Joe smiled. "That may be, but we are in the security business, and it's never a bad idea to make sure you are actually speaking to the people you think you are. ID, please."

The three men in the identical suits looked at each other. The big man nodded, and each man produced a Florida driver's license, which identified the biggest man as Alfred Elspeth and the other two as John Slater and Henry Weller. The information matched what Glenn had been told.

"Satisfied?" the leader asked

"Make your inquiries, counsel," Sleepy Joe told Glenn with a sweep of his hand.

For the next fifteen minutes, Glenn sought to obtain a coherent picture of the American company and their reason for wanting to partner with the General. He learned nothing he hadn't already gleaned from Oliver's documents. When he asked for details about the work they anticipated doing with the General's company, Alfred Elspeth demurred. Glenn sized him up as the leader.

"Our business requires that we never say anything that might lead anyone to our clients. I'm sure you understand. Until we have all signed on the dotted line, that information remains confidential."

"Oh, I do understand," Sleepy Joe interjected. "But I'm not certain you do. This is Thailand. In the end, there are no secrets. Everyone eventually finds out everything. I doubt anyone in the world would contract to provide unspecified services."

"So much for the inscrutable mysteries of the Orient," Henry Weller, the suited man to the leader's left chimed in.

Glenn cast an angry look.

"First of all, no one calls Asia the 'Orient' anymore. We call this part of the world Southeast Asia, to be specific.

"Second, one of the inscrutable mysteries of Southeast Asia is how many foreigners see mystery when everything is out in the open. Companies like ours are called upon only in the most compelling circumstances. We only accept work when we know what it entails."

The third suit, John Slater, who had been silent, finally spoke.

"We're well aware of that, Counsel. You've studied us and our assets. We invited the General to make an offer for forty-nine percent of his company. Surely someone at your firm has a calculator on their phone and can come up with a figure. Thus far we have not received one. We're here to find out what the General wants, and almost certainly we'll pay. What does it matter why we want to buy? If his number is reasonable, we're prepared to transfer the money on the spot."

"I'm not bidding against myself," Glenn replied. *I'm sure glad I learned that personal injury lawyer's phrase from Charlie when I heard him arguing on the phone with insurance adjusters.* "You're the ones making the offer to buy. Give us a monetary offer and you'll receive an acceptance, rejection, or counter-offer. Quite frankly, that's what we anticipated receiving today. Instead, you want us to make the first move. A seller could get badly burned that way. We would have to discuss your idea with the General. It's his decision, not ours."

Elspeth looked to his colleagues, then at the Thai interpreter. None gave the leader any response. He turned to Glenn and Joe.

"We'll leave you two alone to talk with the General. We'll be back in twenty minutes."

Sleepy Joe held up a hand, palm facing the big man.

"We wouldn't think of inconveniencing you. Mr. Cohen and I could use a little time to stretch our legs going around the block, and we can talk while walking." He stood, gently lifted Glenn by his elbow, and the two were out of the room before anyone else could say a word.

~

GLENN AND Joe walked two blocks and then cut into a side soi. Sleepy Joe seemed to know where he was going. After a short walk on the soi, they entered a dingy laundromat with narrow lanes between machines and dim lighting. Two old women folded laundry in the rear. Joe directed Glenn to some beat up old plastic chairs.

"You know damn well they listen in on everything said the moment we entered that room, and tried to hack our phones to boot," Joe said

"Oliver has made sure our phones are as secure as can be, and we didn't say anything to each other. But why do we want to do business with such people?" Glenn asked. "It's like a sell-your-soul-to-the-devil offer. Not saying these guys are devils, but this is definitely not a normal way to do business, not even here."

"We don't want anything to do with these creeps," Sleepy Joe said. "That's what they are and that's what you'll tell the General. I think he'll listen. He sent you to get your take."

Glenn nodded and exhaled a deep breath.

"He's a mixed bag. You never know when he'll listen to me."

Sleepy Joe reached into the inside pocket of his suit jacket and withdrew a joint.

"Care for a smoke?" he asked Glenn.

"Here? In a public laundry? What happens if a cop comes by?"

Joe laughed softly. "In that case, he'll accept a modest bribe, or I'll kill him," he said as he lit the joint.

"With those assurances, who could refuse?" Glenn responded.

A few tokes later, Sleepy Joe stood and stretched, arching his back and touching his toes.

"Harder to do in a suit," he explained. "That's why I have to make sure I'm as nimble and ready as if I were wearing normal clothing."

"Nimble and ready for what?" Glenn asked. "You're worried about three ignorant corporate types and a little man with a pen and paper?"

Joe shook his head.

"Now you see why the General wanted me here. Not necessarily because he thought you were in danger, but because he figured I was the guy to decide if danger was a possibility down the road."

"And?" Glenn asked.

"You're on to the suits not being legitimate," Joe began. "They are not corporate executives, at least not with any normal corporation, security business or anything else. They're thugs, hardcore."

"How can you be so sure?" Glenn asked.

"Because of their body language, which is something guys like me are trained to spot. The way the big man looked at the little Thai guy was a signal that they knew what kind of guy I am. The likelihood of three corporate executives being so big and buff is possible but highly unlikely. But largely it was their hands, especially the big man at the head of the table, who I'm certain is not Alfred Elspeth. Those fingers and knuckles have met quite a few faces over the years, you can bet on that one."

"So that's why they bring along a guy to take notes? Damaged fingers?"
"That little Thai fellow wasn't there to take notes. Good chance he can barely write in English. No, he's there for the same reason I was. Protection."

"Against whom?" the look on Glenn's face was as if he had just seen a two-headed person walking down the street.

"That's a fine question, counselor. No one in their right mind would be afraid of you, and people like me are never the aggressors where I'm not in danger. Either these folks were afraid of something, or *we* ought to be afraid of something."

"Which one?" Glenn asked.

"I've gathered all the raw intelligence my feeble mind could uncover," Sleepy Joe replied. "Putting it together will be your job."

As usual, Glenn thought.

Fifteen

GLENN OPENED the conference room door without knocking. He knew this went against etiquette, but he was more interested in catching the suited men unaware in the hope it would reveal something. At a minimum, it would impart the message that the General's dealings with these alleged buyers were over.

"The General sends his best wishes and trusts you will enjoy your stay in Bangkok," Glenn said while he and Joe stood a few feet from the door. "At this time, he is not interested in pursuing a transaction and won't waste any of your valuable time." *Hope I sound officious enough.*

"I am disappointed, and that is putting it mildly," Alfred Elspeth replied. "We came quite a distance to negotiate in good faith."

"But not enough good faith to make an offer. Coming in here and acting like some grubby insurance adjuster trying to pressure a down-at-the-heels personal injury lawyer into taking a bad deal for their client. Well, I'm not that lawyer, and the General is not that client." Glenn turned and headed to the door while Sleepy Joe slowly walked backwards. Glenn opened the door and walked through. Sleepy Joe continued walking back-wards while staring at the four men in the room one at a time. When he reached the Thai man, their eyes locked for a moment, and then the Thai man dropped his gaze ever so slightly.

"Good day," Sleepy Joe said as he backed his way through the door. "And for your sake, let's hope we never meet again." When he was completely outside the conference room, he slammed the door so hard that several vases on the receptionist's desk rattled noisily.

∽

"No one followed us," Sleepy Joe told Glenn as they paid their motorcycle taxi drivers. Joe had led Glenn out of the Holiday Inn through one of the restaurants on street level, where they hopped on the cycles to Phra Khanong, barely a mile north of Ekamai. The drivers dropped them off at the intersection of Phra Khanong and Sukhumvit. They walked a block down Phra Khanong, turned right onto a narrow side soi, and entered a tiny tea shop with three small tables. Glenn was surprised to find a place in Bangkok that still sold only tea. The city was awash in coffee shops, many excellent, but others not up to Glenn's standards.

"They'll never find us here," Joe said when they were seated. "Doubt they saw us as the motorcycle taxi types, at least not you. Anyway, hard to follow a motorcycle taxi that's driving on the sidewalk, going against traffic, and playing chicken with buses and trucks. We're safe here."

"Why shouldn't we be safe?" Glenn asked. "Why would anyone be following us?"

"That's the ultimate question you're going to answer eventually," Sleepy Joe said. "First you'll have to figure out why a bunch of American thugs and a trained Thai killer would go to such lengths to impersonate a legitimate American company and then pull such an amateur stunt as inviting an offer for a contract without saying a word of what it involves."

∽

OLIVER PROVIDED an answer to Sleepy Joe's question.

"It's because these three Americans are fools," he explained. "No matter who among us showed up, we would spot a masquerade a mile away, and any real security people know this. Joe made them instantly. We ought to be asking what their real endgame is, and why they are in Bangkok."

Glenn had asked for the meeting at his place. He called Oliver and the General. Sleepy Joe and he went directly to the condo, and the other two arrived moments after them. They sat around Glenn's dining room table, a pot of coffee in the center, along with several cups, creamer, and sweeteners. While Glenn poured coffee, Oliver went to his liquor cabinet and grabbed a bottle of Jameson's Irish Whiskey, which Glenn won at a St. Patrick's Day raffle six years before. Oliver poured whiskey into his cup and then the General's.

"Figure you two prefer a joint," he said to Glenn and Joe.

"If you insist," Sleepy Joe said, as he produced one and lit it.

"I have a few questions for Oliver," Glenn said. "Not to question your efficacy in any way, but I do have some questions about the way these guys were vetted. It's clear they are not American business executives."

Oliver arched an eyebrow and smiled. The light from Glenn's chandelier bounced off his shaved head.

"Do you?" he asked. "By all means, let's hear your concerns."

"I didn't say they were concerns," Glenn said. "I said they were questions. Asking questions is what lawyers do, after all."

"Fair enough," Oliver said.

"First, how did these guys manage to convince you that they were American executives? Joe and I saw right off the bat that they aren't any such thing. Did you check them against the pictures on their website?"

"They don't have their pictures on their website," Oliver replied. "They run a security company. Protection and investigation. There's no percentage in letting everyone in the world know what they look like. Unless one needs their services, one need not be aware they even exist."

"So did we just rely on the photos they sent you as really being the company executives?"

"No, we did not," Oliver huffed. "Or at least I did not. I drew on every resource at my disposal, and none could produce photos of these executives. Most had heard of the company, and told me they were what they claimed. I called the company just to make sure they existed, and they do. After he received the first email, I told the General to ask for photos before we met. That's how we got the ones I gave you, which were of the men you met. They are not who they claim, and we don't know why. Perhaps I should have considered the lack of a publicity photo as an opportunity to impersonate the party. I assure you in the future, that will be considered. It's part of what is meant by experience. Sometimes experience is not pleasant, but it is instructive. And it is ongoing."

Glenn fired off his second question.

"Did you see any verification that this company was genuinely interested in becoming minority owners of the General's company? Or did you rely entirely on what the General reported that they'd told him?"

Oliver took a long sip of his whiskey-laced coffee before answering.

"Both parties are in the business of keeping secrets. No written communications or documents were provided to the General, none that would prove their intent. They wouldn't discuss it by phone if they were so insistent on meeting personally. A few emails, that was all. There couldn't be any way of knowing the whole story until we met them. How do we establish that someone really wants to make a purchase, until they do? The email address is legitimate. I have confirmed that my call to the American company was in fact to that number. While they were rather taciturn, they did confirm they were sending three executives to Bangkok to make an offer for part ownership in the General's security business."

The General offered his perspective.

"Is it possible that they hacked your phone so when you called the American company, it was diverted to a different number? Wouldn't it be rather easy for them to have the real company number flash on the screen, even if they were elsewhere?"

Oliver sat up stiffly and his face flushed slightly.

"Are you implying that I was incompetent and didn't do my job, placing us in possible danger? And that these people were digital geniuses? If that's what you think, say it."

Sleepy Joe addressed his fellow Australian.

"No, Oliver, not at all. We have a problem we're trying to solve. Before we can, we have to understand it. Before we can understand it, we need all the facts. We need to figure out who these guys are, what they want, and why they are going about trying to get it so oddly. The General exchanged a few emails, you thought those e mails and your call were legit, but Glenn and I just met some rough-looking chaps who don't seem legit at all. Whoever they may be, they are not an American security company looking to partner with the General for legitimate reasons. You didn't know they were not who they claimed, but that doesn't make it your fault or mean you screwed up. Knowing what you were thinking and why, it might explain how they got past. Might also give us a better idea of what we need to do from here."

"He's right," the General said. Oliver nodded and the redness drained from his face.

"Yes," he said softly. "It would not be difficult to arrange for a call to be shifted elsewhere." The General nodded as if to signal he had figured that out already.

"Glenn will conduct an investigation," the General said. "I don't mean an investigation of Oliver's investigation, like the Republican obsession with Mueller. I mean a serious and thorough examination of these Americans. For starters, who are they? Why the impersonation? What is behind contacting me? What do they really want from me and my company? Why did they fear possible violence enough to have their own Sleepy Joe present? And of course, where we went wrong to allow them to get this far. I want all our mistakes examined, with nothing overlooked, even if it was by me. Like Oliver said, that's how experienced people become experienced."

Glenn grabbed the half-inch joint from Sleepy Joe and sucked on it so long and hard it burned down to an eighth of an inch in seconds. He dropped the remainder in an ash tray.

"I'm a lawyer, not an investigator," Glenn protested. "You have investigators on your payroll, and all your contacts in military intelligence. Oliver is an investigator of a special type, but you have those who knock on doors and look through peepholes. General, you hired me as a lawyer to represent you at a meeting and report my findings. I've done so, and my services are concluded. I don't want anything more to do with this."

The General finished his whiskey-laced coffee and poured a second cup.

"Glenn, this isn't charitable work. I understand money no longer motivates you, as it does the rest of us, but I can offer you much of value in addition to your fee. I promised to help release you from any commitment you feel to Phil Funston when this job is over. I think we can agree it's not over." The General smiled, as did Glenn. The words of the old New York Yankee catcher Yogi Berra echoed through his mind.

It ain't over until it's over.

"Okay, General, we have a deal, provided you also agree to never again try to push one of your mia noi's friends on me."

"I absolutely will not promise that," the General replied.

~

THE FOUR men sat around Glenn's table in silence for no more than twenty seconds, but to each of them it felt like much longer. The General broke the silence.

"Glenn is correct. Normally we would rely upon my company and Oliver. We have deduced today that Oliver and my security were quite possibly compromised to some degree. We have no idea how deep they have penetrated with their hacking. We must assume there are more people involved, as it seems unlikely these thugs had such technical skills. To be safe, let's assume they hacked our systems and know a great deal about us. Oliver can check all of our systems and add new protections, but it will take time. We should lay low until we know for sure our phones and internet are secure and when it's safe to go out in the open. They apparently anticipated us sending Glenn and someone like Sleepy Joe. Who knows what else they have learned about us? Needless to say, the way they have deceived us is a sign we need to be more careful. At least I do.

"There are few people I trust completely. Oliver is one, but we're both temporarily invisible. I have you and Joe, and Wang of course, but he may have other roles to play later on."

"Does that mean we go into this without Wang?" Sleepy Joe asked.

"He won't be at your beck and call," the General replied. "He will be there when needed."

"I am providing you with two highly competent professionals to help," the General continued. "Men outside my business, but men I trust as much as any of you."

"When do we get to meet them?" Glenn asked.

"You already have," the General said. At that moment the intercom buzzed. Lek informed Glenn that there were two men in the lobby who said they had an appointment with him. Glenn looked at the General, who nodded. Glenn told Lek to send them up.

A minute later, Glenn answered the doorbell, and Colonel Somchai and Major Parhat walked into his apartment.

Sixteen

Five Days Later

AT THEIR first meeting with the others, after the Colonel and Major were brought up to speed it was decided that Somchai would conduct an independent investigation of the Americans. After hearing the results, Glenn would use his analytical skills to plan the next step, assuming one was necessary. They would meet without the General or Oliver in a few days.

Parhat liked Glenn, or at least admired him. Unlike the General and Colonel Somchai, his career had not brought him much contact with foreigners, certainly not many Americans. Growing up in Rayong, he attended public schools devoid of farangs. He was honored to be admitted to the Academy, as he craved a military career, but it meant virtually all classmates were Thai. Parhat envied the way the General and Somchai understood the farang mind and were supremely confident in their dealings with them. He wanted to have farang friends as they did, especially an American. *They are the smartest and the most generous, according to the General and Colonel.*

Even though he liked America and its people, Parhat presumed a certain degree of boorishness was inherent in their character. Glenn Murray Cohen disabused him of this notion as being universal. Glenn treated everyone the same, with kindness and generosity. He was not loud or pushy with ordinary Thai people. Glenn was the most sophisticated farang Parhat had ever encountered. He possessed the finest tastes in clothing and food, drank only in moderation, and had extraordinary manners for a farang, The General assured Parhat that Glenn was above all a man of honor and of his word. The General's love for Glenn was obvious to Parhat. He knew Thai men with American business or professional associates, but none who had a truly close farang friend.

"It's too bad he refuses to learn our language," the General told Parhat over drinks at the NJA Club a few days after he'd introduced him to Glenn. "He could almost be one of us."

Glad he said "almost," Parhat reflected later that night.

∼

COLONEL SOMCHAI shook hands with Glenn and Sleepy Joe. When he and Parhat were in Glenn's living room, Major Parhat gave them a wai. *Khun Glenn and this Sleepy Joe creature are older than me*, he rationalized.

"When our young friend has some overseas assignment, he'll learn about shaking hands," the Colonel said.

"Make it America," Parhat said. "I want to speak English like Khun Glenn."

At Colonel Somchai's suggestion, Glenn gave his report first.

"There's no doubt there is indeed such an American security business known simply as Martin, Walker and Associates, though Martin and Walker died years ago. They have executives with the same names as used by our three visitors. Officers and employees of the company do not post their photos or any details not related to their qualifications. I think we can also be quite certain that the real Martin, Walker and Associates has never contacted the General about buying him out, and those three men have no connection with the real thing. Whoever they may be, they are not Alfred

Elspeth, John Slater or Henry Weller."

"Why should we be so certain?" Sleepy Joe asked.

"Because Charlie says so," Glenn replied.

Sleepy Joe's eyes grew wide. "Charlie? That Charlie? The one you hate because every time he calls, something dangerous happens? I like him, and I think Oliver does, the General too, because every time Charlie calls, we all make a lot of money. American dollars. Cash on the barrel."

"The very same," Glenn said. "I don't hate the man, I just don't like danger. But if I'm looking for someone with the appearance of respectability, but willing to cross any line that won't land him in jail, it's Charlie. That's exactly who this job called for."

"And what did this Charlie do?" Parhat asked.

Glenn explained how Charlie had made an appointment to discuss hiring the company's services to locate missing witnesses in civil and criminal cases. Two were local Tampa residents. The third was a Thai-American who was believed to have fled to Thailand. Charlie presented convincing paperwork on all three matters, but not a word was true.

"The company told Charlie they'd be happy to help on the two locals, but they couldn't help if the third fellow was in Thailand," Glenn recounted. "They wouldn't have any legal authority to conduct any sort of investigation, and as we know, they couldn't do any work without the proper visas. They didn't know of anyone in Thailand they could recommend."

Parhat looked as if he had just been given a winning lottery number.

"If they were really trying to break into the market here, Charlie was handing them work on a silver platter," Parhat said. "This would have been a perfect opportunity for them to present work to the General's company, to see if it is a good fit." He nodded in the manner of someone content with their presentation.

"Or as experienced security people, they smelled a potential rat and clammed up," Sleepy Joe said. "You think we're the only ones who ever get suspicious?"

"Of course not," Glenn said. "But in this instance, I agree with Major Parhat. The most likely explanation is what the company told Charlie. Take it from me, Charlie is totally convincing at whatever he does. That's why he gets away with it. It's also why he's a hell of a trial lawyer. I watched him persuade some juries to believe the opposite of all evidence and common sense and acquit his guilty clients."

"The highest honor one can pay you criminal defense lawyers, isn't it mate?" Sleepy Joe asked.

Glenn smiled and nodded.

"Yes, and one reason among many I'm here and not sharing office space with Charlie." He continued his report. "The General informs me that his people have had the three suits under constant surveillance since we learned about them. He used his connections at Immigration to find out when they arrived. His crew tried to bug them, but these guys, whoever they are, were a step ahead of the game. Someone with brains is helping them. They have anti-bugging and scrambling equipment the General's people hadn't encountered before. Any bug would be useless.

"The General's crew were able to plant a miniscule tracker on the car the suits use. Only the Henry Weller imposter drives it. It's leased under a phony name. The tracker has the latest technology, given to Oliver by a grateful Israeli, able to avoid any electronic sweep, too tiny to be seen. As long as the trackers work, we don't have to rely only on tailing, because we can't totally lose them. We'll always know where Weller is when he's driving. As you'll see, it has already given us a lead.

"Once we realized that the General and Oliver were very likely compromised, with their phones and devices potentially hacked, they dropped out of the game, except as resources for us. They'll be back soon as it's safe. Any further surveillance reports will come from Colonel Somchai."

Glenn excused himself to walk to his kitchen and bring the coffee he brewed and almost forgot. He poured cups and added creamer and packets of various sweeteners. He remembered the spoons.

As he assembled the tray, Glenn debated whether to share his theories of the case, or whether such speculation would do more harm than good. He opted for full disclosure.

"There's no doubt about the three suits being imposters who stole the identity of an American company in order to fool the General into thinking they wanted to work with him. Obviously, these guys could not cut any deal on behalf of the real company. They may have actually come here to negotiate, although in a rather unusual manner. There's no law preventing a buyer from asking a vendor how much they want, but the more common practice is for the offeror to give a number, and then the parties bargain over the price. It strikes me that these three mysterious visitors know nothing about business, and were simply going to write a check for whatever the General asked. They thought by being so generous, he couldn't resist. They hadn't thought about the reality, how fees are set, or why the General is so esteemed in security and investigation."

"Maybe we should have demanded ten million American dollars," Sleepy Joe chimed in.

"These guys had no idea how to value a business," Glenn said. "Perhaps the General would have walked away with considerably more than the minority stake is worth, but most likely these guys couldn't come up with the money. If they had the money and the knowledge, they would have made a serious offer."

"Having met them, you are a hundred percent correct," Sleepy Joe said. "Tell us what you think they're really up to."

Glenn poured himself another cup and drank half of it, black, in two slurps.

"I can give you my conclusions, but be advised, they are a work in progress, based on very little evidence. Let's say it's my trial lawyer's sixth sense at work here."

"Always done well for us in the past," Joe said. Turning to Parhat, he said, "He's like one of these Cambodian fortune tellers. He's almost always right."

Glenn continued, "We can assume that there's no way these fellows could actually pay the General in the name of a company they do not own, without anyone noticing. That leads me to conclude they never had any intent to actually be in business. If they wanted the General's skills, contacts, and his people, they would have come in with specific plans and a budget. If they needed him, they could hire him even if he didn't sell. More likely they were here for a specific and secret reason, and not primarily interested in becoming a minority owner of a Thai business. It is not their real reason for being here. I suspect whatever they planned was not something they'd want the Thai or American governments to know about. They are looking for something, and they think the General can help find it."

"As Khun Glenn says, why not just hire the General?" Parhat asked. "Wouldn't that be a lot easier than this charade?"

"Of course," Glenn replied. "We can conclude there is a different reason."

"And what are they looking for?" Parhat asked.

"No idea as of now," Glenn said. "But it has to be very important, because they brought along some serious muscle. Those three guys probably wouldn't have needed the little Thai guy to kidnap the General, though against someone like Sleepy Joe, he'd come in handy. Had the General appeared and refused to deal, they would have grabbed him and pressured him to do their bidding. We threw them a monkey wrench by sending me and Joe. There was no point in kidnapping me. Assuming Joe didn't kill them, they'd still have to negotiate with the General, and they'd be stuck in his town, with him on the loose, and all his irepower lined up against them.

"You've had the pleasure of hearing my uncorroborated theory of the case," Glenn said. "Incomplete of course, as we don't know their motives. I suspect Colonel Somchai will shed more light."

Seventeen

SOMCHAI WORE a dark blazer with a white shirt and no tie. He looked like a rich Thai businessman in casual wear.

He poured himself a cup of coffee and began his report.

"I took over surveillance immediately after your meeting with Oliver and the General, using some of the General's people, ones I have determined have not been compromised in any way, plus a few good people borrowed from military intelligence. I am still able to draw upon their resources as needed."

Just like the General, Glenn thought.

"We learned from the car tracker they were staying in a condo way down on Soi 49. We later saw Weller drive there and park in the building's covered lot. We spoke with the condo unit owner. He listed it on Airbnb and received an inquiry from someone claiming to be an American real estate investor. He told the owner they needed the place while they were negotiating the sale of property in Bangkok. They wired him three month's rent plus a security deposit. I doubt they have any intention of staying three months. That was part of their cover. Makes them seem like normal businesspeople hunkering down for a long haul, not unusual in business dealings over here."

"Do we have the name and other details they used to rent the condo?" Glenn asked.

"Worthless," Somchai replied. "Total fakes. The name used to sign was a man who died forty years ago, and the American address is a closed pizza parlor in Detroit. They didn't use the names they borrowed from Martin, Walker and Associates."

"Can we trace the wire?" Parhat asked.

"We did. An account was opened a few days before the transfer, and closed as soon as the money was sent. The account was in the name of a different dead man."

"Allow me to continue," Somchai said. "We have been following them constantly. We haven't learned a thing. Other than that condo and the car. These guys are masters of avoiding electronic surveillance, or whoever helps them is, so we can't listen in on them. One of our men did follow the fake Mr. Elspeth around one morning, and when the big man stopped for a coffee, our person was able to retrieve the cup and we sent it off for a genetic evaluation. You know, there are a million companies doing it these days, but we used a government lab here that has the latest American technology. Turns out the leader, the biggest one is ninety-one percent Serbian."

"How the hell is Serbia involved in any of this?" Sleepy Joe asked. "I wasn't aware Thailand and Serbia had any issues between them."

"Because there are no issues," Somchai said. "It is purely coincidental that this guy, and presumably his two friends, are Serbian. Our ethnology and anthropology experts have examined the photos and agree. It just means that someone hired Serbians. We are trying to find who did that hiring, and for what purpose."

Glenn raised a hand and Somchai nodded, understanding Glenn had something to say and Somchai wanted to hear him.

"I'm starting to think when the smoke clears, we're going to learn that it was a government behind this. I know it sounds crazy, but whoever is behind this has the capability to direct phone calls and protect against eavesdropping, and they're so good, they even fooled Oliver. That's not the three Serbian clowns I met. I think the General suspects the same, which is why he didn't want to attend the meeting. I'll accept that he genuinely and sincerely believed there was no danger to me and Joe, potentially only to him, but he was wrong, and this assessment does not inspire great confidence in his understanding of this whole affair."

"I doubt the General would disagree with the last part of your statement," Colonel Somchai said. "The first part is incorrect. The General has never suspected a government was involved, foreign or our own. If he believed so, he would have taken the appropriate measures, which means reporting this to the authorities. He absolutely did not believe nor have reason to suspect Glenn or Joe would be in any danger. Those were logical conclusions, considering what he and Oliver reasonably believed to be the facts."

"There's no point wondering what someone might or might not have believed in the past," Major Parhat said. "We should focus on making certain our conclusions from now on are solid and supported by facts. Can we be sure these gangsters are Serbians? Khun Glenn says they spoke perfect English. I wish I could speak English without a funny accent."

"So does Glenn," Sleepy Joe said, and everyone laughed.

"Thank you for a moment of lightness, Joe, but I must return to my report," Somchai said. "I have a meeting in an hour with a foreign intelligence contact I've known since I was a captain."

Somchai recounted in greater detail how his crew followed the Serbians by tracking the car electronically and lots of good old-fashioned tails on foot. The Serbians did what farangs do in Bangkok: eat, get massages, shop, drink. They stopped in a few of the bars on Soi Cowboy, had a few drinks, ogled and pawed the girls, who were not complaining based on the drinks they bought and the tips they left. But they never went further and never stayed more than a half hour. They made certain to speak only in English.

"But they never did anything with all three together. One of them was always alone, tailing a farang. Literally monitoring him twenty-four seven. Not always the same Serb, but always one of them, even watching his hotel when he was sleeping. One of our people got a clear photo of the man they are following. I sent it to Oliver's Israeli associates, who will use their most excellent facial recognition software to see if there's a match. My contacts at Immigration can also search, but it's always a good idea to check on their information. I bet Oliver's Israelis get us the details a lot quicker, and in a pinch, I'd go with them. In the meantime, I have another photo of interest."

Somchai displayed his phone screen to the others. It showed a hard-looking man in camouflage cradling a semiautomatic rifle. It was the leader of the three Serbs, the fake Alfred Elspeth. Much younger, but the same man.

"I was able to get this through some old contacts in the Australian military intelligence community. Seems like some Serbian-Australians were overly sympathetic to the Milošević regime when they were massacring Bosnians and persecuting Albanians. The Aussie government keeps their eyes on these folks, and when they saw our immigration photo of the big guy in the suit, our Mr. Elspeth, they made a match. He uses a lot of differ-ent names, and absolutely no one knows his birth name. There are at least three conflicting birth certificates floating around. For the sake of convenience, let's use Alfred Elspeth, the name on the American passport used to enter the Kingdom. A passport that is legitimate, by the way. Don't ask how it was issued. When we find out, we'll let you know."

"My mate and fellow Aussie Oliver could have gotten the same info," Sleepy Joe sniffed.

"Undoubtedly," Somchai replied. "Who do you think originally introduced me to my old contacts? I met Oliver back in my days as a military attaché in Canberra. He'd occasionally do a job for the Australian army. Sometimes we worked on joint projects."

"Speaking of joints," Sleepy Joe said as he produced another.

Major Parhat threw him a look of annoyance.

"Ganja is highly illegal in Thailand. Tolerating your drug abuse may be a necessary evil at present, but must it be continuous?" he asked.

"Actually, yes," Sleepy Joe replied. "And quit trying to sound like a fancy lawyer, like Glenn. No one calls smoking weed 'drug abuse' and no one calls it a 'necessary evil.'"

"Sleepy Joe is right," Somchai said. "Now allow me to continue." He showed them a photo of the Alfred Elspeth from the meeting, looking younger and dressed in military fatigues.

"This photo was taken outside Srebinica, in 1995, when Serbian paramilitary troops massacred five thousand Muslim males of all ages. That's the kind of man we're dealing with."

"Do we know exactly what he was doing there?" Glenn asked. "Maybe it's just the old criminal defense lawyer in me, but if we're calling a man a war criminal, we ought to have some proof."

"I haven't heard of any confessions, or any eyewitnesses identifying him, but he was Serbian paramilitary not far from where his colleagues committed genocide," Colonel Somchai replied. "If he weren't a violent man, he would not have been there in the first place."

"That doesn't make him guilty of genocide," Glenn said. "How far was he from the massacre? Any evidence he knew or should have known it was going to happen? What did he do when he learned?"

"Glenn, if I'm ever in trouble, I want you as my lawyer," Parhat interjected. "But let's move on."

"He's not only violent," Colonel Somchai continued, "he's also more intelligent than you think. After the Balkan Wars ended, he put together a little crew of mercenaries and hired them out to any government willing to pay. They're not ordinary hitmen, and they aren't garden variety thieves or looters. Governments hire them to do things they can't do on their own, for any number of reasons. But they all require skills, brains and courage."

Glenn understood what Somchai meant.

Sort of like the way the CIA wanted me to kidnap a Russian gangster, because no one would suspect me, and the Thais wouldn't care so long as it couldn't be pinned on the U.S. government. Except even these Serbs know their stuff better than I ever did.

"The same reasons people hire the General," Sleepy Joe said.

"In a sense," Somchai replied.

Glenn turned to his friend.

"Joe, are you saying these fellows are willing and able to threaten, kidnap, kill if necessary?"

"All of the above," Joe said. "I know the type. They'd love to be like I was in the army, but they lack discipline and real courage. They get information using some methods Oliver does not. His information is still light years better than theirs."

The four men sat around Glenn's table for a full minute, drinking coffee, mulling over what they'd learned from each other. Parhat was the first to break the quiet.

"I appreciate the opportunity to learn from experienced experts," he said. "If I understand what Colonel Somchai and Khun Glenn have explained, a foreign government has hired a group of Serbian gangsters to impersonate an American security company so they can partner with the General and use his company for some unknown purpose, which is probably illegal. Am I right so far?"

"A hundred percent," Glenn replied.

Parhat nodded, a look of satisfaction across his face.

"And we have identified their mission as being related to a farang they have been following, but who they have not even attempted to contact, let alone harm."

"You're getting an A," Sleepy Joe said.

"And if we can find out why they are interested in this farang, we will likely know which government hired them, and what this farang has that is of such interest to them?"

Colonel Somchai's phone bleared an alert. He checked the message.

"At least we know this mysterious farang's name," he announced. "Cross checked with my contact at Immigration and Oliver's facial recognition buddies. Actually, the Israelis were able to get into our Immigration system and do the cross check. Good thing they're not our enemies, or we'd be in trouble with only our own security systems."

Glenn asked Somchai the foreigner's name.

"Thomas Boston."

Eighteen

Glenn put the pieces together.

The Serbs were bird-dogging Thomas Boston, and by serendipity, Oliver came along in time to save the American epidemiologist from some embarrassing, expensive, and potentially painful consequences of poor judgment.

Sirens must have sounded when they realized Oliver was connected to the General. Dollars to donuts Oliver's been under surveillance ever since.

Glenn understood this made it even more dangerous to have contact with the big Australian, but since Oliver was the only one of them to have met Mr. Boston, he had to be shown the photo of Boston and confirm it was the man he rescued. He explained this to the others.

"We have to figure out a way to show Oliver the image and get his response without letting the bad guys know we're on to them," Sleepy Joe said when Glenn was done. "Is there anyone we can really trust or count on? How can we communicate with Oliver on something like this, if we have a government-sponsored gang following him around, maybe even having access to his phones and computers?"

Parhat asked if they could be certain Oliver was being surveilled.

"There's nothing so unusual about one farang getting into that kind of trouble, and a wiser farang helping them," he said. "Why would these foreign government agents divert time and manpower to follow a total stranger who doesn't seem to have anything to do with their task?"

Somchai raised his hand, and Parhat stopped speaking. Colonel Somchai waited a few seconds before speaking.

"I agree with Glenn. They surely followed Oliver after he saved Boston. Those Serbs didn't understand any better than we do why a man like Boston would set foot in a Patpong go-go bar. They weren't going to let it go without a look. For all they knew, Oliver might have been a contact, or an agent of some other government doing the same as them. These guys are pros, even if not the very best, and pros don't discount any possibility. When they found out Oliver was with the General, they didn't stop following him. And they won't until they get what they want, whatever that may be."

Parhat blushed.

"Thank you for the instructions on intelligence surveillance," he said in Thai. "I just wish you did not have to say it in English in front of these two strangers." Parhat used the Thai word for "stranger" because Glenn and Joe would know he was speaking of them if he said farang, the slang word for foreigners, specifically Westerners.

Somchai patted Parhat's arm. He spoke again, their language.

"These two are not strangers, at least not to me or the General. Besides, these two will never be ordinary strangers. They knew what I was thinking before I said a word. Keep that in mind. You can learn a lot from them. Neither Americans nor Australians are hesitant to speak their minds. You'll almost always know what they think, and that's good for everyone. They'll say important things most Thais might not want to say. One reason the General and I want you here. To learn."

Parhat reflected on his mentor's advice. *Maybe I can learn from these farangs. The monk in my local temple once told me that a person may be able to pass on the teachings of the Buddha even if they do not live by them. That describes the American character perfectly. Teach things that are right even if you don't live by those words. Probably Australians as well. Even some Thais.*

Glenn waited for the two Thais to finish their conversation. Glenn was accustomed to the Thai practice of switching from English to Thai when they didn't want foreigners to understand. This was usually reserved for something so important it couldn't wait. Glenn could not understand the Thai, but the Colonel's voice and manner indicated that while Parhat felt this was such an occasion, Somchai did not.

"I have a way to show Oliver the photo of Boston without using a potentially compromised internet or phone," Glenn said. "Assuming he makes a positive identification, we can question this Mr. Boston to learn why he has people after him." No doubt Somchai and Parhat were told of the way Oliver encountered Boston. Somchai and the General, like him and Joe, were able to connect the dots to the people surveilling the scientist. Glenn was nevertheless concerned Parhat was too thick and myopic to do anything except sit there looking out of place among smart and experienced people. *This guy did not rise through the ranks on merit, like the General or Somchai. He must come from a rich family, and he was useless for their businesses, so they palmed him off to the military.*

"I'm going to go down to the lobby and speak with Lek," Glenn said. "Five minutes, tops."

∽

"So, Major, ever see combat?" Sleepy Joe asked Parhat when the door closed behind Glenn. Joe knew his friend would not appreciate his goading the arrogant young officer.

"Not exactly," Parhat replied. "I have been called upon to quell several demonstrations."

"I don't consider beating up students and strikers to be combat," Sleepy Joe said. "Let me be blunt: have you ever killed an enemy soldier? Or at least tried?"

A heavy silence hung over the table for a few seconds. Colonel Somchai spoke: "The Major has spent most of his career on the administrative side," he explained. "Some time in intelligence, some in strategic planning. Quite important, and in fact, a likely path to promotion. He requested a posting in the South, where he will be responsible for several anti-terrorist units. He will see quite a few armed encounters with the insurrectionists and terrorists down there. I personally vouch for his bravery."

Sleepy Joe smiled and extended his hand.

"Well, then, if the Colonel vouches, it's more than good enough for me. No offense intended, Major, it's just how I am." Parhat hesitated for a moment, then clumsily shook Joe's hand.

These people are crazy, Parhat thought as he released Joe's hand.

∽

GLENN RETURNED five minutes later, as promised. He told the others that Lek's cousin would be working with them. Sleepy Joe raised a hand, palm forward, and held it up until Glenn pressed his own palm against it.

"Worth a high-five, isn't it mate? Calling in the calvary!"

"What is he talking about?" Parhat asked. He remembered Lek, the Isan man in the condo lobby, who was pleased when Somchai identified the two as friends of Glenn. "I know Lek works here, but what does his cousin have to do with anything?"

"We're bringing in the calvary, mate," Sleepy Joe repeated. "The Boys in Brown. You want to get anything done in this town, you've got to have the police on your side."

Glenn explained that Lek's cousin was a police lieutenant working in the nearby precinct. He'd assisted the General on several matters in the past, and was skilled in merging police and personal matters.

"I appreciate he is a police officer, but has he been properly vetted?" Parhat asked.

Colonel Somchai joined Glenn and Sleepy Joe in laughter. Then he explained to Parhat, "Major, we need to remember Glenn is in charge here, personally selected by the General. Under those circumstances, it's most unwise to question his judgment on something like this. Besides, he told you this police officer has worked with the General. If that's not sufficient vetting, I don't know what is. Continue, Glenn."

"The Lieutenant and his team are going to bring us both Oliver and the leader of these Serbian imposters," Glenn said. "We'll soon find out who Mr. Alfred Elspeth really is."

"I knew he'd think of something," Sleepy Joe said, throwing a thumb in Glenn's direction. "Always does."

"You mean a bunch of Bangkok cops are going to use their legal authority to grab two foreigners off the street?" Parhat exclaimed. "Couldn't we have used our own people to do that?" he asked, turning to Colonel Somchai.

It was Glenn who answered. "Uniformed or plainclothes military snatching farangs off the street would be rather unusual. It would draw a lot of attention, surely from the local and Western media, maybe even from embassies. Definitely not the attention we want as we try to gather the facts. On the other hand, there's nothing especially unusual about a Bangkok cop rousting a farang. Could be for any number of reasons. The person could have run afoul of some law, immigration or otherwise. Or maybe it's just the typical police income supplementation. In any event, our Serbian friends won't know what it means or that Lek's cousin is with us. Oliver will immediately know he's in safe hands and will most surely be relieved."

"Won't they just follow the cop car, and see that it brings them here?" Parhat inquired.

"I thought of that," Glenn said. "The police will bring the big man in the suit, the guy calling himself Elspeth, and Oliver to separate stations. Oliver will have seen the photo and confirm it is Tom Boston. They will wait a few hours and then be lead out to the sally ports in the rear, and brought here in unmarked cars. They'll come through the condo's service entrance in the rear. I am not at all convinced the Serbs know where I live. I'm pretty sure Joe and I shook off any tails, and I'm not big on leaving paper trails. Even if they know we're here, and even if they find out Oliver and Boston are here as well, what are they going to do? They want Boston alive. We can all agree if they wanted him dead, he wouldn't be walking around today."

"I told you, he thinks of everything," Sleepy Joe said.

"We don't have to worry about the General," Glenn explained. "He's constantly surrounded by armed men, and he's quite capable of defending himself as well. There's no way anyone gets to the General here in Bangkok. The problem is communicating with him, since for the time being we must presume his phone and any Wi-Fi network he uses were compromised by his contacts with these people. We'll communicate in a rather low-tech manner. We'll exchange written notes with him through the good services of the Lieutenant. He'll have his most trusted plainclothes officers disguised as gardeners, FedEx delivery, utilities, grocery deliveries, you name it, they'll get to him and pass the messages and return the written response. When the time comes for the General to join us, we should be able to sneak him out with one of these plainclothes covers."

"In fact, after that, the General and his men can watch out for us as well," Somchai said. "At this point, it's Boston these imposters are focusing on, not the General."

"Why didn't we just contact the police when this started?" Parhat asked.

"Who said anything about *the* police?" Sleepy Joe said. "We're talking about *our* police. Big difference."

"One more thing," Glenn added, "which should ease some of our fears of the three bad men in dark suits. When the officers drop off Oliver and the leader of the Serbian suits, they're taking two new passengers with them. That'll be Sleepy Joe and Major Parhat. Their assignment is to get Mr. Boston and bring him to a safe location. By any means necessary. I was thinking of one of the General's safe houses."

"No offense to you or to the General," Joe piped in. "But the last time we used one of the General's safe houses, the North Koreans found us and blew open the doors, killed one of the General's best men, and would have killed you if my sweet ex, Nahmwan, had not taught you how to use a pistol."

First time he's mentioned her in a long time, Glenn thought, then asked Joe if he had any other options.

"I've got a great hideout," he said. "I can keep him there until it's safe to bring him here to meet with all of us and Oliver. We'll just need the

General's or Lek's men to provide protection after he gets here, unless you want to waste me or Parhat babysitting a scientist."

Parhat sat up.

First nice thing he's ever said about me, he thought.

"Why don't we just have the police pick up Boston as well?" Parhat asked. "Seems like a lot less trouble."

"Maybe," Glenn replied. "But Tom Boston has information we don't want to share with anyone at this time, not even the Bangkok police. They're not all trustworthy and are easily bribed. There's a limit to how many completely trustworthy people even the Lieutenant can provide. I want Sleepy Joe to be present when we get Boston." Glenn saw the hurt look on Parhat's face and continued.

"With you at his side the entire time, of course." Parhat was satisfied with the addendum, but could not resist asking one more question.

"We're going to grab the leader of the bad guys, and Sleepy Joe and I will surely run into the Serb who is tailing Khun Tom. What about the third Serb?"

"We want the big man above all," Glenn said. "The other two probably don't know anything he can't tell us, though we'll eventually question all three. I fear Joe is going to have to take out the Serb who is tailing Boston. No doubt that guy springs to action the minute he suspects something is happening to Boston. Not that I am looking forward to violence."

"But I am!" Sleepy Joe yelled.

Nineteen

MAJOR PARHAT and Colonel Somchai sat on the couch in Glenn's living room, watching the news on CNN. Glenn and Sleepy Joe were out on the terrace. Glenn was enjoying one of his dwindling Romeo y Julietta 1875s, occasionally taking a hit off the fat joint Sleepy Joe rolled as they watched the early evening Bangkok traffic. Glenn did not call it rush hour, since to him, almost all Bangkok traffic was rush hour regardless of the hour. He did notice more horn-honking when people were driving home.

Watching traffic taught Glenn a great deal about the different strata of Bangkok society. The affluent sat in the back seat of imported cars as their drivers nudged their way through the morass. Those who had no car and driver but could afford taxis passed the time in lesser but air-conditioned comfort. The daring might own a small 125cc motorcycle or pay the equivalent of a dollar to be taken home at record-breaking speed by an orange-vested motorcycle taxi driver. For somewhat less money, there were the air conditioned BTS Skytrain and the underground MRT subway. They worked if one was going where there were stops, constantly being added. There were a few air-conditioned buses, which cost more than the inexpensive battered old gas-belchers which ward off heat prostration by removing windows and doors.

The poor rode those crudely ventilated buses or walked. Bangkok did not have the inexpensive *songtheaw*, pickup trucks with planks for seats lining the sides of the bed, widespread elsewhere in the Kingdom. The tuk-tuk, a motorcycle towing a passenger side car behind it, was a common person's transport in other parts of the country, but in the Green Belt of Bangkok, they existed to charge tourists outrageous prices, and hopefully drag them off to buy Chinese-made junk at inflated prices, with the tuk-tuk driver getting a kickback. When one of his Thai girlfriends took him to the Klong Toey market to buy fresh fish, Glenn learned there were often tuk-tuks in the Thai parts of the city used as normal transportation.

∽

"I'M GLAD to be getting out into action again," Sleepy Joe said while Glenn rotated his cigar a half inch above his lighter.

"Have to properly toast the foot before lighting," Glenn explained for the hundredth time. "Then rotate it a bit closer until it catches."

Joe knew his friend well enough to understand that the ritual was as enjoyable to Glenn as the occasional puffs of smoke he took and exhaled slowly after savoring their flavor in his mouth. Nevertheless, he was pleased to hear Glenn was winding down his cigar smoking days. It would mean more time for Glenn to smoke weed with him.

"I don't envy you having to nursemaid that brat of a Major," Glenn said as he exhaled his first puff of cigar smoke. "The General must have some reason for insisting he join us along with the Colonel, who, by the way, is a hell of a guy."

Sleepy Joe patted Glenn on the back.

"We've given the kid no quarter, and he's learned from what we said. My guess is the General sees something in Parhat, but knows he's a work in progress, a diamond that needs polishing, if you get my drift."

"Well, he didn't give me a lot of time to whip him into shape," Glenn said. "Believe me, I wasn't thrilled about sending him out with you. But let's be honest. We can't risk alienating the Colonel, who seems to have confidence in him. Somchai is a cross between Oliver, the man who can find out anything, and the General, a brave and wise warrior. You're going to need someone to help you, be a lookout, and call for backup if needed. And give this Parhat this much, he is smart, and a lot of the questions he asks make sense."

"I notice you didn't say he could help me in hand-to-hand," Joe said.

"That's what I'm afraid of," Glenn replied. "I know there's no reason to fear for you, but this guy's not even close to what you would need if things went bad."

Joe released a plume of marijuana smoke, weaker and thinner than the thicker rings and clouds Glenn exhaled every minute or so.

"Don't be too afraid," Joe said. "Parhat has mastered several martial arts, and he works out like a madman every day. Solid muscle, not a gram of fat. And he is an excellent marksman as well."

"You could tell all that just by sitting in a room with him for an hour?" Glenn asked.

"You're smoking the wrong stuff," Joe said. He gently pulled the cigar from Glenn's fingers and replaced it with the burning half joint in his own hand. "Of course I can tell that and more by just sizing him up. That's why I'm Sleepy Joe. Don't worry, I'll bring him back alive."

﹏

"Orders are orders," Colonel Somchai told Major Parhat when the latter asked if there was any way he could avoid working with Sleepy Joe. The Major suggested either Somchai replace the Australian, or Parhat go it alone.

"Both out of the question," Somchai said sternly. "I'm too old to fight men twice my size. And you've never done anything like this. You'll learn from Sleepy Joe, just as you say you are learning from Glenn."

"Khun Glenn is different," Parhat argued

"The General will be glad to hear this," Somchai said. "But he also likes Sleepy Joe."

"I don't think that's really the case," Parhat replied. "I wouldn't call their relationship one of affection. The General sees what Sleepy Joe is, and he has a constant need for such a person. No doubt This Sleepy Joe creature is very good at what he does, which appears to be killing people."

"That's part of your job as well," Somchai said. "And like your job, there's a lot more to what Sleepy Joe does. He is extremely intelligent and perceptive. That's really his secret weapon. That's what gives him such an incredible advantage in any close combat situation."

"He's a filthy, vile ganja addict," Parhat retorted.

"All of which makes him even more effective," Somchai said. "Scattered all around the globe you will find the graves of people who thought that's all he is."

"I'm not so sure that's how I want to be known," Parhat said.

"Probably not. But you won't mind being known as someone who is alive because of Sleepy Joe. If your life is ever in danger while with him, that's exactly how you will feel."

"Let's hope that is not my fate," Parhat snapped.

"Why not?" Somchai asked. "It seems rather auspicious to be one of the few people who could make such a claim. Probably means an even better life when you're reborn. Probably be Chief of Staff."

Parhat looked into the Colonel's eyes and locked with them for a brief moment.

"Hard to believe that any relationship with a farang like him could be seen as the kind of merit you're talking about. Who you associate with makes a big difference in this life and the next. With all due respect, Colonel, when it comes to matters of military intelligence, you're the best I know. But when it comes to the Dharma, I'll rely on my uncle, the head monk in a temple near Rayong."

"I know your uncle well," Somchai replied. "As you know, before he entered the *Sangha* he was a career military man. When he retired after twenty years, he changed his way of thinking and put on the robe. But he never disconnected from his old life. It was he, after all, who asked the General to use his pull to get you into the Academy. But don't feel bad. At least half your class got in the same way."

He has so much to learn, Somchai thought. *I truly hope he does.*

Twenty

PARHAT STRUGGLED to close the orange vest. Sleepy Joe had gone to the store just above On Nut that sold them to Bangkok's motorcycle taxis and asked for the biggest size. Major Parhat was taller and far more buff than any motorcycle taxi driver Glenn or Joe had ever seen. The goal of a motorcycle taxi driver was to deliver every passenger as quickly as possible, return to the designated stand, and pick up a new passenger if luck did not produce one along the way. The smaller and lighter the driver, the faster one could move, and it was easier to maneuver in the narrow lanes between the cars, trucks and buses the drivers weaved between as the often-terrified passenger hung on for dear life. With the vest closed and the helmet placed on his head, no prospective passenger would care or even notice that this one was out of place.

"You ready to duel these maniacs driving those big bruisers?" Sleepy Joe asked. He and Parhat were in the room Joe referred to as his "safe house."

"You're the first person I've ever brought here," Joe said. "The General doesn't even know it exists. Not even Glenn has been here."

"I'm honored to be placed on a level above even your closest friends," Parhat said.

"Don't be," Joe replied. "There's a lot of bad people who might be looking for me, and I would not want anyone I cared about to be present if they found me here."

When Joe saw the horrified look on Parhat's face, he quickly informed him he was only joking, and laughed. *For a Thai, he shows his hand way too easily.*

"Aussie humor. Ask the Colonel," Joe said. Parhat's horrified look evaporated.

Minutes later they were cruising down Rama IV, a busy commercial boulevard with constant traffic. Parhat drove, with Sleepy Joe as his pas-senger. As they turned down one of the odd numbered sois towards Sukhu-mvit, Joe shouted to Parhat.

"Get me there on time and there's a nice tip," he yelled.

If Colonel Somchai had not assured me this man is the kind of professional he dreamed of having when he was serving with military intelligence, I wouldn't consider working with him. Can anyone this crazy really be any good? Not that I had a choice.

Somchai's people had followed Tom Boston ever since the Colonel learned of him. They had a huge advantage over the lone Serbian thug tailing the American epidemiologist: they knew about the Serb, but he had no idea they existed.

The surveillance showed Boston was a creature of habit. Every morn-ing he left his hotel and walked a half-mile to the Amazon coffee shop on Thong Lor. Why he elected to pass dozens of coffee spots on the way remained unclear. The studied opinion of Somchai and Glenn was that there was nothing mysterious; Boston enjoyed killing time by walking the streets of Bangkok. Glenn explained to the two Thai army officers that when a farang first arrives in Thailand, they find everything amazing, and this includes street scenes Thais might not even notice.

"When does this feeling end?" Somchai asked.

"Never," Glenn replied. "The amazing thing about Thailand is that after many years here, it is still amazing."

∽

"He usually gets here around nine thirty," Sleepy Joe said when Parhat stopped the bike on a side soi a few blocks from the coffee shop. "I'm going to slowly walk there now. In four minutes, exactly four minutes, you leave this spot and pull up in front of Amazon. I mean right in front. Be ready to leave immediately and move as fast as you can."

Parhat nodded and looked at his army watch.

"Four minutes exactly," he said.

∽

Tom Boston was pleased with himself for choosing a hotel plan without breakfast. He didn't eat much in the morning, and making coffee in the hotel room was no way to start a day. He enjoyed the sights, sounds, and smells of the streets, and Amazon made a hell of a cup. He had enjoyed that morning's walk and anticipated the cappuccino he would enjoy momentarily.

He did not notice the large man in a dark suit trailing him from a quarter block away since he'd left his hotel room. Boston was unaware that this was the man's morning routine just as much as it was Boston's.

As Tom Boston was about to open the door to the coffee shop, he felt a tap on his shoulder. When he turned around, he saw a rail-thin man only a few inches taller than he. With his long stringy hair pulled into a ponytail and his worn jeans, the man looked like a refugee from Haight Ashbury circa 1967. Boston detected an odor he recognized as marijuana, which he'd last smoked as an undergraduate, but one never forgets the smell.

"You are Mr. Boston, the American epidemiologist?" the strange man asked in a soft tone that sounded like one of the nurses at Bangkok Hospital confirming she had approached the right patient. Boston went there for a checkup after his encounter on the Patpong sidewalk. There was no damage. The hippie's accent reminded him of Oliver's, but rougher and harder to understand.

"I am, but how do you know me?" Boston asked. He knew a coffee shop on Thong Lor was not the same as a bar in Patpong, but his dangerous encounter there made him wary.

The odd man smiled.
"I'm a friend of Oliver, my mate who saved your ass from some goons looking to rob or beat you, maybe both. Remember he said he'd contact you to get together? Well, this is it."

At that moment, a motorcycle taxi drove right onto the sidewalk, stopping a foot from Boston and Sleepy Joe.

"Hop aboard," Sleepy Joe told Boston in the same soft voice.
"Not until I find out a little more," the epidemiologist said, almost as softly as Joe.

"I said get on right now!" Joe said, in a voice that was definitely not soft like before. When Boston hesitated for a moment, Joe picked him up by the waist and hoisted him onto the back of Parhat's motorcycle. The moment the little American was securely seated, the big man in the dark suit approached. Joe recognized him as the Serb who was impersonating John Slater of the American company. When he was ten meters away, he started moving fast, in between a trot and a run. Parhat pulled away from the curb as Sleepy Joe blocked the big man from the motorcycle. Parhat edged the bike over the curb and, seeing a clear space of several car lengths, turned into traffic and roared away. The big man grabbed Joe by the neck of the

Grateul Dead T-shirt he wore. Joe could see he was not carrying a firearm. There were no bulges anywhere.

There was no indication the Serb recognized Joe rom the office meeting. It would not have mattered if he had, because as soon as the Serb was within arm reach, Joe grabbed the big man's hands and pushed them back hard enough so that it would be days before those wrists stopped hurting. The man screamed in pain. Joe delivered a right hook that caught him under the chin, and the Serb fell to the ground.

"You're only a watcher, so I'm letting you off easy," Joe yelled at the prone Serb. "Consider yourself very lucky."

A small crowd had gathered around the men, and several patrons spilled out o the coffee shop. Joe did not run away. Instead, he walked right through the knot o people, with the look o confidence worn by a man who has just totally disabled an opponent twice his size and was now walking among people shorter than he.

Joe walked off the sidewalk, onto busy Thong Lor. Traffic was moving and the light at the intersection with Sukhumvit was green. Joe ran to a cab that was picking up a passenger, a Thai businessman, and followed the man into the back seat.

The driver said something in Thai, which Joe did not understand. The businessman spoke in English, telling Joe he had the cab first.

"Well, now we've both got it," Joe said. "I'm going the same place you are, and I'll be happy to pay. Big tip," he said loudly, which the driver understood. The businessman nodded his assent, and the driver managed to make the light. Two blocks later, when they were stopped at another light, Joe pulled a five hundred baht note rom his pocket, tossed it onto the ront seat, and left the taxi.

"*Khob khun khrup,*" the driver yelled as Joe scurried off.

"I can never understand these crazy farang," the businessman told the cab driver. "But they are good for the economy," he said.

∼

Tom Boston didn't say a word the entire ten minutes of the breakneck-speed ride. Most of the time he had his eyes closed so he wouldn't have to see how close he was to huge buses and trucks as Parhat weaved through traffic. When the ride ended, and they were in front of Sleepy Joe's safe house, Boston asked the Major if he really was a motorcycle taxi driver.

"No," the Major replied, "but when I was in the Academy, they sent me to a course on defensive motorcycle driving."

"I assume you got an A," Boston said.

The Major patted Boston on the back as they entered the lobby of the building, using the key Joe had provided.

"Flattery will get you everything," the Major said. "Isn't that an American saying?"

"It's actually 'flattery will get you *everywhere*,' but the sentiment is the same, and any American would know exactly what you mean. Don't worry. By the way, your English is excellent. You speak like an American."

"Flattery will indeed get you everywhere," the Major replied.

∼

Sleepy Joe opened the door for Parhat and Boston. On the outside, it looked like any other wooden door in the city. Inside it was a thick steel door with multiple locks. The room was small, but had a bathroom, a tiny kitchen, a big screen television taking up half of one wall, a couch, and a bed and nightstand nestled in a corner.

"Let me show you the best part," Joe told Parhat when he saw him taking in the room. He punched in numbers on a combination lock and opened the closet door. Inside was a rung ladder on a wall. The door was also steel from the inside.

"We're on the top floor for a reason," Joe explained. "If anyone starts banging on the front door, this gives me an extra few minutes to get up on the roof, and I have a camera that lets me know if by any chance they have anyone up there."

"What would you do if there were?" Parhat asked.

"If there were three or less, I'd go and kill them with my bare hands. Otherwise, I'd grab this machine gun and mow them down," he said, pointing to a weapon hanging on the wall. "Though I prefer to use my hands. I really don't like blood and gore. I'm a sensitive guy in that way."

This farang *is very crazy,* Parhat thought. *But he is good. Now I understand what the Colonel meant when he said I'd learn from him. He's still a madman, but like he himself said about the police helping us, he's our madman.*

"This is quite a place," the Major said, his admiration clear in his voice.

"Enjoy it for now," Joe replied. "We have to consider it compromised now."

"Why?" Parhat asked. "We were not followed."

Sleepy Joe sat down on one end of the bed and motioned for Boston to sit on the other end and for Parhat to pull over the chair in the kitchen.

"I believe our American friend can confirm my history. Wasn't it Benjamin Franklin who said that three people can keep a secret if two of them are dead?"

"That's correct," Boston said.

"Well, I'm sure none of us wants to be those two unfortunate bastards. As I see it, the only option is to end the secret and find a new safe house."

Parhat absorbed every word Joe said.

Amazing. A man in his line of work needs a place to hide, and this is perfect. Yet he gives it up when Glenn asks him and because it involves the General. I know Glenn is a farang *with honor, and this is his best friend. Perhaps a violent* farang *psycho can also be a man of honor. Okay my Colonel, I am learning.*

Tom Boston became more animated as the shock of his mystery ride wore off.

"I thought I was meeting Oliver," he said.

"Sorry to disappoint you," Sleepy Joe said. "I'm Sleepy Joe, Oliver's mate and a fellow Aussie. Oliver sends his regards and will see you not too long from now. I mentioned his name so you would understand we were friends, not people to fear."

"I believed you since I had no choice," Boston said.

"The scientific method at work," Joe said.

Twenty-One

OLIVER KNEW his dear friend Glenn would never believe him, but the truth was his favorite massages did not end in orgasm. With a live-in girlfriend, a mia noi, and at least two *giks*, more casual relationships than the first two, these days Oliver had little need to seek out sexual release in dark and dingy upstairs massage cubicles. To the contrary, Oliver almost always sought out the best masseuses, and his favorite in Bangkok was a fancy spa one hundred meters off the corner of Sukhumvit and Thong Lor. A patron began the session by alternating between shower and sauna, and then when softened and relaxed, was taken to a private room where an experienced masseuse brought relief to every muscle and tendon in the big Aussie's body. Oliver liked the aromatherapy massage, the scents of Thai herbs affording an extra layer of relaxation and soothing.

An hour and a half later, Oliver handed his masseuse an outsized tip; as Glenn was prone to say, everything Oliver did was outsized. Glenn, being American, strongly approved of large tips, something Europeans and Asians, especially Thais, deemed foolish, frivolous, and unwise. Oliver and his friend Glenn were secure in the knowledge that whatever epithets an angry Thai might someday hurl at them, "Cheap Charlie" would never be among them. While this was one of the very worst names a farang could be called, when it came to tipping there were no cheaper people than the Thais, otherwise among the most generous people on earth. As the confused or exasperated farang expats say, "This is Thailand," usually shortened to "T.I.T."

Oliver walked to the corner and crossed Thong Lor. A few meters up on that other side was the best mango stand in Thailand. Whatever the variety, they were larger and healthier looking than other mangoes anywhere, even the super-expensive grocery stores near the Embassies. Oliver was a mango aficionado, almost as serious about this fruit as Glenn was about coffee. (And for a few more weeks, cigars as well. Sadly, the mango season in Thailand ran from March through July, and this being the middle of December, the selection, largely imports, would never meet his standards, not even at this stand. He decided to walk home instead.

The traffic light at the intersection of Sukhumvit and Thong Lor took an eternity to turn green, but Oliver was not about to join the small throng of nimble Thais who chanced the oncoming traffic when the light was still red. *If a Thai driver hits a farang, even when the* farang *is in the right, that poor sucker gets hit with the repair bill to the driver's car. And probably has to bribe the cops so they don't file a phony charge against the unlucky farang.* Oliver knew of instances where the police had gone directly to the hospital, hoping to extort the injured party while they were weak and hopefully drugged. *Good thing we have Lek's cousin to protect us against these thugs.* Oliver did not openly laugh at his own thoughts, but enjoyed an internal chuckle. *In Australia, we call upon the police to protect us from criminal thugs. Here, the criminal thugs sometimes are police. I love it here anyway. And actually, there's little crime, aside from touts pulling scams and cops wanting bribes.*

At that very moment, a police car with a siren blazing forced its way between the cars waiting for the light. When the police car was not more than ten meters from Oliver, a uniformed officer emerged from the front passenger side and strode towards him. Oliver recognized Lek's cousin, the Lieutenant. The look on his face was officious and stern. When he was within a meter of Oliver, all Thais had cleared from the sight of the intent-looking officer moving towards them.

"Make like I'm taking you into custody," the Lieutenant whispered in the Isan dialect, in case any of the handful of farangs lingering nearby understood standard Thai. Thai people would never interfere with a cop arresting a farang. "I'll make like I don't understand English very well."

That shouldn't be too difficult for you, Oliver thought. He then uttered a few vague protestations in a voice that went from annoyed to frightened, as he called out "What are you doing?" followed by "I want to call my embassy." He complied with the Lieutenant's gesture to place his hands behind his back. The cuffs were set so loosely that Oliver could have pulled even his thick wrists through the loops.

When they were inside the car, the cuffs were removed by the cop in the rear seat and the Lieutenant told Oliver of the plan, this time speaking regular Thai. "We've got a nice lunch waiting for you, with a pint of cold Foster's. Regardless of what you may have heard, we treat our prisoners very well." The driver and the other officer in the back seat laughed when they heard this.

～

OLIVER ENJOYED the Japanese bento box Lek's cousin had waiting for him when they reached the station. Oliver ate at the Lieutenant's desk while he left to pick up the leader of the three Serbs, the Alfred Elspeth imposter. Oliver learned over the years that Thais and farangs had long ago agreed that Japanese was the happy medium that each could enjoy. Oliver was no exception, and he devoured pieces of sushi and chicken teriyaki between slugs of beer.

"I don't have to worry about you sneaking a look at anything on my desk," the Lieutenant said as he left the office. "You're Oliver. You can find out anything you want."

We'll see, Oliver thought as the Lieutenant closed the door behind him.

∽

WHILE OLIVER enjoyed his Bento box, the Lieutenant and his most trusted sergeant and corporal battled traffic on Soi 49. The plainclothes officer posted outside the Serbs' condo called and informed Lek's cousin that the leader had not left the apartment.

"Do we just wait until this farang feels like leaving?" the sergeant asked. "What happens if he sleeps until dawn, like so many of these people?"

"Don't worry," the Lieutenant replied. "We thought of that. Or should I say Khun Glenn thought of it."

The police car was two blocks from the condo when the plainclothes officer entered the lobby and spoke to one of three employees behind the desk. The officer had long ago developed an ability to sense who was in charge in any situation. No doubt it was the middle-aged man in a suit, not either of the two very attractive young women. The plainclothes officer explained he was from the Bangkok Safety Department and was investigating a report of a leak in one of the apartments, which happened to be the unit occupied by the Serbs.

The unctuous Thai man in charge looked at the plainclothes officer as if he were a stain on the floor requiring a mop and bucket. He identified himself to the plainclothes officer as the concierge.

"I would have been notified of such a problem," the man told the officer. "I'm not familiar with your agency. May I see some identification, please?"

The undercover officer flashed his badge.

"I hope you don't insist upon seeing my gun as well," the officer said. "Because then I'd have to shoot you. Now you and I are going upstairs, and if anyone is home, you are going to introduce me as a public safety technician investigating a gas leak. Am I clear?"

Minutes later the two men stood before the door of the Serbs' apartment. The chastened concierge rang the doorbell and called out his name and title as ordered. The officer heard heavy steps which grew stronger as they approached. A loud, American-accented voice asked who was there, his anger clear. The concierge explained the reason for the visit.

"Come back later," the voice yelled through the closed door.

The undercover officer knew enough English to understand. He told the concierge to inform the tenant that Thai law allowed a public safety technician to enter with or without permission when danger was imminent. There was a pause, and then several loud clicks emanated from the door as the locks were undone. The door opened and the two Thais faced a six-foot-three-inch farang wearing a T-shirt showing off his huge biceps and chest. It was the make-believe Alfred Elspeth, same man in the photo the Lieutenant had shown the undercover officer.

"I smell no gas," the big man said without attempting to hide his annoyance. "You must have the wrong apartment." The Serb watched intently as the alleged safety officer reached into his coat pocket. *Probably going to show me some document in Thai which I won't be able to read.*

"Afraid not," the undercover officer said as he fired his taser at the big man's chest.

When Lek's Lieutenant cousin and his colleagues reached the building, they were greeted by the ashen-faced concierge, who followed the undercover officer's instructions and brought them up to the Serbs' apartment. The Serb was lying on the floor, handcuffed, legs tied with a piece of rope. A gag permitted only the faintest, most muffled sounds to emanate from his mouth.

The Lieutenant nodded at the undercover officer.

"Good work," he told his colleague. "Take the rest of the day off." He looked at the corporal and sergeant, who pulled the big man up by his armpits. When he began to struggle, the corporal smacked him in the head loud enough to shock the concierge. They dragged him out of the apartment, dressed only in his T-shirt and workout pants. When they were gone, the Lieutenant spoke to the concierge, who was sweating and mumbling.

"If anyone asks, you tell them this farang was arrested for financial fraud. This apartment remains sealed to all except me and anyone I authorize. We'll let you know when you can put it back on the rental market." He told the man to call him if anyone tried to enter the unit. He handed his card to the concierge, and then showed a photo of the third Serbian, the only one they hadn't encountered.

"If this farang shows up, call me at once," he said. The Lieutenant was not worried about the fake John Slater, the one that Sleepy Joe disabled on Thong Lor; the Lieutenant had him followed after Joe bent back his wrists and fractured his jaw. The man was currently recuperating in a small private hospital which provided excellent care and didn't ask many questions. He wasn't badly injured; his wrists would be fine in a few days, and the jaw fracture was not large. One of the orderlies was the Lieutenant's informant, and a nearby police station could have backup there in minutes if he tried to leave.

～

No Bento box or private office awaited the big Serb at the little substation on the far edge of Bangkok. The taser wore off and he was fully conscious. He was handcuffed and manacled at the waist, free to use the toilet that constituted the only fixture in the small cell, aside from the weak bare bulb dangling from the ceiling. There being no furniture, the big man was forced to either stand or sit on the filthy floor. He sat and leaned against the wall, only his rump and his upturned heels touching the floor. His toes pointed upward at a slight angle. He had been in the game a long time, but he couldn't understand his situation. He had no idea why Thai police would care about him tailing an American suspected of embezzling from his employer back home.

Whoever it is that sent these cops, it's certain it wasn't that little thief from California, he thought. *Maybe he's not the nerd we thought.*

The cell door opened. Four Thai uniforms entered. One of them pulled a hood over his head. Less than a minute later, he was most unceremoniously tossed into the backseat of a police car which promptly pulled away and snaked its way through traffic.

Twenty-Two

WHEN GLENN learned Boston's tail was disabled and under surveillance and the second Serb, who he believed the leader was captured, he decided it was safe to allow Oliver to roam about freely, especially since Sleepy Joe, finished with his first assignment, was free to guard his fellow Australian.

"A pleasure to be working with a man who will take the occasional toke with me," Joe told Glenn.

"*Occasional?*" Glenn asked with exaggerated surprise. Oliver was not a ganja smoker on the level of Glenn or Joe but was a reliable toker.

The concierge at Soi 49 was waiting for them when Oliver and Joe arrived. Lek's cousin had called him and emphasized the importance of cooperation.

"These are not regular farangs," the Lieutenant explained. "They live here, they understand us really well, and have some powerful Thai friends. And they are my good friends. You would not want me to hear any complaints about lack of cooperation."

"I assure you there will be none," the concierge croaked.

The concierge used his key to admit the two Aussies into the apartment. They told him to wait outside until they were done, and if anyone tried to enter, get away as quickly as possible.

When the door was closed, Oliver looked around and took a deep breath.

"I was beginning to wonder if we'd ever get this far," he confessed. "After the way I almost blew it."

"You're doing a good job right now," Joe said. "After a somewhat shaky start, I might add. For a lot of us as well. But right now we're doing fine. We know who the bad guys are, and we know who they are looking for, and unless we are missing something, it has to do with Boston looking into the virus. What we don't know is just who they are working for, or if it is a foreign government, as Glenn, the brains of our group, seems to think. There is no evidence pointing to anyone thus far. These guys, who terribly botched posing as American businessmen, and gave us our first opening in the case, can't be the brains of the operation. You and Glenn are going to figure everything out, and the General and me will take care of the bad guys. With a little help from our local police, of course."

"Thanks for the vote of confidence," Oliver said. "There were times I felt like I was losing my edge."

"When that happens," Sleepy Joe said, "it is absolutely imperative that you have a hit." He passed his joint to Oliver, who took one long draw and blew the smoke up towards the ceiling.

"Sometimes you come up with the best solutions," he said.

"I've got another good idea," Joe said. "While you ransack this apartment, I'll make myself comfortable on the sofa and see if there's anything good on cable."

Oliver said he thought that was a fine idea. He handed what was left of the joint to Joe and started his search. The apartment came furnished, and Oliver saw no sign that the tenants had added any personal touches. He methodically searched all cabinets and drawers, pulled off bedsheets and couch covers, and looked under every chair, in every container of salt, sugar, and coffee. While Oliver worked, Sleepy Joe made himself comfortable on a couch Oliver had searched, turned on the television, and lit another joint. Joe didn't like the twenty-four-hour racing channel that came on when he powered up the set, so he began flipping through the channels. It was the usual set of channels a farang is afforded in the better rentals: CNN, BBC, Sky, HBO, Showtime, and all the Thai soap operas and *American Idol* knockoffs a farang would ever need.

∽

JOE WAS at home with any set of television controls on earth. He was soon scanning channels, hoping for a good movie or decent music. He zipped through channels of no interest. Halfway through, the guide grid turned into a black screen with bright blue writing. Joe didn't understand the words because they were in an Asian language. Looked more like Chinese than Thai, of that Joe was sure. He called Oliver. The minute the big Aussie saw the screen, his eyes opened wide despite Sleepy Joe's weed.

"This is not right," he said. "I'm certain it's Chinese." He took a picture of the television screen with his camera.

"I think it's safe to send this to the General," Oliver said. "Our devices and networks were swept, cleaned, and secured better than ever. We have to know what this says."

"I didn't know the General can read Chinese," Joe said.
"He's got one Chinese grandparent on each side, and his parents grew up with a lot of the culture. He told me on more than one occasion how he went to a special Chinese school after regular school a few days a week. That must be where he learned how to read this gibberish. I'm glad he did.

Once the General figures out what this is, he'll tell Glenn, and those two will get to the bottom of this. With my help, of course."

Sleepy Joe was surprised at this piece of the General's family history.

"I never knew the General was part Chinese. He never mentioned any of that to me."

"Haven't you ever heard him say that he has Chinese blood himself but still can't stand the Chinese?" Oliver asked. "If I had an Aussie dollar for every time I've heard him say that, I'd be almost as rich as him. Of course, no doubt he is referring to those hordes from the People's Republic. I know for a fact the General holds in the highest of regard the Chinese people of Singapore, Taiwan, and just about every country except Vietnam and Communist China. Thai and Chinese-Australians are on the good list, needless to say."

"If the General ever said that when I was around, I wasn't paying attention," Sleepy Joe said. "Unless he specifically demands my attention, I'm never listening to what he is talking about."

I don't believe that for a minute, Oliver thought.

～

FIFTEEN MINUTES after Oliver sent the screenshot of the television to the General, the nervous concierge called to inform him that the man himself was on the way up to his apartment. Oliver immediately knew that if the General was casting any remaining caution to the wind, this screenshot must be important, and said so to Sleepy Joe.

"He may take comfort knowing we've disabled one Serb and snatched another," Joe noted. "Now we've made it into their lair and discovered their connection to a foreign government, as Glenn predicted. He should feel safer."

"It's their instructions," the General told Oliver and Joe the instant he was in the Serbs' apartment and the door closed behind him, his bodyguard behind him with an assault rifle. "Telling them that the mission is over, close everything and go to wherever they're supposed to hide when things go bad. They surely know by now that Boston and the big guy are in someone's custody and this Slater imposter is in the hospital. "

Oliver explained he had completed his search and said there was nothing else of value in the apartment.

"Let's go to Glenn's and speak with Dr. Boston," Oliver said. "After that, Sleepy Joe will question the big Serb."

The concierge was most relieved when he saw the three men leave his building.

∽

TOM BOSTON and Glenn sat at the dining table drinking coffee. Lek's cousin stood by the door and would decide who got to enter. Several plainclothes officers were outside the building, on the roof, and on random floors.

"I can assure you that Oliver's questions will be directed solely at your expertise," Glenn said. "He needs for you to put everything in some sort of order so he can pass it along to his experts."

"I thought I was his expert," Boston said.

"Oh, you are indeed," Glenn said. "There are different kinds of experts. What you say may help other experts to take whatever steps are needed. It all starts with you."

There was a loud knock on the door. Glenn heard Oliver speaking Thai, so loud that his voice passed through the thick door. The Lieutenant welcomed him into Glenn's apartment. The General and Sleepy Joe were right behind Oliver.

Boston smiled when he saw the man who saved him on the streets of Patpong.

"Your chance to return the favor," Oliver said.

Oliver told Boston he was to dictate a voice memo that detailed everything he had learned about the mysterious virus, and in chronological order. He was to mention everything he had picked up from his talks with local epidemiologists and from any other sources. The recording would be sent to people in the Thai, Australian, and American governments, people Oliver could trust to keep the information confidential for the present. Boston would explain the tape's contents to the others in plain English after it was sent off.

Oliver turned on the voice memo feature on his phone and set it on the table. Boston began to speak and kept going for fifteen minutes. He mostly spoke in scientific terms, numbers, and references to events which were unintelligible to all but an epidemiologist. When Boston was done, Sleepy Joe asked if he wanted to smoke weed.

"No thanks," Boston said. "I never use drugs."

"That's a shame," Sleepy Joe said. "You really ought to give it a try. It's a lot safer than hanging out in rip-off whorehouses."

"We need to keep his mind clear so he can do as Oliver said and explain that stuff he just said. I didn't understand a word of it," Glenn said.

"My peers would be sorely disappointed if you did," Boston said. "Let me try to tell you what it means in ordinary English."

The four men sat in silence as Tom Boston explained that all indications were that a new strain of virus had emerged from Wuhan, China. It was almost certainly a variation of the SARS virus.

"That's sort of good," Boston explained, when he saw the look that the mention of SARS brought to the faces of his audience. "It means we have understanding and experience." He continued, telling them that the information he gleaned was not corroborated because it was impossible to obtain a single lab report or any other document from China.

"Don't they have to cooperate with the World Health Organization on something like this?" Glenn asked. "I remember them being involved with SARS."

"Word is that WHO is either being manipulated, stonewalled, or co-opted," Boston said. "My guess is stonewalled and ashamed to admit it."

Boston then said that the virus seemed to attack the respiratory system, based on scarce anecdotal evidence passed on surreptitiously from Wuhan.

"Internet and cell phone service have been restricted, so getting a real handle on what's going on is almost impossible."

"Doesn't that tell us the communists think they have a real problem on their hands?" the General asked. "If they got it under control quickly, they'd be bragging about it. When they screw up or can't fix a problem, they either lie or say nothing."

"In that case, we are waiting for the lies," Boston said.

OLIVER SENT Boston's voice memo to his contacts in the Thai government's forensic lab, used for law enforcement and public health, and then to his contacts in Australia and America. He sent a copy to Colonel Somchai, who would see that Thai military intelligence experts on biological warfare took a look. "Maybe they've come across something similar in their work," he said. Glenn frowned and shook his head.

"In their work," he said, in a failed attempt to mimic Oliver's Aussie ac-

cent. "The things some people have to do to get by."

"I'm with Glenn," Sleepy Joe said. "Killing people with germs is cheating."

Oliver explained to Boston that for the time being, he himself was done with his questions, but Sleepy Joe had a few.

"Don't mind his scraggly appearance," Oliver told Boston. "He's Australian, meaning he's okay."

Boston nodded.

Joe showed the epidemiologist the photos of the three Serbs. Boston did not recognize any.

"Either they're better at surveillance than they might seem, or you aren't thinking about being tailed. You were not out of their sight for a second until we rescued you."

"Rescued me from what?" Boston asked.

"Well, mate, or should I call you Doctor?" Joe said. "Our General tells us these three were working for China. You're here to find out what is going on in that country, and it seems China is not interested in anyone knowing the truth. What do you think these fellows had in mind? Think of what almost happened to you over a bar bill. Imagine what might happen if you got on the wrong side of a bunch of commies."

Oliver interrupted. "Excuse me, Joe, but may I pose one additional question to our friend? Something just came to mind."

"Go ahead, mate," Joe said.

Oliver posed his question. "Dr. Boston, if distinguished scientists like you and your colleagues at your institute were convinced there was a potential danger from this virus in China, why didn't you take your concerns to your government? America is in the World Health Organization, and you have your own rather powerful Center for Disease Control and National Institute of Health. Not to mention you have the CIA to gather intelligence. So, no offense Dr. Boston, but why send a research scientist with no intelligence skills and no familiarity with this part of the world?"

Boston looked at the faces of the four men around the table. *They all want to know the answer to that one.* "I knew sooner or later I'd have to address this," he said. "So please listen carefully, and take what I'm saying as a scientist's analysis, and nothing more.

"You gentlemen must understand that America right now is not always the same America you knew before our current president took office. He's dead set against any international cooperation except with Russia. Even worse, science is looked upon mostly with disfavor, and decisions that should be science-based do not even take science or medicine into account."

Oliver listened to every word. "Dr. Boston, is this really the case, or are you another left-wing Democrat like our friend Glenn here? Not that I have anything against these people, except their ideas. I still love Glenn."

"No politics here," Boston replied. "Just giving you the facts. There was a White House Pandemic Response Team set up during the Obama Administration, but May of last year President Trump disbanded it. We also had an epidemiologist from our Center for Disease Control embedded in the Chinese equivalent, but just this July, President Trump eliminated the position. As a result, we're operating in the dark. Information and data are the epidemiologist's greatest tools, and when it comes to viruses from China, where so many emanate, we're now operating in total darkness."

"This is your president doing this to you?" Major Parhat asked.

"As I said, we scientists are disfavored by this current administration,"

Boston continued, a clear trace of anger in his voice. "We can't get him to admit climate change is real. Even more distressing, like politicians anywhere, our current president is going to weigh the economic impacts of the public being aware of a potential pandemic. Epidemiologists would be compelled to recommend certain precautions and restrictions to contain the spread. Some economic activities will necessarily be impacted, some possibly shut down completely until the threat ends. This president is up for reelection this coming new year. He probably doesn't want to run when the economy is slowing down and restrictions are imposed on the public, even if those are the right and necessary steps."

"You mean he'd rather risk people dying of this virus you're talking about?" the General asked. "I cannot believe any American president would ever feel that way."

"Up until January 20, 2017, I'd have agreed with you fully," Boston said. "But from what I can see, this guy does not care at all about human life. My specialty is epidemiology, not psychiatry or psychology, but nevertheless, I have no issue calling him unstable and without any morals whatsoever."

"And that's of course purely scientific, and not political," Oliver said. He smiled to show Boston he was not upset.

"If I've said anything that's incorrect, please inform me," Boston replied. "You're the answer man, so surely you'll correct me if I'm wrong. We'll take your silence as confirmation of my facts."

A man after my own heart, Glenn thought.

And Oliver remained silent.

Twenty-Three

"Our large and menacing Serbian friend will be here in minutes," Glenn told the others after he read the text from Parhat. He told Tom Boston to go to the guest bedroom and remain there until further notice.

The man calling himself Alfred Elspeth was brought into the apartment by Colonel Somchai and Major Parhat, and two rifle-toting soldiers. His hands were still cuffed and his legs manacled. He wore the undergarments he had on when apprehended.

"Must have created quite a stir in the lobby and in the elevator," Sleepy Joe said.

"We took the service entrance and elevator," Parhat replied. When the Serb was close to the table, Parhat pointed to a chair and ordered the big man to sit.

"I assumed you've already questioned him," Glenn said to Parhat.

"We have not," the Major replied. "The Colonel and I agree that it would be more productive if you interrogated him with Oliver's assistance. Your background as a lawyer is well suited for this."

"Isn't the Colonel's background as a military intelligence officer even better suited?" Glenn asked.

Colonel Somchai responded. "It is that very experience that tells me a farang with your brains is going to have better luck with this farang than the Major and I could hope for. My specialty was with terrorists and spies. Yours is with gangsters and thugs. Far more suitable."

Glenn nodded. "Unshackle him."

Parhat stared at Glenn.

"Khun Glenn, this is a very dangerous man."

"And I've got a police officer and four soldiers to protect me if he tries anything, just in case Sleepy Joe hasn't killed him first. This is my call, isn't it?" He asked the Colonel to arrange for clothing to be brought to the big Serb, and if they couldn't find anything to fit him, Oliver's wardrobe surely contained large enough items. The condo on Soi 49 remained off-limits until the investigation was complete.

Colonel Somchai said something in Thai. One of the rifle-toting soldiers handed the weapon to Parhat while he used a key to free the big man from his restraints. The other soldier pointed his rifle at the man's head.

"Do you prefer Mr. Elspeth, or may I call you Alfred?" Glenn asked the man when he was unshackled, referring to the name of the American executive this mysterious man had appropriated and used on an American passport. "Or are you going to tell me your real name?"

"Why does that matter?" the man asked.

"Because we want to see if it's one of the names on the list of war crime indictments over at the International Criminal Court," Sleepy Joe shouted. "First you murder men, women, and children, now you're trying to stop scientists from finding out if there's a deadly new virus out there. And who are you doing this for? The damn Chinese government!"

The big man scanned Sleepy Joe from head to toe.

"You were with Glenn at the office. I almost didn't recognize you without your suit. But I have no idea what you're talking about. There's no scientists and no Chinese involved here. My associate and I were hired to tail an embezzler. He stole millions of dollars from friends who thought they were investing in a hedge fund guaranteed to return huge profits. An investment firm hired us to follow him around Bangkok for a few weeks and report back to them regularly. No danger, no violence. We're not even armed."

"You still haven't told me your name, or why you used someone else's to enter this country," Glenn said.

The man sighed.

"I guess there's no harm in telling you what you're bound to find out anyway. My birth name is Mikhail Gordanovich. I haven't used it in at least thirty years. I've used a lot of different names in a lot of different places, but the few people who know me, really know me, use the name Mick Gordon. Feel free to use that one. And call me Mick if you like."

"Thank you, Mick," Glenn said. "We're off to a good start. You still have to tell me about the stolen name and the passport."

"We were given the passports for this job and told that if we were ever discovered, to claim that we were American executives here on business. Once we got here and saw we liked it, we decided to try and stay. My friend and I are tired of roaming the world, collecting a paycheck and then moving on before we can even enjoy the money. Not to mention that following a little American around Bangkok is a lot less dangerous than being in a firefight. We spent years protecting bad guys and hoping no other bad guys attacked them while we were on the job. It was me who figured out we should try to make some connections, and security and investigations seemed like something for us. It's not hard to hear things in Bangkok. Just hang out in bars. I picked up some talk about the General's business, so we targeted that, hoping to buy or work with a Thai security firm. My friend and I have some money saved up, and things aren't that expensive around here. Good idea, but I guess we didn't know what we were doing. Look how it worked out."

Glenn stopped Mick before he could continue rambling on.

"Something strikes me as odd," Glenn said. "You keep talking about your 'friend' in the singular. But there are three of you. One is in the hospital and one is still on the loose. Tell us about him and how we can find this missing Serb." Glenn showed Mick the photo of the man Sleepy Joe had disabled, who used the John Slater passport, and a photo of the missing man, who was going by the name Henry Weller. Mick said that the man they knew as Slater had been calling himself Anthony Harper for many years. "Just call him Harper," he said.

"What about the third guy?" Glenn asked. "What name does he really go by? Hopefully not a difficult Serbian name."

Mick let out a short but loud laugh.

"First of all, he is not a Serb. He doesn't speak our language and he's nothing at all like us. He's from the company that hired us on behalf of the law firm. He doesn't stay at the apartment with us, just comes by to see how things are going. He handles all the finances for this job, including our final payments. Hope you find him because we're owed some money. I don't know what name he has on his passport, but we've always known him as William Flanders."

Glenn continued questioning Mick. The big man said he didn't have any idea that China was involved and had no knowledge of the mysterious Chinese message on the television screen.

I believe him even though I shouldn't.

"Was it this fellow Flanders who got you the American passports?" Glenn asked.

"Indeed," Mick replied. "And he flew here with us. From Florida."

"What were you and your friend doing in America? I thought you were Serbian war criminals hiding out in Australia. And I'd also like to know how it is that you speak American English without any trace of a foreign accent?"

Mick scowled at Glenn.

"I told you that is total bullshit!" he yelled. "I don't know where you got that from. I spent a few months in Australia earlier this year, and that's it. We thought the Serb community there would accept us since they were living in a democracy. But the old guard has people everywhere, and it wasn't safe for us. As for being a war criminal, if you did any checking, you'd find out that when we learned what was happening in Srebrenica, Harper and I told our own men not to take part and in fact to leave the area. Most of them did. When we joined that paramilitary group, we were told we were fighting to save Serbian Christians from Muslim terrorists. That was of course a lie. I received a request to send some of my men to join the main force surrounding Srebrenica. I didn't like the idea of having fewer men to defend our own position, so I sent out two men to assess the situation first and then decide whether I would send any fighters."

Major Parhat interjected. "Did you have the authority to disregard the orders of a superior officer? I'm assuming that's who made the request. At that point you didn't know war crimes were being committed."

This Serb and this Thai speak far clearer English than Sleepy Joe or Oliver, Glenn thought.

Mick explained how things worked back then. "That is a good point, Major. I hope you can appreciate that we are not talking about real armies, like the one you serve in. Anyone could form a militia back then. So long as one had weapons and a desire to kill Croatians, Bosnians, and Albanians, there was a place at the table. We were all in charge of ourselves, but everyone took orders from Milošević, who was totally in charge then, and he had ways to make his wishes known. He had people everywhere and knew everything going on in Srebrenica while it was happening.

"My scouts returned, and when they told me what was happening in Srebinica, I gave orders to disband and leave. Most did, but sad to say, several went to join the murderers. There was no way we were going help murder innocent civilians. I saw it was all lies I'd been told and that we were the ones doing the killing. I signed up to be a soldier, not a murderer. Harper and I have been lucky since we left the Balkans. We've been able to make a living and stay out of the way of some really pissed off Serbians."

Glenn looked at Oliver.

"Can we check this out?" he asked. "All we were told by the Aussies was that this guy was in their country hanging around with some bad guys. He's given us an explanation that could very well be true."

"Give me fifteen minutes," he said. "I'll be on the balcony making some calls."

∼

WHILE OLIVER did his due diligence, Glenn continued probing Mick. "Tell me how you and your friend happened to be in America and how you were hired for this job in Bangkok."

"Flanders met us in Australia, said he was a Serbian who immigrated to America and changed his name. We didn't believe he was Serbian. He didn't speak the language. We didn't believe he was an American either, but we were being paid a lot of money, so we didn't think about it all that much."

"Why didn't you believe him?" Glenn asked.

"A lot of reasons," Mick said. "For starters, he had a trace of some foreign accent, definitely not Serbian. The few times when I tried to talk to him about American sports, baseball, football, he knew almost nothing. When Harper and I spoke about our favorite television shows from when we were growing up, in America and Serbia, Flanders gave us blank looks. We're pretty certain whoever he is, he's not an American or a Serb. But in our line of work it is not unusual for people who hire us to be completely deceptive about their background. As long as they paid us, we didn't care."

"You aren't American," Glenn said. "Yet you could pass for one any time. You speak just like any of us Yanks, and from what you're saying, you know all about our sports and our popular culture. How did you learn all of this?"

"Same way you did," Mick replied. "It's called growing up in America."

꩜

MICK'S PARENTS were Serbs who didn't care much for Marshall Tito or communism, and when his biologist father was awarded a two-year fellowship in post graduate work in America, twelve-year-old Mick and his family moved to Arizona in 1985. When the two years were up, they disregarded Yugoslavia's insistence they return home, and spent four happy years on visa extensions. By 1991, Yugoslavia ceased to exist, and the family returned to the newly independent nation of Serbia with great hopes.

"I don't think anyone except Tito ever believed there was such a thing as Yugoslavia or Yugoslavians," Mick said. "But we definitely considered ourselves Serbs.

"I was eighteen when we returned," Mick explained. "I felt thoroughly American, but a few months after returning, like all other Serbs, I was caught up in the thrill of independence and nationalism. I wanted to enroll in university, but after six years in America, my Serbian was not good enough. In America, I was a kid who insisted on speaking English when my parents spoke to me in Serbian. Funny how English speakers are surprised that it's not my first language, while Serbs are forever asking me where I got that funny accent."

"But good enough to join the paramilitary," Glenn said.

"Don't need to speak much for that," Mick replied.

A year after returning to his homeland, Mick joined a local paramilitary headed by one of his mother's cousins.

"I started off as a sergeant," he said. "I earned money, because even though we weren't officially part of the government, it was them who paid us."

"See any combat?" Sleepy Joe asked.

"No," Mick said. "My mother made certain to instruct her cousin to never allow me to be in danger. That's not completely possible in war, but he did keep me several miles from any combat. There wasn't really much risk in those days. We were rolling over the Bosnians. There was some serious fighting against the Croats, but I wasn't anywhere near it. Most of the time they had me protecting the top officers. Most of them were just thugs. Anyone who was willing to kill for Milošević could start their own army and the government would arm them and send them to kill Muslims. Ninety-five percent didn't know what they were doing. Later on, when the Bosnians got better at warfare, these paramilitaries lost a lot of men. You didn't really have to have courage or skill to do what they did. They never fought when there was a risk to them, only when they were up against poorly armed or unarmed peasants. I was actually protecting them from each other, not Muslims or Croats. They were all a bunch of gangsters, still carrying on their illegal activities, and they were more afraid of rival gangs than the enemy. There was a lot of competition between criminal gangs over looting and who got to sell cigarettes and alcohol to the volunteers. Most of our commanders spent the bulk of their time running their criminal enterprises."

Glenn glanced at his notes. "Okay, Mick, I think we have a line from you going from Yugoslavia to America, back to a newly minted Serbia, and then into a paramilitary force with a no-danger assurance to your mother. And unless Oliver tells me otherwise, I will accept that you were shocked by what you learned at Srebinica and cut your ties with the paramilitary and your country. What we need to do now is complete the journey so that we know how you wound up hired by China to follow Mr. Boston around Bangkok. Why don't you start by telling us what you did when you decided to leave Bosnia."

Mick poured himself a glass of water from the pitcher on Glenn's table. He took a long drink before answering.

"We made our way to the nearest Serbian town. We ditched the uniforms and told everyone we were refugees displaced by Muslims. We paid a truck driver to bring us to Belgrade, where we got our passports from home and flew to Russia. That was one of the only places it was easy to get to during the war. We told everyone in Russia that we were former Serbian paramilitary who served in places other than Srebinica. After a year, someone offered us security work protecting a cabinet minister in one of those African dictatorships. That lasted a few years, until he was assassinated, and then we found work doing the same thing a few dictatorships away. Believe it or not, most of these guys trust foreigners more than their own citizens.

"A few years ago we were well-paid guards for a rich businessman in Africa. He was kidnapped while asleep in his own bed at home and even though the ransom was paid, he was killed. It was an inside job; the maid and the chauffeur were in with the kidnappers, and there was not much we could have done. We were hired as armed guards, not investigators. But you can imagine what this did for our reputation. We decided our African safari was over."

At that moment, Oliver returned to the table. "My friends in the Australian intelligence community can say only that Mr. Mick Gordon, as he prefers to be known, was Down Under for a month earlier this year, associating mostly with the local Serbian communities. Several of them knew him to have been in this particular paramilitary unit stationed outside Srebinica, but there is no evidence that he participated in the genocide in a direct or supporting role. It is believed he cannot return to Serbia. He was not involved in any political activities."

"What exactly were you doing in Australia?" Glenn asked. "And how did you get in?"

"Looking for a place to settle," Mick said. "We had passports from the last country we worked for, which is quite standard when you're doing security for foreign leaders. We saw a few immigration lawyers in Sydney, and they all said our only hope was to ask for asylum from the Australian government. They warned us it could backfire and the Australian government could decide our story isn't true and think we were actually part of the groups that did the massacre. When this job in Bangkok materialized, we jumped on it."

"Where were you hired?" Glenn asked.

"While we were in Australia, we met Bill Flanders at a Serbian party. He told us he was a Serbian-American in Sydney on business. He claimed to be the chief security officer for an investment company. Like just about every Serb in the country, he knew Harper and I were ex-paramilitary, and from the way he talked, he believed we were war criminals who'd committed genocide at Srebinica. We tried to explain, but he didn't seem to care at all if we were murderers. We started running into each other at parties and bars and pretty soon we were meeting for beers every now and then. One day he asked if we were interested in doing some overseas work that didn't require carrying a gun and involved no violence at all. We were getting bored in Australia, and we didn't like being treated as heroes for all the wrong reasons, so a job somewhere else sounded perfect.

"Flanders explained we'd have to spend a few days in America because the job required that we leave from Florida. Hey, Florida sounded great to us. We flew in using the African passports we already had. When we got to America, Flanders met us and gave us the U.S. passports."

"You didn't have any qualms using a fraudulent American passport?" Parhat asked.

"None at all," Mick said. "I must have used two dozen passports in my life, and except for the one I was originally issued in Belgrade, not a single one should have been issued."

Glenn reviewed his notes to see if he had any more questions on how the two Serbs were recruited. Satisfied there were none, he moved to a new area. "Your claim is you were hired to tail an American who embezzled from a company back home. Doesn't it seem strange that the company would hire two Serbs with questionable reputations, and them being in Australia, of all places?"

"Maybe it should have, but it didn't," Mick said. "We all happened to be in Australia, we were all Serbs, at least Flanders claimed he was. We were always being hired in one place for a job somewhere else, and dictators aren't the only ones who trust foreigners more than their own countrymen. To the extent I gave it any thought, I figured he liked the idea that me and Harper are tough guys, and even though he promised no violence, hey, fights break out all the time."

The General spoke for the first time since Glenn had begun the questioning.

"Let me assure you, Mr. Gordon, you were working for China. They were communicating through your television set."

Mick leaned forward and shook his head vigorously.

"Are you crazy? Have you been watching too many fantasy movies? We watched television just like anyone else, mostly sports and action movies, to tell the truth. I hate the news."

The General showed Mick the photo of the television screen with the Chinese message.

"You recognize your own living room, and I'm sure you can figure out this is Chinese."

"I have no idea what you're talking about," Mick said.

Glenn raised his hand to let the others know he was running the meeting and leading the questioning.

"Mick, I tend to believe you, and I want to believe you. I know you've been straight with us all the way. Let's keep it that way.

"You've told us that this Flanders fellow doesn't live at the condo on Soi 49 with you and Harper. If that's the case, and you know nothing about the China connection, why would the messages be delivered to your television and not his?"

"We always had the impression Flanders had no fixed address and moved around a lot," Mick said. "We believed he was based in America and that he operated in what we can call a gray area, bending the rules and breaking the law when he had to. We weren't born yesterday, and when we got those American passports and he gave us the cover story for our identities, we knew this was not the kind of man who kept records and paper trails."

"Did Flanders have access to the condo?" Glenn asked.

"Of course," Mick replied. "His outfit was paying for it. He came by a few times when we were around, just to say hello, make sure there were no problems."

"According to the concierge, Mr. Flanders also came around when no one was home," Colonel Somchai said. "We can easily imagine Mr. Flanders dropping by to check for messages and not worry that the other two would see or understand it."

"I have a question about the circumstances under which we met," Glenn said. "I get that you and Harper are close friends going way back to Serbia, and I can even understand why you would come to Bangkok and quickly decide it's where you want to live for the rest of your lives. Hey, plenty of foreigners, me included, have gone through this. But what I don't understand is why you brought Mr. Flanders and the Thai man if this was going to be just the two of you buying in."

"Flanders came to us and said he understood we were interested in buying a business, and he knew what type. No idea how he knew. He said that we might be good in the field, but we would do better with an experienced businessman with experience in the security field like him helping us negotiate. He added that if the price were more than we could afford, he might be able to help us. It seemed sensible. He never told us why he brought the Thai fellow, and we never asked."

"Of course this Flanders knew of your interests in the General's company. You were being eavesdropped twenty-four seven. He didn't want you two doing anything without him in the mix. If it worked out, China would have an important new asset," Colonel Somchai said. "Standard operating procedure for the Chinese."

Glenn had no more questions for Mick, nor did anyone else.

Mick would be brought back to the station, provided with new clothing. He would be kept in an unlocked cell guarded by several of the Lieutenant's trusted men. Mick asked how long he had to stay at the station. Somchai said a few days at most, and he would enjoy unlimited access to television and take-out food. Mick smiled upon learning this.

"Hopefully there's a channel with some football," he said, referring to soccer. "I follow the sport. But I'm looking forward to enjoying Bangkok."

"Let's get our hands on Flanders before we let you and Boston go running around Bangkok."

"What are the odds of catching him?" Mick asked.

"Pretty good," Colonel Somchai said. "Every police officer in Thailand is on the lookout, as are our connections in Immigration. The police are us-ing their network of informants, which includes restaurants, hotels, bars, massage parlors and nightclubs. The General is sending his own team out to look. If he's in Thailand, we'll find him soon, or know he's outside our control."

Mick frowned. "Does that mean I could be in trouble?"

"Not while under the custody of the Lieutenant," Glenn said.

Glenn asked Parhat to question Harper in the hospital. He would go to the police station with the Lieutenant, and once Mick was safely ensconced the two would head for the hospital. Glenn explained that if there were any issues with the medical staff about questioning a patient, the Lieutenant was skilled at negotiating them.

I'm learning some good American slang working with Khun Glenn. Someday I'll speak English just like the General. Parhat thanked Glenn, bid farewell, and left.

Mick shook hands with everyone and left with the Lieutenant and his men.

∼

"IT LOOKS like our friend Mick told us all we need to know about Harper and Flanders, but of course, we have to question Harper to see if there are any significant discrepancies in their stories. And who knows? Maybe Harper picked up on something Mick didn't. Let's face it, these guys aren't the brightest bulbs in the lamp."

"He'll get some valuable experience seeing how investigations are put together," Glenn said to the General and Somchai after Parhat was gone. "It will be useful when tracking down terrorists in the South."

"For which His Majesty's Army thanks you," the General said. "He's a good kid. Reminds me of myself at his age. Took everything very seriously, didn't understand there were the official rules and the unofficial rules, and they could be interchanged at any time."

Colonel Somchai chuckled. "You didn't take everything all that seriously, as I recall. Many girlfriends lodged that complaint."

"Who knows, maybe they were right!" the General rejoined.

Glenn didn't follow. *This is where the Thais always lose me.*

∼

AFTER THE Lieutenant and his two subordinates left with Mick and Parhat and the General left to oversee his dragnet for Flanders and the Thai equivalent of Joe, Glenn spoke to Somchai, Joe, and Oliver before leaving on music business.

"I have no doubt Mick's telling the truth when he says they thought Boston was an embezzler and Flanders represented a company trying to recoup what he stole. It's an easy story to pass off, and it's really what most investigations are all about. There's no way in the world these two bozos concluded that Boston was an epidemiologist looking into a viral outbreak in Wuhan and the People's Republic of China was trying to silence him."

"What is going on, Glenn?" Sleepy Joe asked. "The commies are trying to hide a possible deadly virus outbreak from the rest of the world? Even from their neighbors?"

"They wouldn't be commies if they acted otherwise," Oliver said.

Glenn raised is hand to silence the group.

"Let me finish, and then you can have a free form bull session as long as you want." "There's no question China is involved. The television message ends any doubt. There's no one other than Flanders who would have access to the message, so it's rational to conclude he speaks and reads Chinese and that he's an agent of the People's Republic."

"He certainly doesn't look Chinese," Oliver interjected. "At least not from the photos. Glenn and Joe saw him close up. Did he look Chinese? Our experts said he is Serbian, just like Mick and Harper."

Glenn raised his hand again. "Guys, we'll never get through this if you keep interrupting. Just let me finish." The entire table signaled their agreement by nods and grunts.

"We actually had DNA from Harper, and we have the history from Mick. So those two are Serbs, no question. As for Mr. Flanders, all we know is that he's a white man. He doesn't speak Serbian according to

Mick. No one has linked him to Serbia or the war. He does, however, speak Chinese, and he works as an intelligent operative for the People's Republic. My best guess is he is one of the many minorities living in China. They've got a whole bunch. Some we hear about because they don't want to be part of China, like the Uighurs and Tibetans. They've also got Koreans, Central Asians, Russians, communists from other Asian countries. Why wouldn't they be happy to have them? Think of how useful someone can be if they can pass as a Westerner but inside are totally loyal to Beijing.

"I've no doubt that this is a PRC operation and that it's headed by Flanders. He hired Mick and Harper to follow Boston because they were like oxen who would plow ahead as ordered, and if caught they didn't have any information that would expose China's involvement. They weren't going to be involved in actually grabbing Boston. They were keeping tabs on him and reporting back. When Flanders decided the time was right, my bet is they were going to carry it out themselves, using their own highly skilled operatives. The Thai who showed up at the meeting was one. Sleepy Joe made him on the spot. They'd most likely take him to their Embassy here, and then on to China. From what I read, China uses their embassies and diplomatic privileges for whatever purpose they need.

"As all nations do," he added before continuing his analysis.

"Their cover's been blown, and there's an opportunity to learn a lot about how they insert spies overseas, spies who don't cry out 'China' when you see them. I believe their main goal now is to silence anyone who might help with that line of inquiry. That means Harper and Mick. Colonel Somchai told the Lieutenant to have two police guarding Harper at all times. We can't be too careful with the Thai version of Sleepy Joe running around looking for him. Mick should be safe back at the station even when the Lieutenant is at the hospital. The General has men surveilling the streets around the station, and the men and women who work there are all believed loyal to the Lieutenant. Still, I'm having Sleepy Joe get over to the station to be available just in case.

"This condo is well-guarded, as is the NJA Club. Little chance anyone is out looking for us. If the Chinese are trying to fly under the radar here, the worst thing they could do is set off a dragnet for the killers of Westerners and Thai military officers."

"That's about it for now," Glenn said. "The Lieutenant will take Mick back to the station, and Tom will remain here. I've got that music business to take care of, and I'll be back here in a few hours. Make yourself at home while I'm gone."

"We'll enjoy some of your remaining cigars," Oliver said.

～

GLENN AND Joe left the condo together. Glenn told Lek that while he was gone, Oliver was in charge.

"Khun Oliver speaks Thai and Isan just like the real people," Lek said.

"You mean I'm not real?" Glenn asked.

"Sorry, Khun Glenn," Lek said. "You are a real farang, same like Khun Oliver, but he knows how to sound like a Thai person."

"It's a good thing to hope for," Glenn replied. "But I'll be very happy if someday I speak Thai as well as you speak English."

"I think this Yank should first learn to speak English as well as you do, mate," Sleepy Joe said.

Farang *jokes aren't really funny*, Lek thought as he watched Glenn and Joe leave the lobby.

Twenty-Four

THE TWO police officers, both corporals, were bored with their assignment. They knew the farang inside the hospital room was someone important, and because of this, he was important to their Lieutenant. All they had to do was make sure no harm befell the farang on their watch, and they would be in the Lieutenant's good graces. They both yearned to be sergeants, and being in the Lieutenant's good graces was a big help towards that goal. The food in the hospital cafeteria was decent, and the young ladies who brought it to them quite attractive. There were worse paths to a sergeant's stripes.

They were finishing their lunch when the man in the funny clothing came out of the elevator down the hall and walked towards them. He was wearing black from head to toe, from the tightly closed black collar to the bottom of his toe-length cossack. A round black hat, not quite as high as a baker's, sat atop his head. A large cross hung around his neck. He had a long black beard. He stopped in front of the door the two soldiers guarded. The shorter soldier blocked the doorway.

"And who are you?" the taller soldier asked. "No one is allowed to enter."

"Oh, I'm not Mr. No One," the man said in Thai, smiling. "My name is Father Antonius. I'm an Orthodox priest. This man is of my faith, and it is my religious duty to minister to him in his hour of need."

"Well, this man is not hurt that badly," the tall soldier said. "Lightly busted jaw and sprained wrists. He'll live. And how come you speak Thai so well?"

"It's not that hard a language," the priest said. "And my ministry is not only for the dying. It's for anyone who suffers."

"Like you must be suffering in that black suit," the short soldier said. The priest ignored the comment.

"Our Christmas holiday comes in a matter of days. It should be a joyous time for those of our faith, but some, like this man, will spend it in a hospital. I am here to bring him cheer. I want to give him a blessing and remind him that others care about him. I need a brief time alone with him. Our religion requires privacy for this blessing."

The two soldiers looked at each other.

"Of course, I have special permission to enter hospitals to minister to those in need," the priest said. He reached inside his cossack and produced a letter from the Foreign Ministry, in Thai, with several official seals. It granted the Bulgarian Orthodox priest, Father Antonius, the permission he claimed.

"Okay," the tall one said after he and his colleague read the document. "Can you make this blessing in a few minutes?"

"That's all I need," the priest said.

The short soldier stepped aside, and the priest entered the room.

"You think this would be all right with the Lieutenant?" the short one asked. "He said let no one in the room."

"I'm sure it would be," the tall soldier said. "This man is like a Buddhist monk, except our monks are smart enough to wear cotton and keep their heads and faces shaved. Besides, he has that letter. Even an officer like the Lieutenant must do as the Foreign Ministry says."

~

"Who are you?" Harper asked the priest when he saw him in his room. He was groggy from painkillers, and it took twenty seconds to focus his eyes and mind. "I didn't ask for any priest." He spoke in English. The priest answered in the same language.

"I am here to offer my compassion for your suffering," the priest said.

"Thanks, but I'm not religious at all," Harper said. "No offense, but I just don't believe in it anymore."

"No offense taken," the priest said. He moved to the side of the bed and loomed over the prone Harper. When Harper recognized Flanders' face, he tried to scream, but the fake priest's hand clamped quickly over his mouth. His severely sprained wrists were wrapped in elastic bandages, and to move them at all caused unbearable pain. Pain from his fractured jaw broke through the painkillers. Flanders looked down on him.

"I'm sorry, Harper, I really am. I enjoyed working with you, and I came to like you and Mick, much in the way one has affection for a pet. And none of this was your fault, or Mick's. If anyone is to blame, it is me. I never should have allowed you to go forward with that crazy idea of buying part of the General's company. The one in a billion chance that Boston meets Oliver was not your fault either. But my orders are to close everything down, and in this case, that means you and your friend. We can't leave anyone alive who knows why Boston is here.

"It's funny, Harper. I'm supposed to be the priest, and you ought to be confessing to me, but here I am confessing to you. That's because I feel bad, and because you won't be able to tell anybody."

Flanders' hand blocked any sounds from Harper's mouth. His eyes bulged as he watched Flanders use his free hand to quickly pull off his crucifix from around his neck and plunge its sharp pointed end at his chest.

"*At least you didn't feel a thing.*"

~

"IT'S BEEN more than five minutes," the short corporal said. "We better get him out of here now. The Lieutenant could stop by any time and see him. So could that pretty girl when she comes back for our plates."

"I'll take care of it," the tall one said. He knocked on the door. When there was no answer, he knocked harder. After being greeted with silence again, he tried to open the door. It was locked. He reached into his pocket for the key the Lieutenant gave him and walked into the room. He scanned it. He immediately saw the crucifix sticking out from Harper's chest. He gasped, caught himself, and continued scanning the room. His eyes stopped when he saw the bundle in front of the open window.

A black cossack and round black hat. And a fake beard.

~

THE TWO corporals stood by the open window. The short one peered out and studied the rope that dangled from a clamp attached to the windowsill. The corporal pulled on the clamp hard as he could, but it did not budge.

"This rope only goes down four floors" he told his taller colleague. "We're on the eighth floor, so we can assume he didn't drop to the ground. He could have entered a window on any of those four floors below us. This is a big hospital. It wouldn't be hard at all to blend in with the crowd of visitors and workers and walk away."

"Don't you think we ought to check on our friend in bed over there?" the short one asked, jerking his thumb towards the bed. His colleague nodded.

"Do you really think he's alive?" he asked. "What are the chances someone dresses up like a Christian priest, sticks a Christian cross in a man's chest and climbs out a window on a rope without making sure the victim is dead?"

"I'd say zero," the short corporal replied. "Maybe we should just call the Lieutenant and wait for him."

This time the tall man shook his head. "No, I'm sure the Lieutenant would want us to check to see if maybe he's still alive. We are in a hospital, so maybe he can be saved."

"I don't know," the short one said. "I watch all these American crime shows on television, and they're always talking about not touching evidence at a crime scene."

"Really?" said the tall corporal. "That makes no sense. What if you have to change things to make it easier to prove what happened?"

"I don't think they're allowed to do that," the short man replied.

"That's also crazy," the tall one sneered. "No wonder they have so much crime over there."

They moved next to the bed. The tall corporal flinched when he saw the priest's crucifix stuck deep into Harpers' chest, a trickle of blood across his hospital gown. Pinned to the top was an envelope addressed to the Lieutenant.

"No doubt he's dead," he told the short corporal when he recovered his bearings. "I'll call the Lieutenant, and we don't touch anything!"

∽

FLANDERS SILENTLY thanked his trainers as he landed on the window ledge two stories below the room where he'd just committed a murder. Holding the rope with both hands, he delivered a swift kick to the window, reached a hand through the broken glass, and released the latch on the inside. Seconds later he walked through the room, passed a sleeping patient, opened the door, and walked into the hallway, dressed like any farang visiting a friend in the hospital. If anyone asked why he was there outside of visiting hours and without signing in, he would apologize profusely for any misunderstanding and leave. So long as the murder wasn't yet discovered, security wouldn't be called over an unauthorized visit.

He took the stairs and hurried down. He was in the street less than two minutes after he terminated Harper with the crucifix. He'd gotten to know the deceased well enough to understand Harper was an atheist who would not have taken any offense to what some might see as blasphemous disrespect of a major religion, even so close to Christmas.

Were the decision left to Flanders, he would not have killed Harper.

"He's nothing more than a follower, a simpleton who does what he's told," Flanders argued to his handler when they met soon after Boston was abducted. "He knows nothing about who we are or the real reason we're interested in this American. He thinks Boston is an embezzler."

"True," their handler replied, "but he has seen and heard many things which he may not understand are important, but such information could be valuable to skilled investigators and intelligence agents."

Flanders did as ordered. He always did as ordered.

When he was two blocks past the hospital, Flanders turned right and circumnavigated the block. He then walked three blocks north and did the same. Confident he was not being tailed, he walked another block and turned into a narrow side soi intersecting the street halfway up the block. Twenty meters down the skinny soi was a steel door to the left. Flanders pressed his palm against the door for fifteen seconds. When it swung open, he entered the two-room apartment. Seated at a small table in the first room was the small Thai who had accompanied Flanders and the two Serbs to the aborted meeting with the General's people.

"All went well, I assume?" he asked Flanders in Chinese. Flanders nodded.

"In that case, why don't you pour yourself a drink, watch some television, and then get a good night's sleep in the bedroom? I'm going to leave and take care of Mick. When I'm done, I have to make a report. I'll do that elsewhere. You stay here. There's no need to leave. There's plenty of food and booze. I'll be back tomorrow afternoon."

"How do you even know where Mick is being held?" Flanders asked.

"Same way I knew where Harper was recuperating," the Thai replied. "Paid contacts in the police department. It's really not all that hard to do in this country. Even back home, police are bribed all the time. Why would it be different here?"

"Even easier for you," Flanders said, "you being part-Thai and knowing the language since birth." After ten years as Sun's partner, he knew only the parts of his background necessary for the job. Included within such detail was that Sun's grandfather, a Thai communist, came to China during the Second World War to fight with Mao's troops. He never returned and married a Chinese woman.

Sun told him years ago how his grandfather's progeny married among other members of this mixed community, which numbered into the thousands after an influx of Thai communist volunteers during the Korean War. Flanders surmised this was because pure Chinese disdained anyone who wasn't like them, especially part-Chinese "mongrels." As a second-generation native-born communist, Sun never thought of himself as anything other than a citizen of the People's Republic of China. Like any minority wishing to succeed, he carried a Chinese name and spoke fluent Mandarin, even if Thai was spoken equally in his childhood home.

Thankfully. Otherwise, I would not have been selected for this assignment. Half the people in this city are part-Chinese and look like me.

"You haven't done too bad with your looks either," Sun said. "It got you sent to America and then here." When Flanders had first walked into the orientation for future overseas agents, Sun was as surprised as the other students to see a blue-eyed white man among them. They soon learned that Flanders' great grandfather was a White Russian officer who'd fled across the border to Xinjiang province, where the family remained. By the time Flanders was born, all the anti-communism was long burned from the family, and Flanders was a loyal citizen of the People's Republic of China.

Flanders knew he was a perfect overseas agent, used by China to gather information about Russian activities in Silicon Valley, Brooklyn, and Miami. The intensive English-language training he received in China enabled Flanders to perfect his American accent, though among the Russians in Silicon Valley, he made certain to speak with a heavy Russian accent. Flanders and Sun met in California when assigned as partners there. Sun was assigned to spy for China, seeking out potential assets, Chinese background or not, who could provide technological secrets. Flanders kept tabs on the local Russians, reporting their activities to his handler. Occasionally, he helped to recruit Russians to work as agents for China.

When the PRC felt the need to send experienced agents to Bangkok for this assignment, those two were natural choices. Sun would fit in with the Thais, especially the wealthy Thai-Chinese, while Flanders, with his perfected English, would pose as an American. Flanders was given an intensive course in Thai three years ago when he was sent to spy on Russians in Pattaya and could speak it well. This posting in Bangkok was an important assignment. China had its eyes on Thailand, seeking to create a subservient and compliant neighbor, difficult with a nation that prided itself on never being colonized. Skilled agents were needed on the ground to make certain this transition proceeded smoothly, and any problems for China were to be promptly resolved.

Problems like Tom Boston. Right now that problem was not being solved and was growing worse. Flanders was supposed to end a problem, not create new ones.

Flanders recalled the years in America, which involved no violence. He and Sun identified and cultivated people to provide classified technical information through bribery or compromising situations, usually involving sex or drugs. Once Flanders or Sun softened up a target, the handlers took over. It was an easy posting, filled with endless parties, dinners, and trips to Tahoe or Vegas. Bangkok was a lot different. China was a lot more aggressive in their own backyard. In America, the orders were to never kill. In Bangkok it was an option, the last perhaps, but an option nonetheless.

"I hear what you're saying about me being lucky to have inherited these Russian good looks," he told Sun. "But maybe that happened because the Han don't want to marry Russians, so we've kept the race pure."

"Makes you unique," Sun said. "Never can lose you in a crowd back home."

"Is that really something good?" Flanders asked. "When we go back home, you're going to fit right in. How many people even realize you're part-Thai? You fit in with the Thais here, and with the Chinese back home. I'm always a foreigner."

"You only look like one," Sun said. "You're as Chinese as me."

"No, I'm not," Flanders said. "When we were in California, you were accepted as Chinese. Here, you're a Thai-Chinese. Back home, you're just Chinese. But me? I was a Russian in America, an American in Thailand, and guess what: in China I'm just a white man who speaks perfect Mandarin, a freak of nature. I was more accepted in America and by the farangs here than by Chinese in my own country."

"Flanders, let me ask you this: when we go back home, you're going to be treated like a hero. How do you think the Americans would treat you if they caught you?"

"Probably better than our government will when they find out we keep digging ourselves into a deeper hole," Flanders said.

"Not to worry," Sun said. "I'm taking care of this. That's where my training comes in. During our last six-month rotation back home, I was given the most intensive training in what we might call 'urban survival skills,' or maybe we ought to call it 'the Chinese Sleepy Joe program.' The first time I saw that Australian killer trying to pass himself off as a lawyer I realized what kind of person our program was modeled after."

"I still find it hard to believe he's someone we should be afraid of," Flanders said.

"He put poor Harper in the hospital before his morning coffee, and if he's working for the General, he's got to be top of the line. Our intelligence has very little on him, but I eyeballed him myself and had no doubt then or now. You don't want him to find you, so you stay here until I return."

"Can I ask you something?" Flanders said. "Not as an agent, but as a friend."

Sun looked at Flanders as if studying him and nodded.

"We screwed up. We were supposed to follow this Boston fellow, see who he connects with, and then someone else would take over once we could tell them where to do it without getting caught. Instead, Boston is being protected by some of the toughest people around, Mick is in custody, I had to kill Harper against my own wishes, and I'm hiding in a back alley, scared to death that a psycho is going to kill me. Tell me, Sun, what do you think is going to happen to me when I get back to China?"

"You'll be debriefed and receive a new assignment," Sun said.

"You don't sound all that convinced," Flanders said. "Remember, I'm not the grandson of an Asian communist who came to China to fight with Mao. I'm the great grandson of Czarist White Russians who killed communists and came to China because they thought it would never be communist. I don't get the same leeway they give someone like you. With me, they probably think they were wrong to ever trust a Russian."

"China is our home and our country," Sun said. "Everything we do, we do for China, and China appreciates it. I told you it's not our fault things went differently than expected."

"One more thing," Flanders said. "It's going to come out we walked right into the General's hands when Harper and Mick were stupid enough to think they could buy into his operation and we allowed them to try. That's our fault. We should have known how stupid that was and stopped it from ever happening. It was you, me, Harper, and Mick. Harper is gone, and Mick is next. It was not supposed to end like this. We better get our story straight and make sure there's no differences when we're questioned."

Sun was quiet for a few seconds. He looked at Flanders, who looked back at him.

"I hadn't really thought of it that way," he told Flanders. "I suppose if there were only one of us, that problem would not exist. The survivor could say they were not there and had no knowledge of that meeting. It's not like Sleepy Joe and Glenn are going to tell them different."

Flanders saw the revolver only after Sun had it pointed at his face. The silencer muffled the sound of both .22 caliber bullets fired into his forehead.

Twenty-Five

One Hour Later

GLENN WAS more relaxed knowing Mick and Harper were no longer threats, assuming they ever were. Flanders and the mysterious Thai from the meeting were still at large, but they were no match for Sleepy Joe, Parhat, and the combined men of the Lieutenant and the General. *I hope not.*

Glenn left on his music business. "I think it's safe now," he told the other three. "At least I hope so," he added.

~

GLENN WAS rarely in this part of Bangkok, and almost never took the MRT, Bangkok's subway system. Rong suggested the restaurant where he wanted to meet, and Glenn was amenable to a brief vacation from the recently stressful Green Zone. Fortunately, the artificial intelligence voice that announced each stop named the station and cheerfully reminded passengers to "mind the gap between the platform and the car."

The street signs weren't in English in that part of town, but Rong's directions were excellent, specifying how many blocks or traffic lights to walk before each turn. Glenn had no trouble finding the restaurant. Glenn saw the young Thai seated near the rear of the restaurant, studying his cell phone. He didn't notice Glenn until the American was seated next to him. He had already ordered food, which sat before him. *I understand, I'm a half hour late*, Glenn thought. He didn't think it would take so long to walk from his condo to the MRT station at Asoke, but it gave him time to think about how to persuade Rong that the time had come for him to take over as Phil's manager.

"Hope I'm not interrupting you," Glenn said.

"Hello, Khun Glenn. Sorry, I was caught up by what I was reading."

"Which is what?" Glenn asked.

"Just some Thai stuff," Rong responded.

"I'm sorry I'm late," Glenn said. "Tell me what you wanted to talk about."

Hopefully he'll start the ball rolling by asking when he gets to have my job. We both know that's where this has been heading.

Rong hesitated before explaining.

"It's about Phil, of course. I really appreciate the opportunity you gave me to act as his manager while you do other things. You need to know what I have seen, and what I think."

"Let's hear it," Glenn said.

Rong stared at the plate of food in front of him then looked at Glenn. "I'm not a doctor, but I think Khun Phil suffers from mental illness," he said. "No sane person would continually undermine their career by acting like an asshole whenever he has the chance."

"What did he do this time?" Glenn asked.

"Someone requested a song the other night, some old American rock song I never heard of. Phil yelled out that he wouldn't play 'a piece of shit meant for morons.' The man got angry and told Phil that song was playing when he proposed to his wife in New York City many years ago. Phil tells the guy to pick a new song and a new wife. Next thing I know, the man is up on the stage lunging at Phil. Normally, the other musicians would jump in to protect their bandmate, but these guys just stood back while this angry American started swinging at Phil. The club's bouncer managed to separate them, but by that time, nearly everyone in the audience got up and left. We're never being hired there again, and those musicians won't get on a stage with Phil. What do you think this is doing to my reputation? Or yours?"

The waitress took Glenn's order, giving him a chance to formulate a response.

"What do you suggest we do about this?" he asked. "I've been dealing with Phil Funston for thirteen years, two and a half as his manager, and I haven't figured out how to control him. That's why he's still stuck at the same local club circuit level, no tours, no invites to join bands, no studio work. It's my job to manage him and that means no more than getting small gigs forever. I'm doing a terrible job."

"Oh no, Khun Glenn, you are doing a good job," Rong said. "The fact that he is still performing and not in jail or deported is because of you."

Glenn smiled.

"Sounds like I'm back to being a criminal defense lawyer." When he saw Rong did not understand, he explained that back in America, he defended people accused of crimes, and his job then was to keep them out of jail.

"Sooner or later you may have to do it again for Khun Phil," Rong said. "Which is why I have decided that it is best if both of us step away from him. He is nothing but trouble. He is not worth my time, and definitely not yours."

"Your time is as valuable as mine," Glenn said. "I'm sorry if you feel I've wasted any of it."

"Oh no, Khun Glenn," Rong replied. "You gave me a chance to break into the local music scene in a better way than selling guitars and accessories to people who mostly aren't real musicians. I got to play with some great musicians, including Phil. I'm not just a practice bass player anymore. I will get more work than Phil. I am sure I will go on to better things than he ever will. I thank you."

"In other words, you're done with Phil as of right now?" Glenn asked.

"Yes, it's time for me to move on. You should too. Don't blame yourself for Phil's situation."

Glenn told Rong he would think about what he had been told, and he wished him the best in whatever he did. They moved on to other topics, mainly Glenn telling Rong what groups from the past he recommended, and Rong doing the same with contemporary artists.

"Stay in touch," Glenn said as he and Rong left the restaurant.

He's a lot smarter than me, Glenn thought on the escalator down to the MRT platform.

How could anyone as smart as Khun Glenn not know all this already, Rong asked himself.

∼

"THE KID is right," Sleepy Joe said when Glenn recounted his meeting with Rong. "Fire Funston's ass as your client, and then I can chase the bastard out of the NJA Club forever."

Glenn put down his coffee mug and looked down at the floor.

"We can't do that, Joe. Even if he deserves it. It's bad enough I'm walking away. Without a manager, he'll be back to the rare job."

"Yeah, mate, and that's his fault, not yours," Sleepy Joe said. "The man is a dickhead of the highest order, and he's never going to change. You promised him six months and now it's two and a half years. You're free to walk any time."

Glenn stood and walked to his stereo.

"I'm in the mood for Jeff Beck today, how about you?" he asked Joe.

"I'm always in the mood for Jeff Beck," Joe replied. "No one has mastered the Stratocaster like Mr. Beck. He took over where Jimi left off."

Phil plays a Gibson Les Paul, Glenn recalled. *Bought it with my four thousand dollars. I can kiss that money goodbye. Maybe it's worth four grand to kiss off Funston.*

"It's not about any legal obligation I might have," Glenn explained. "It's not even a moral obligation. I doubt anyone has ever done as much for Phil as me."

"Then what is it?" Joe asked.

"I hate failure," Glenn said. "I hate not getting the job done."

"Well," Joe asked, "what about doing the best job anyone could do?"

"Really not good enough," Glenn said.

"It's going to have to do," Joe said. "I rarely insist you do anything, mate, but I insist you ditch Phil Funston and you do it tomorrow. End of story."

Glenn thought for a moment then smiled.

"I guess I have no choice. I wouldn't want to wind up in the hospital like Mr. Harper."

"And I went easy on the poor fool," Joe said.

∼

SINCE MEETING Rong, Glenn had not been present at as many of Phil's performances as in the past. His past reason for attendance was to be on the scene for any problems Phil created. Rong, a Thai, was better equipped for such instances, and Glenn felt less need to spend as many nights watching a man he despised.

By serendipity, Phil called Glenn the night before and said he wanted to meet him at the Club the next day, allowing Glenn to piggyback his last two meetings as manager.

As he walked the last block to the NJA Club to meet Phil, Glenn ran through his prepared remarks.

It's been a great experience, Phil, it really has been. But I promised six months, and we're now at two and a half years. I've done as much for you as I possibly can. I'm not a rock and roll manager and we both know it. I helped establish you as a regular on the Bangkok club circuit, enabled you to make a living, and now it's time for me to move on. I have other things in my life, and I think if you get a new manager, it should be someone younger and hungrier for money.

Unfortunately, the person Glenn had in mind for that role of a "younger and hungrier for money" manager had just informed him he was inextricably opposed to the idea.

I was hoping Rong would step in, but unfortunately he has other matters to take care of and is no longer in my employ. You've got gigs booked for the next two months, which gives you plenty of time to find someone new.

Knowing Phil Funston for years, Glenn understood this news would not be well-received. If Phil reacted badly, there was no safer place for Glenn than the NJA Club, especially since the General had extra security in the immediate vicinity.

When Glenn was near his table, Phil started drumming loudly with his knuckles. The noise caught Glenn's attention and he sat next to his soon-to-be-former client.

"Glad you could find the time," Phil said as soon as Glenn was seated. "I just needed to see you alone for this, not that skinny runt you've been palming off on me."

Glenn stiffened and stared at Phil. *I'm done with this asshole. I can tell him whatever I want.*

"Rong is a fine young man. He's been a better manager than I could ever be. He also happens to be a hell of a bass player, and he's made you a better guitarist by playing with him so often. If you're thinking about trying to get me to fire Rong, let me advise you that . . ."

Phil rose and spoke in a loud voice that betrayed the several beers he'd consumed. His face and bald pate turned a deeper red each second. He leaned towards Glenn and interrupted him with an angry snarl.

"I don't have to tell you to fire Rong. I'm doing the firing, and it starts with firing your ass. You're out as my manager Glenn, you and that runt are out of my life. I just got an offer to tour China with an American band. Three months, playing clubs, hotels, resorts. Beijing, Shanghai, Hong Kong. I'll make more in a night than I make in a month around here. I got this on my own when their manager heard me playing at one of the General's son's clubs. You weren't there, you sent the little kid. You're out and you are not getting a cent of the money from the China tour. Did I mention they were paying in dollars?"

Glenn slumped back into his chair, every muscle in his body relaxing. *Here I was worrying about what to say, and he made it so easy. But he's forgetting something.*

"Well, Phil, if I wanted to, I could press a claim for my ten percent, being as no matter what you say now, for two and a half years I carried your sorry ass until you got yourself in a position where someone discovered you. At a gig I got for you, I might add, after I negotiated a better deal where you don't kick back to the General and his fat-assed gangster wannabe son. But you know something, Phil, what's a lot of money to you is chump change to me. Keep your ten percent if it makes you feel better. But of course, because we're trying to cut clean and cut now, you'll want to repay me the four grand in dollars I loaned you for the guitar that made this all possible. That's almost a hundred thirty thousand baht at the current rate, Phil. I doubt you carry that much with you, so how about you bring it by the Club tomorrow at noon?"

Fat chance I'll ever see a baht from him, but this should keep him out of my life forever.

"You'll get your money when I get back from China," Funston yelled before storming his way from the table and out the door.

He hasn't seen that much money in years, and he's not going to see it any time soon.

〜

OLIVER AND the General sat in Glenn's living room with Tom Boston. The General returned from his oversight of the dragnet, reporting that if either of the subjects tried to leave the city by air, rail or bus, or passed by any of Bangkok's countless surveillance cameras, they would eventually be caught. Glenn had returned from being fired by Phil but didn't say anything to his friends. *Not the time for personal matters,* he thought. Sleepy Joe was heading to the station, and the Lieutenant and Parhat to the Hospital. The men turned to Glenn when he entered the room.

"We've been listening to the news on CNN, BBC, Sky, RT, and the main Thai stations," Oliver said. "Not a word from any about a virus."

"I suppose no news is good news," Glenn said. "What say you, Dr. Boston?"

"I don't really care about the news or lack thereof," the epidemiologist said. "I'm interested in facts, scientifically validated facts. Right now, there aren't any. Officially, there's nothing to report aside from rumors, which could cause panic. I don't think that's something the business interests of the West or the East for that matter care to spark off. Nor do epidemiologists, for that matter. We find false alarms and mismanaged release of information are very counterproductive.

"But if you're asking me what I think, the answer is not pleasant. Here in Bangkok, colleagues who have some contacts in China are reporting exactly what we heard in America earlier this month about an outbreak of a coronavirus variant in Wuhan, China. It was mostly coming from one doctor in Wuhan, and the Chinese government and WHO claim no knowledge of any public health threat. I've already explained why governments and economic interests would not want the truth to come out, at least not until they think there's no choice. By the same token, I can think of no reason why a doctor would make up a lie that tricked dozens of epidemiologists into believing it. What he describes, and what others are starting to confirm, though thus far no lab reports or medical records made available, sounds like a highly contagious variation of what we saw with SARS. We don't know for certain where it came from or where it's heading. I can assure you that if it is indeed a new variant and it has gotten out into the broader community, we are going to see it everywhere. How much it spreads, how many people die, that depends on how quickly and how efficiently the governments of the world acknowledge the problem and mobilize to fight it. So far what I'm seeing is denial, which is going to hurt us more than you can imagine down the road."

The others sat quietly for half a minute, reflecting on Boston's words and struggling to understand them.

"Are you telling us that there's a good chance we're looking at a worldwide epidemic of a deadly new virus?" Somchai asked.

"Yes, Colonel, that's exactly what I'm saying. The scale is dependent upon how governments react."

"What should they be doing?" the General asked.

"Working together to contain and eventually eradicate the virus. That might mean wide ranging travel restrictions, banning large gatherings, keeping distances from each other. Right now we don't even know how the virus is transmitted. If it is airborne, we'll need masks over the mouth and nose. If airborne, it could take anywhere from two days to two weeks to become ill, depending on the patient's prior health and how much they were exposed."

"Then that's what every government should order right away!" the General said loudly, pounding a fist on the table.

"Easier said than done, General," Boston explained. "I've already explained how governments, especially presidents up for reelection, do not want to run during an economic shutdown they imposed, combined with restrictions on what people are allowed to do. These things are never popular with the public, and without government endorsement, there's little chance of compliance. There's always a tension between we scientists and doctors on one side, politicians and businesses on the other. As people of science, we cannot allow political or economic considerations to interfere with our studied medical advice. Sounds like all too many governments don't want to take human lives into account."

"What's your recommendation to all of us, who now are aware of this possible outbreak?" Oliver asked.

"Epidemiologists can never please everyone," Boston said. "If we recommend too much, we get blamed for hurting business if it turns out the epidemic wasn't as bad as it could have been. If we recommend too little, and it turns out to be worse, we get blamed for the deaths. The safest and wisest recommendation from a scientific standpoint is to recommend maximum protection. That would mean staying away from crowds, as that's where it's most likely to be spread, whether it is airborne or by direct contact. Since we have no hard evidence the virus even exists, let alone spread beyond Wuhan into Thailand, no one is going to follow such a recommendation, not even people like you, who understand what I'm saying. My recommendation is to follow the news, stay in touch with me when I'm back home, and take your advice from the America's Center for Disease Control and National Institute of Health. I have no doubt Oliver can call Thailand's leading epidemiologists and get the best local facts."

"For the right price," Oliver said.

"Until then," Boston said, "try your best to stay out of big crowds, even smaller ones filled with people you don't know for sure are acting responsibly or just got back from China. If the virus is really as contagious as I hear, it's only a matter of time before it's in Bangkok and someone in a big crowd is infected."

"One question for you, Dr. Boston. Assuming it is a contagious virus, and it does break out beyond China to the rest of the world, what might we be looking at? Is this going to be like the Spanish flu of 1918, or even worse, like the Black Plague? Will it be with us for a long time, like smallpox and polio? Will it be very deadly?"

"Those are all excellent questions, Glenn, the very ones we epidemiologists are asking. I have to reiterate that at this time we do not know."

"Is it 'que sera, sera?'" Glenn asked.

Boston smiled for the first time since he'd begun his presentation.

"At this moment, I suppose that's as effective an approach as any other I might offer."

"Would you be able to join us for New Year's Eve on Koh Phangan?" Oliver asked Boston. "At my place. I've got quite an event lined up. We'd love to have you, and I assure you, no one who has been to China will be in attendance."

"That's very kind of you, Oliver, but I could never explain to my wife why I wasn't home for New Years. If I'm not back by then, I'll have more than a virus to fear."

Wonder if the wife knows about your interest in Patpong go-go bars, Oliver thought.

"Even after we eliminate any threats from Flanders or his Thai version of Joe, it's still not safe for you to be here," Oliver said to Boston. "You could really hurt China if you went public at some point, assuming you have enough to do so. When we get the word that they're down, you'll be taken to the airport under guard, and our best people will remain with you until you board the plane."

"No offense, but I can't get home too soon. It's been an experience, playing medical sleuth, getting jumped by thugs in Patpong, followed by Chinese agents, rescued by a military officer and a violent hippie, hiding out with you guys. I long to return to the staid life of an epidemiologist."

"Doesn't sound like it's going to be very staid much longer," Oliver said.

Twenty-Six

THE LIEUTENANT and Parhat sat in the back seat with Mick between them as they were driven to the station by two police officers. Once Mick was safely installed in his unlocked cell and provided a fine lunch, the Lieutenant and Parhat left for the hospital. He told the sergeant at the front desk he'd call when he was done, and if there were any problems, call him immediately. The Lieutenant, though in uniform, drove in an unmarked car.

The Lieutenant parked in a no parking zone near the entrance, and he and Parhat went into the hospital lobby. The Lieutenant explained at the information desk who he was and who he wanted to see. He turned ashen when told the patient had died violently, and that it was now a police matter.

"I am the police," the Lieutenant shouted. "Can't you see my uniform?" He demanded to be taken to the room, which was now the crime scene.

I don't have to guess who did this, he thought as the elevator ascended. *The Chinese now feel free to commit murders on our soil.*

Parhat did not say a word during the encounter at the information desk. He was in absolute shock that a key witness like Harper could be killed in a hospital while guarded by police. He spoke up as they rode the elevator.

"No offense intended, Lieutenant, but something like this could never happen in the military,

"No offense taken," the Lieutenant replied. "Two different worlds. Your military would not last five minutes on the streets of Bangkok these days."

The two corporals stood in front of the room, the looks on their faces reminding the Lieutenant of the looks he'd seen on condemned prisoners. Two technicians from Forensics stood to the side. Parhat followed the Lieu-tenant and said nothing.

"We would not allow anyone to enter until you arrived, Lieutenant," the taller one said.

"I wish you had followed that protocol before someone walked in and killed him," the Lieutenant said. He motioned to the two technicians to follow him into the room.

One of the technicians handed the Lieutenant a pair of disposable gloves. He put them on while eyeing the pile of clothing by the window. He approached the bed and saw the crucifix embedded in Harper's chest and the letter held in place with the same.

"Would I be damaging the crime scene if I removed this from the corpse?" he asked the technicians.

"I doubt it," said the one who gave him the gloves. "There's not likely to be questions about what killed him, and we'll have the weapon handled only by your gloved hands."

The Lieutenant pulled the crucifix from Harper's chest and slid off the letter. He handed the cross to the technician. He sat down on the only chair in the room and opened the envelope, still wearing the gloves. The note was handwritten in Thai.

Lieutenant, our dispute is not with Thailand or the police. We are defending our country against foreign enemies who are about to launch a terrorist attack against China from your soil. We regret not being able to notify you earlier, but there was no time, and we could not take chances. Hopefully your government understands. We just ask that you stay out of our way for the few days more it will take us to fix this problem. We'll compensate for any damage we cause by mistake. Please make sure the General understands this.

This was not the kind of matter the Lieutenant dealt with as a crime-fighting Bangkok police officer. This was foreign affairs, intelligence, diplomacy.

Colonel Somchai will know what to do. This Major doesn't have a clue.

On the way out of the room, the Lieutenant passed the two ashen-faced corporals.

"You're to go the station immediately, wait in the break room, and not talk to each other or anyone else about this event. I want you in front of my office in one hour." He called the station to send a car.

"In the military, those two would have been arrested on the spot," Parhat told the Lieutenant. "I cannot believe your leniency."

"I cannot believe your naivety," the Lieutenant replied. "They are guilty only of stupidity. We require their cooperation to get a full description and whatever details we can get them to recall. We don't run our police force like the army. That's why we get things done. Like I said, you military people wouldn't last five minutes here. If the crooks didn't kill you, your own men would and no one would blame them."

∼

SLEEPY JOE hopped off the back of the motorcycle and handed the driver a hundred baht note for the sixty-baht ride. He told the driver to keep the change, which brought a smile and a khob khun khrup. Joe started the two-block walk to the police station. The sergeant at the front desk knew he was coming and the Lieutenant had shown him a photo of Joe he'd taken on his phone. Joe was taken to see Mick.

The big man was drinking beer and watching television when Joe arrived at his unlocked cell. Mick was glad to see him.

"They're treating me well, guarding me all the time, but I'll still be glad when this is over, whatever life brings me then."

Joe declined the offer of a beer.

"Not while I'm working," he explained. He told Mick that he was safe and in good hands, and he himself had to leave. *I want to make sure Glenn is safe, and that is best accomplished by me at his side. Besides, I want to get stoned and watch television at his place.*

Shouldn't be long, Joe assured himself as he walked through the door of the building. *I can report Mick is secure in his temporary digs, television working fine, beer and good food delivery. I'll be back on Glenn's balcony smoking weed with him in no time.*

Twenty meters from the entrance, Joe spotted Sun getting off a motorcycle he parked across the street. He wore a helmet with a visor that obscured his face, but Sleepy Joe had no doubt who it was by the height, body build, and the scent a fellow warrior emits even from a distance, detectable only to fellow warriors.

I'd recognize that walk anywhere. It's the walk of someone who does the work I do. There are only two such people in Bangkok fitting that bill, me and him. That isn't me, so it's him. He's not here to make sure Mick has the best television and food delivery.

Joe fell a dozen steps behind Sun. When Sun was at the foot of the steps leading to the station house door, he pulled the strap on his helmet and started to remove it. He didn't see Sleepy Joe come from behind but felt the strong grip on his neck while at the same time his right arm was pulled farther back than he thought physically possible. Sun knew that arm was now useless. The helmet clattered against the floor. Sun didn't have to see a face to know his assailant.

Sun concentrated all his strength in his right leg and left shoulder as he cartwheeled right, pulling Sleepy Joe into the air. They landed on the ground with Sun on top of Sleepy Joe. The Australian had his left hand gripped tightly around Sun's throat and his right hand held Sun's left arm against the ground. Joe's shoulder pressed against Sun's other arm to limit mobility. Sun knew that even if he managed to use his left hand to free his throat, his enemy would have him at his most vulnerable and would kill him.

Instead, Sun moved his left arm as far as he could and maneuvered his left hand into his pants pocket to withdraw the .22 with the silencer. The chamber held seven bullets, and he'd used two on poor Harper. He needed at least two for Mick, to make certain he was dead.

With Sleepy Joe on top of him, and his diminishing air supply pulling him into unconsciousness, Sun was still able to press the pistol next to Joe's shoulder. If he could tilt and aim properly, he could unload a bullet or two into Joe's chest. Sun used his remaining strength to lift the gun as far as he could and pulled the trigger.

In the absence of noise, it took Sleepy Joe a few seconds to realize he'd been shot. The initial pain was no different from the pains one experiences in hand-to-hand combat. He felt blood coming from the wound in his shoulder, wetting his shirt. When he was unable to move the shoulder, he knew Sun had shot him.

Small caliber, or I'd be dead or bleeding out by now. His hand remained around Sun's neck. Sun had ceased all movement.

"Had to shoot me, you punk? Weren't willing to fight it out man to man? You think you're tough, but you're nothing but a commie punk!"

Sun showed no signs that he heard Joe.

Sleepy Joe realized he was slowly falling asleep. He looked at his shirt, which now had a half inch wide stripe of blood running from his shoulder to his waist. He tried to stand but could not.

"Just sit. I already called for ambulance," the Lieutenant said. The Australian looked up at him from the sidewalk.

"Didn't know you could speak English," Joe said.

"A little. I learn more being with all you farangs. Still think it be better you learn Thai. We are in Thailand."

"What can I say?" Joe asked. "You're right."

"I think he's still alive," the Lieutenant said. "I felt a small pulse."

"Yeah, the bastard shot me before I could choke him to death," Joe said.

"Good you don't. We can find out a lot from him."

"I couldn't agree with you more, mate," Joe replied. "Any man who gets far enough to shoot me can teach us a few things."

Parhat stood next to the Lieutenant, eyes wide open. He had just returned to the station from the hospital, where Flanders was killed, and where Sleepy Joe had disabled Sun but was shot in the process.

Maybe the Lieutenant is right about we military not lasting five minutes in this place.

The ambulance arrived. The Lieutenant spoke with the driver briefly and watched as the emergency medical technicians gently placed Joe in a stretcher.

"I can walk," Joe said. "I was shot in the shoulder, not the leg."

"You've lost blood, and we can't be a hundred percent sure there isn't a little .22 slug somewhere else," one of the medical technicians said in flawless English.

"I hope they're not taking me to the same hospital where Flanders got killed," Joe said as he was loaded into the ambulance.

"We're taking you to the Police Hospital," the technician said. "No one gets shot there unless the police want it to happen."

The Lieutenant heard and understood the exchange. He didn't find it funny.

Parhat smiled.

∼

THE TWO corporals stood silently in front of the Lieutenant's office when he arrived. Parhat had left for Glenn's condo. This was strictly police business. He opened the door and motioned them to sit inside.

"Your instructions were as clear as water," the Lieutenant said when they faced him across his desk. "Yet you allowed a man to enter and kill the prisoner you were guarding."

The two men remained silent.

"Is there any reason you should not be dismissed from your positions immediately? Why should the public follow orders if the police refuse?"

The shorter corporal spoke up. "He was a farang priest. We thought it was like allowing a monk to see someone. He had a letter from the Foreign Ministry."

"Who told you that you had permission to allow monks to enter that room?" the Lieutenant asked. "When I say 'no one' that includes monks and farang priests. By the way, this one was not a priest. He was a communist Chinese agent. He killed a man with a Christian cross and escaped by dangling out the window. I'd say that's not what we expect from a farang priest.

"Or maybe it is," he added.

"As for that letter, tell me, officers, is there a single soi in Bangkok where we couldn't find someone selling one if we needed it?" The two corporals looked at the floor.

"In any event," the Lieutenant continued, "I've decided not to sack you, though it would be entirely justifiable. You two have been with me for a long time, you're honest, don't take bribes, and you both have good military service records. So as disgusted as I am with the loss of intelligence your disobeying orders has caused this nation, I'm only suspending each of you for ten days without pay. This will delay any opportunity to be promoted to sergeant for at least two years, and that will only happen if your records from this day on are spotless. Am I understood?"

"Yes, Lieutenant," the corporals said in unison. The Lieutenant waved them out of the office.

Two more in my debt forever, he thought as he watched through the glass window of his door as the corporals walked down the hall.

~

SLEEPY JOE spent the night in the Police Hospital. His wound was cleaned, the slug removed, and he was fed intravenous antibiotics to ward off any infection. In the morning, after a pretty nurse changed his bandages and brought breakfast, he was discharged. The Lieutenant stopped by early in the morning to make certain Joe was recovering and receiving any amenity he wished other than lighting up a joint. He told Joe that he saved Mick's life and the big Serb was safe in one of the General's hideouts. Joe didn't need to ask the Lieutenant if that was because he feared Chinese spies in the Bangkok Metropolitan Police.

The BTS stop was nearby, and ten minutes later Sleepy Joe, looking none the worse for being shot in the shoulder, was in the lobby of Glenn's building. Lek greeted him with a broad smile and a wai.

"I am so happy to see you, Khun Joe. My cousin told me you were shot, but he said it was a small caliber gun and you are fine. But I still worried, and Khun Glenn did also. I told both, 'don't worry, Sleepy Joe is an amazing guy.'"

"Thank you, mate," Joe said. "Your cousin is pretty amazing too. A few days ago he didn't know more than a few words of English, and now he's carrying on serious conversations. He has a way to go to be perfect, but he's off to a great start."

Lek looked at Joe as if he had mumbled nonsense.

"Khun Joe, there is some mistake. My cousin speaks English perfectly. He studied English language in college. He first came to be a police officer because the department needed English-speaking officers with college degrees when cases have farangs from America, Canada, Australia. The Lieutenant was first person to teach me English."

Sleepy Joe felt as if he'd received a mild electrical shock.

Wonder what the hell I said around him when I thought he didn't understand.

Twenty-Seven

A Few Days Before Christmas Day, 2019

It was Glenn's thirteenth Christmas in Bangkok. The holiday grew more pronounced each year but without a trace of religious symbolism. Thai people treat Christmas as another excuse to have a good time. Shopping malls and plazas display Santa with his elves and reindeer, but a creche or cross would be hard to find. The go-go bars entice expats with alluring young women in skimpy red blouses and shorts, Santa hats perched on their heads.

All of this suited Glenn. He was not a Christian and had no plans to ever become one. In America, he was never averse to holiday season parties, but he shied away from singing carols and wouldn't consider attending Midnight Mass. Growing up Jewish in New York City, Christmas Day meant either Chinese restaurants, Radio City Music Hall, or movie theaters with holiday releases. In San Francisco, perhaps America's least "Christian" city, the holiday was not all that different from Bangkok: a celebration, but not of the birth of the man Christians believe was a deity in human form. As far as Glenn was concerned, Christmas was an annoying time of year, filled with bad music, fake cheer, and obnoxious, semi-mandatory gift-giving. The only upside was the large increase in drunk driving cases, much needed by criminal lawyers facing end-of-year bills. To Glenn,

Santa Claus was a client who was busted driving under the influence after a party.

Thailand was a Buddhist nation. Glenn's Thai friends explained how Thailand practiced its own distinct version of what the Buddha taught. This strand was called *Theravada*. Glenn never understood the doctrinal differences between Thai Buddhism and the Zen traditions of China, Vietnam, and Japan, or the heavily layered and well-organized Tibetan form. He knew the others referred to Theravada as *Hinayana*, or "lesser vehicle," and their own was termed *Mahayana*, or "greater vehicle." Glenn believed it had something to do with who you save first, yourself or others, but wasn't certain. He was told by Thais that some of the other branches were dismissive of Theravada. *Goes to show even Buddhists have prejudices.*

Glenn found the near-absence of Christianity in Thailand comforting, though he'd never said this to any farangs of that faith. The thought that he was escaping the most persistent religious foe the Jewish people have ever known was not on his radar screen when he landed in Thailand on a whim, lacking even rudimentary knowledge of the country. Over the years, he came to appreciate the nearly invisible Christianity as one of the Kingdom's endearing features. While the occasional ignorant idiot used swastikas or Hitler in ads or on T-shirts, this was a function of Thailand's insular and nationalistic education system, which ignores most things outside its borders. Antisemitism was virtually unknown in Thailand, practiced and expressed exclusively by a handful of foreigners. Glenn was aware of the clear disdain in which Thais held Christian attempts to convert them. *Just like we tell them to get lost.* The Kingdom was the only Asian nation to escape colonial rule, and the only one where Christianity never secured even a toehold. Glenn believed this was no coincidence.

Even in liberal strongholds like New York City and San Francisco, Glenn felt the sting of antisemitism. There was the Catholic boyhood friend who, when they were listening to the Mets losing and striking out, yelled "Jew" and "rabbi" as curse words. The boy immediately became an ex-friend, but the lesson was never forgotten: you can never be sure with them. There was of course Oliver, born Catholic but a devout atheist of the highest order.

∼

IT WAS a few days before the actual holiday, eighty degrees Fahrenheit after dark. The malls and shopping squares along Sukhumvit from Ekamai to Nana displayed trees without crosses or creches, and jazzed-up carols were right at home in a Christ-less Christmas. *Far less obnoxious than back in America, and it's over in a few days. Then we start the countdown to New Year's Eve,* a noncontroversial holiday for Glenn, who looked forward to the annual celebration with his friends.

This year, Oliver invited the gang down to his large home on Koh Phangan to ring in 2020. Sleepy Joe would be there, as would the General with his latest mia noi. To Glenn's displeasure, Oliver invited Edward. He couldn't understand why Oliver would invite someone who had caused him so much trouble in the past. *Then again, Edward's a semi-retired money launderer with CIA connections. Oliver may need his services once in a while.*

"Doesn't the General's wife expect her husband to celebrate the New Year with her?" Sleepy Joe asked Glenn.

"Come on, Joe, you know Thais have their own New Year, and they also have Songkran," referring to the raucous water festival in April. Glenn had been soaked with water and his face painted white on many Songkrans.

"I'm not certain many older Thais get excited about December 31. Maybe we misjudge, since there are so many foreigners where we go."

"Or maybe she's happy to be rid of him for a few days," Joe said.

~

GLENN HAD an appointment for his monthly massage. He always went to the same place because they offered only traditional, nonsexual massages. Sleepy Joe delighted in massages with "happy endings," anything from the masseuse masturbating them, performing fellatio, or hurried intercourse. *To each his own,* Glenn thought, but he found the notion disgusting. At least Joe didn't trumpet it like Phil Funston. Sex in a small, dingy upstairs room where they couldn't wait to usher you out and bring the next guy in was not Glenn's idea of relaxation. His masseuse, Kai, had been soothing muscles for twenty years, and was a devout Buddhist who played sacred music while working. When she saw Glenn walk through the door, she rose from her chair to greet him.

"Khun Glenn, *sawadii kha? Sabai dii mai kha?*" (Hello, how are you?) Those were among the few Thai words Glenn understood.

"*Sabai dii,*" he replied, using much of his remaining Thai to tell her he was fine.

Kai took Glenn's hand and led him to a middle-aged Thai woman who washed his feet. When she was done, Kai returned and led him by the hand upstairs to a massage room, a simple cubicle curtained on three sides and set against a windowless wall. Most Thai massage parlors, like this one, had the client lie on a mattress on the floor; only the more expensive had raised tables. Kai waited outside while Glenn changed into his massage clothing, not much more than blousy pajamas with drawstring pants.

After ten years, Kai knew her client's preference was a two-hour Thai massage, medium-hard pressure. Khun Glenn was a regular and a good tipper, and Kai felt good knowing he was always pleased with her massage.

Kai didn't look anywhere near her age, forty. She was thin, perfectly proportioned, and always upbeat and friendly. Her hands were soft for one who worked with them all day. Her eyes were bright and her smile wide. Her English was passable, but Glenn preferred to enjoy a massage by allowing himself to drift into that pleasurable space between sleep and consciousness. Much to Glenn's chagrin, the touch of Kai's hands on his body as she applied her masseuse skills caused him distinct erotic stirrings. He suppressed them using an old trick he learned in law school to prolong the time before ejaculation: he would slowly recite the names of the fifteen people who have held the post of Reporter of Decisions of the United States Supreme Court, the individuals responsible for assuring that all decisions are accurately recorded for posterity. When Glenn graduated law school, the Court was on their fifteenth Reporter. He'd read somewhere that his successor was the first woman to be appointed, and Glenn felt it was about time.

Glenn sometimes heard conversations from other massage cubicles, but he preferred to remain quiet and relaxed.

Tension floated away with every twist of an arm or leg. The second time Glenn ran through the Reporters, he lost consciousness two-thirds of the way through and the next thing he heard was Kai's voice telling him to sit up for the final backbend, where he sat, and she pressed her knees into his back as she pulled him backward. When it was over, she clapped her hands on his back and shoulders and rose to leave. It was understood he would see her downstairs, where he would hand her a large tip after he enjoyed a cup of tea.

Just as Glenn was about to step into his pants, a voice came from the other side of the curtain. It was man's voice, bit soft and slightly high pitched.

"Mr. Glenn Cohen?" the voice asked. "I know you are in there."

The accent was not Thai, and no Thai ever called him "mister." In the Kingdom, he was Khun Glenn.

"Could you please come back some other time," Glenn said. "As you can see, I'm busy."

"Yes, we know you are clever, Mr. Cohen. But not so clever as to see when you are being used and tricked."

"Who the hell are you, and what are you talking about?" Glenn asked. He struggled to put on his pants so he could step out and face the man.

"Mr. Boston is a fraud," the man said. "Everything he says is a lie. Enjoy the holidays, send Mr. Boston away, and forget everything else."

"Hang on, I'll be right there," Glenn said as he stepped into his shoes and pushed aside the curtain.

There was no one there.

∽

KAI AND the rest of the staff assured Glenn no one could have walked upstairs without being noticed.

"Only customers go upstairs," Kai reminded Glenn. "Anyone else, we call security." This was the first Glenn had heard of a massage parlor having security, but it made sense. *Not that it did me any good.*

"Are there any windows upstairs?" Glenn asked, thinking of what Lek's cousin had told him about Harper's killer escaping by rope.

"No windows upstairs," Kai replied.

I know I spoke with a man up there, but if I make a big deal of it, they'll think I'm crazy.

"Okay, maybe I just heard people talking in one of the other rooms," Glenn said, hearing in his own voice a lack of sincerity. He left a larger than usual tip and bid Kai farewell until the following month.

"Are you okay, Khun Glenn?" Kai asked, concern on her face as she watched her longtime customer so deeply lost in thought it appeared he might have fallen into a trance. She was relieved when he responded.

"Oh, I'm fine, Kai. Just thinking about New Year's. My friend invited me to a party at his place in Koh Phangan. It's really beautiful and relaxing."

"Yes, you looked worried," she said. "Sorry if the massage did not relax you. I feel bad."

"Oh no," Glenn said. "The massage was wonderful, like always. I was just thinking of how nice it will be when I'm by the beach for several days, watching the sun go down. And up as well, because I'm usually up with the sun. Maybe I was a rooster in my past life."

Kai laughed. "Maybe I will call you 'Rooster' from now on."

"See you next year," Glenn said.

"You have said that many times," Kai replied.

Something about the way Kai referred to Glenn saying the same thing every year resonated within him. He sensed a hidden message in her words. *Let's not overthink this. Do something.*

"You're right," Glenn said. "And it's time we celebrated a New Year with more than my stupid greeting. I'm going out of town to visit my friend Oliver this New Year, but as soon as I'm back I'd like to take you out for dinner so we can finally actually talk." The few seconds it took Kai to respond seemed like an eternity to Glenn.

"That would be very nice," she said. She got up, went to the front desk, wrote something on the massage parlor's business card, and gave it to Glenn.

"I wrote my cell number on the back," she said.

Glenn smiled and put the card in his pocket.

"I'll be counting the days," he said as he walked to the door. As he stepped outside, his thoughts returned to the strange encounter upstairs, and he hoped for a safe walk home.

∽

As soon as he was on the street, Glenn called Oliver and told him about the strange man outside the curtain. Glenn asked Oliver to call the General, Somchai, and Parhat to meet at Glenn's place as soon as possible. He called Sleepy Joe and gave him the full account. Joe appeared to have recovered from the bullet he took in his shoulder, which fortunately struck neither a major artery nor a muscle. The doctor told Joe he'd possibly feel periodic pain there, to which he replied that he regularly felt periodic pain anyway. Sleepy Joe said he wasn't far away and would meet Glenn not more than one block from where he called. A minute later, Sleepy Joe was walking at Glenn's side, and Glenn felt secure.

"Sounds like he's just blowing smoke, trying to scare you," Joe said as they walked to Glenn's. "Hoping we'll write off Boston as a nut and that will be the end of it all. They must be really desperate if that's all they have."

"Whatever, but it's not comforting to know I'm being tailed by Chinese communists, and they can get to me wherever I am. How the hell did that guy get upstairs and back down without being seen by anyone in a crowded massage parlor?"

"There are tricks to be learned, and anyone in intelligence work or surveillance learns many. The thing to remember is that most people aren't paying attention to anything. The second thing to know is that when people do see something, they really don't see it all. They pick up on certain markers that stand out to them. That's why it's rare that two people describe the same event exactly alike. Third thing is that even if a person sees someone or something, if they're not intentionally looking, minutes later they probably forgot what they saw. Someone who knows this and masters the techniques can walk in and out of a lot of places and not be noticed, or at least not recalled. This was just to scare you and the rest of us."

"It definitely succeeded," Glenn said.

Sleepy Joe stopped dead in his tracks. He turned to Glenn and placed a bony arm on Glenn's shoulder.

"Glenn, there is nothing to be scared of. We've been through much worse. We've faced people who wanted to kill us and almost succeeded. The Chinese government is not going to kill a bunch of farangs in Thailand, especially not an epidemiologist. If they want to avoid the spotlight, that's a terrible way. All they have left is fear. But the real fear is theirs, not ours."

Glenn reflected on his friend's words for a moment. "May we then assume that even in the lack of hard evidence or corroboration, there is indeed a viral pandemic that will overrun China and then the rest of the world?"

"That's something Tom Boston can confirm. Maybe the military guys or Oliver found some more info he can work with."

They walked the remaining two blocks in silence. In the lobby, Glenn asked Lek who was in his apartment. He'd authorized entry to all the essential people.

"Just Oliver, the American doctor, and three of the General's men."

He told Lek to expect the General, Colonel Somchai and Major Parhat. The list continued to impress the concierge.

"You know many important people, Khun Glenn."

Sort of like the Chinese curse, "may you live in interesting times."

Twenty-Eight

"This is getting to feel like home," Colonel Somchai told Glenn as he took a seat at the dining room table.

"Make yourself at home," Glenn replied. "All of my friends."

"Seems like I already made this place my home," Boston said.

"Like I do," the General said, as he cut the cap off one of Glenn's last half-dozen Montecristo Robusto Largos. He arrived with Somchai and Parhat a few minutes after Glenn.

"Good idea, General," Oliver said as he reached into the wooden humidor on the nearby side table. "Mind if I smoke this Ashton? It's the most expensive in the collection."

"Actually, the Davidoffs cost more," Glenn said.

"Okay," Oliver said. "I'll smoke a Davidoff."

Glenn wasted no time getting to the reason they were gathered. He told the group about his strange encounter at the massage parlor, including Sleepy Joe's thoughts on how agents were trained to come and go without being noticed.

"That CIA guy, Rodney Snapp, was the best I've ever seen," Oliver said. "How many times did he show up in your apartment, then disappear without a trace? I'm with Joe. People who learn about human perception and recall can do amazing things."

Maybe Rodney's experiences as an African-American taught him a thing or two about getting into places you're not wanted. Glenn had very mixed feelings about the CIA agent who once tried to warn him of danger, but also killed without inhibition when he alone thought it necessary. Glenn knew of at least one such case: his old friend and subsequent North Korean agent, Gordon Planter. No matter how evil Gordon may have become, dealing heroin for North Korea, having his wife killed, and his willingness to sacrifice Glenn and friends, which certainly qualified as evil, he deserved due process of law. Rodney broke Gordon's neck and dumped his body in a filthy canal because he grew tired of chasing him and holding him in place until he could be taken to America. *How is it that criminal lawyers and their clients are expected to follow the law, but the government does not? And now we have Donald Trump in charge.* A voice of authority woke him from his ruminations.

"I share the opinion of Joe and Oliver," Colonel Somchai said. "I agree that this was only an intimidation tactic, a free pass for them with nothing to lose. If we ignore them and accept Dr. Boston's reports as true, they are no worse off than before, and have suffered no further deaths or captured agents. I also believe our Western friends are in no danger of being killed by communists. China does not wish to place a spotlight on Wuhan, and that's what would happen if they started killing Western scientists like Mr. Boston or affluent foreign residents like Khun Glenn and Khun Oliver. It is clear they are watching Glenn at all times, probably because he attended that meeting. Anyone keeping an eye on the General or Oliver would be led to Glenn. They haven't figured out we're using the oldest trick in the book: hiding the doctor in plain view. I suspect this mysterious visit was a last-ditch attempt to frighten us into abandoning the doctor and letting them grab him, or perhaps just raise doubts as to his reliability. They don't know we've already made plans to get him out of Thailand. After Dr. Boston is safely gone, they'll suspect he is still somewhere here in Bangkok, and will waste no time looking for him."

"What do we do now?" Glenn asked. "Where do we go from here? How do we keep Dr. Boston safe? How do we make sure that he reaches people who can prevent a pandemic? A lot of questions, I know, but they need answers. I'd like to hear some suggestions first from our Thai mili-tary officers, who know this country far better than we farangs. Colonel Somchai and the General are retired but have more connections than any active-duty officers. Major Parhat has seen this unfold from the beginning. After that we'll hear from Oliver and Sleepy Joe. Then we're going to make our plan and stick with it. Let's hear first from the General." Glenn knew that Colonel Somchai, as a recently retired intelligence officer, had a better grasp of the overall threat, but the General held rank, prestige, and a place in Glenn's heart.

"I agree this was an attempt to warn and scare us, and there is not any serious chance that even Chinese communists would kill respectable foreigners on our soil at this time," the General said. "But every patriotic Thai should be disgusted that we would even consider it a possibility."

Can't argue with that, Glenn thought. Then he remembered a similar warning in the letter Flanders pinned to Harper's chest with a crucifix. *After that murder, they tried to kill Mick and Sleepy Joe. Maybe this is more than a mere intimidation tactic.* Glenn expressed these thoughts to the group.

"I see your point," Major Parhat said. He looked to the General, who nodded, signaling that it was now the Major's turn. Parhat continued.

"Let's examine who was being killed. Harper and Flanders because they were insiders the Chinese thought might be weak links. Same reason they went after Mick. These guys were all Chinese agents; even if Mick and Harper didn't know, and they had no country looking out for them. They were no longer Serbs that the Belgrade government would help, and those African passports were useless to them. The only reason Sun attacked Sleepy Joe was because he coincidentally interfered with the plan to kill Mick. Sun had to decide whether killing Mick was worth the consequences of killing an Australian citizen close to the General. Sun decided it was. Turned out to be a mistake. I learned just before I got here that Sun died. He never recovered from whatever Sleepy Joe did to him. A real shame, as he would have been a source of much information. However, he did tell us his name was Sun and that he had killed Harper He even told us where to find the body. We even recovered the .22 pistol with a silencer he used."

"How did you get him to talk?" Oliver asked. "These Chinese are trained to resist anything, even the most intense pain."

"We have our ways," Colonel Somchai interjected. "We don't have the same restrictions as the U.S."

"Not that our current government abides by any of them," Glenn added.

"One less communist terrorist on our soil," the General interjected.

"One more notch on my belt," Sleepy Joe said.

Major Parhat resumed his presentation. "I don't see any Chinese agent thinking that killing any of us is worth the trouble it would cause. With Dr. Boston, that's also true, because he's an American, and I'm pretty sure they want him alive. They just want to know what he learned and what the West will soon know. It's conceivable they'd abduct him, question him, possibly as part of some fraud or ruse, and let him go. Once they know the word is out about the virus, they will focus on protecting their country from the virus, and the reaction to any deceptions. Once they get all the information Dr. Boston possesses, killing him creates new and unnecessary problems."

"Who says they can go around kidnapping visitors?" the General asked in a louder than usual voice.

"No one," Major Parhat replied. "They're doing it anyway, and we expect them to keep trying."

"I thought I was going to be put on a plane back to California," Boston interjected.

"Right after we're done here," Colonel Somchai informed him. "Hope you're packed."

"Been packed for days," Boston said.

Major Parhat concluded his assessment. "I leave the actual intelligence analysis to the Colonel. Once Mr. Boston is out of here, if China is hiding things, the damage to them will be done. Their focus will shift to the genuine problems they face from the virus and their actions in hiding it."

Colonel Somchai nodded in approval when Parhat was finished.

"There is nothing I can or would want to add to this outstanding briefing, Major Parhat."

Glenn was impressed as well.

I never knew he had such an analytical mind or knew how to interpret what Oliver calls "'raw intelligence." His English gets better day by day, with an American accent getting close to the General's.

Glenn had a question for the Major.

"Sun used a pistol with a silencer to kill Flanders and was going to use it to kill Mick, but didn't use it to kill Harper. Instead, he pierced his heart with a crucifix. Am I to understand that was part of their campaign to terrorize us? As if running around Bangkok killing people wouldn't do the trick?"

"That's what I think, Khun Glenn. They do two things at once. They eliminate a security threat, and they heighten the fear by letting us know they have no limits and no respect for anything. Or at least they tried. Based on my studies, many Chinese agents are as confused about how Americans think as you are about how they think. My assessment is that they see all Americans and most Westerners as religious Christians, and they know the importance of the cross in that world, so they figured this would send a message that scared you Westerners. I assume they believed the thought of anyone so depraved as to use this religious symbol to kill would let us know we are dealing with people who have no limits and no decency."

"Boy, did they pick the wrong representative sampling," Sleepy Joe said.

"I'm thoroughly convinced they have no limits and no decency. Let's hear from Oliver," Glenn said.

"None of my contacts have any information about intelligence agents coming in from China recently, so whoever frightened our friend Glenn was already in Bangkok, most likely a stringer, maybe not even Chinese, just someone able to operate without being seen, who can sound menacing behind a curtain. Asia is full of such people after all the wars and espionage of the past seventy or so years. I'd suspect the Chinese called one when they realized Glenn was going for his massage. Even if caught, what could he say? Someone whose name he doesn't even know paid him to do this? That's all they would get because that would be the truth. I agree with the Major. The Chinese tried and failed to head off Boston at the pass. If nothing else, the Chinese are great pragmatists. They know this game is over, and it's time to put up walls and defend against the virus and the outrage from the rest of the world when the truth comes out.

"Our little adventure is over. Major Parhat will escort Dr. Boston to the airport, accompanied by three highly trained counter-terrorism soldiers and Wang." Everyone understood that Wang, the NJA Club owner and cook, was stepping in because Sleepy Joe had been shot and his shoulder wound needed more time to fully recover. His line of work demanded full physical capabilities. It was known to this group that Wang had been a celebrated soldier against the communists many decades ago, and still retained the ability to kill when necessary. Glenn and Oliver had seen him stare down a posse of armed Russian gangsters who were clearly afraid of him, and he saw him shoot dead a rogue CIA agent who tried to kill Glenn and Sleepy Joe. Oliver turned to the wounded Australian.

"Anything you'd like to say, Sleepy Joe?"

"Yeah, I've had to smell these cigars the last twenty minutes. Anyone got a light for my joint?" he asked as he produced it from a shirt pocket. Oliver passed him a lighter.

"And lest we forget, in a matter of days, we'll be ringing in the New Year on my little retreat on Koh Phangan," Oliver said. "I'm so glad to have everyone who can make it, especially Glenn, who needs more time away from the problems he encounters in Bangkok."

"I'll be in the far South by then," Major Parhat said. "Let's get ready to make your flight, Dr. Boston. The rest of your escort is already downstairs. I wish all of you a Happy New Year and I thank you for what I have learned."

"I'll be resting up back in my hometown," Colonel Somchai told the group. "It's been a real pleasure getting to know all of you."

EVERYONE LEFT except Glenn and Sleepy Joe. Tom Boston thanked both of them and promised to stay in touch. He said he'd be sure to warn them of any dangers from the virus he perceived threatening Thailand.

"My shoulder feels fine," Joe said. "I could have gone to the airport with them."

"You're lucky no real damage was done by that little .22 slug," Glenn said. "Let the Thais handle security at their own airport."

"Yeah, since they do such a great job keeping out Chinese killers," Joe replied.

Sleepy Joe rolled a joint which they smoked on the balcony. Halfway through, Glenn raised the issue that had been on his mind since his meeting with Funston.

"Joe, I've got a moral dilemma," he said,

"I'm probably the last guy to consult on that," Joe snorted.

"But you are my best friend and I value your judgment. Hear me out."

Joe nodded, and Glenn once again explained how Phil Funston had fired him because he had a new gig touring China.

"Based on what we know, don't I have some moral obligation to warn him?"

"Like hell you do!" Joe shouted. "What do we know? That smart scientists are pretty sure China is hiding a pandemic that's on the way, but no one has any hard information beyond that. You're going to tell him to pass up this job based on that? He's going to think you're angry and trying to screw him. Besides, who cares about what happens to him? He cost you time and money, and he's a waste of human tissue. You get him in a place where a gig like that comes along, and he kisses you off? I couldn't care less what happens to that son of a bitch. Besides, the guy to ask about the seriousness of the danger was Dr. Boston, not me, and that train just left the station."

"Maybe not," Glenn said. "This time of day, we'd get to the airport before Parhat and company get there by car. Obviously, them taking the Airlink train with Tom Boston is not a realistic option. Traffic means we get there before Boston has boarded his flight. I can ask the doctor when I get there."

"Yes, and how do you get to the gate, considering we don't have tickets?"

"I have Major Parhat's cell number," Glenn said. "I'll call him when we're at the airport and he'll get me through."

"Why not just call and have him put Boston on the phone?" Joe asked.

"I don't want to say anything other than get me through the gate. There's no time to have Oliver check my phone again to see if it is compromised. Parhat will know what to do. Nothing else need be said. Who knows how safe it is to talk on the phone? Especially after I was visited at the massage parlor. If I wait until we are at the airport to call Parhat, even if someone is following me or listening in, they won't have time to plan anything. Remember, besides Parhat and the other guards, Wang is there, and now you too. I'll find out what I need to know, and Dr. Boston will be safely on his way home. If I called now and tipped off the Chinese, they'd have time for an ambush before anyone even got to the airport."

Sleepy Joe nodded in agreement.

"I hadn't thought about that possibility. Must be the painkillers. I'm going with you anyway," he said.

"No, you're not," Glenn said firmly. "You're staying here and taking your pain meds and smoking yourself into oblivion so you don't do something to irritate a wound that seems to be healing well."

Joe had none of this. "The General wanted me to be with you, and be with you I shall," Joe said. "All I'm doing is taking a train ride."

Glenn realized that even if he left alone, Sleepy Joe would be out the door minutes later and on the way to the airport.

"I guess it's better if I have you in my sight every minute," Glenn said.

"Actually, it's supposed to be the other way around, Counsel."

"We can be there in forty minutes if we get moving," Glenn said.

∽

MAJOR PARHAT was pleased to receive Glenn's call and looked forward to meeting the American one more time before leaving for the South. He signaled to an airport security officer and instructed him to meet Glenn and Joe at the entry gate and bring them to him. Parhat wore his full dress uniform, so anyone at the airport would understand they were dealing with a Major in His Majesty's army. When he told the Immigration people to allow Glenn and Joe entry, they were not being given a choice.

Glenn fit his idea of what a proper farang ought to be like. *Khun Glenn respects Thailand and Thai people,* Parhat thought. *Too bad he insists on bringing that Sleepy Joe.*

∽

WHEN GLENN and Sleepy Joe followed the security officer and made their way to meet Major Parhat and Tom Boston.

"Personally, no matter what I knew, I wouldn't tell Funston. The man has no honor. None whatsoever."

"You're not me, that's for sure," Glenn said.

They saw the gate number on its sign when they were twenty meters away. They turned into its seating area where Parhat and Boston were seated in a row all their own, Wang and the General's security team keeping anyone else at bay. They allowed Glenn and Joe to approach.

"Thank you for this great help, Major Parhat," Glenn said after Parhat greeted him warmly and invited him and Joe to sit. "I only need to ask Dr. Boston one question, and then I'll leave."

"It is my pleasure to be of assistance, Khun Glenn. Ask Dr. Boston what you wish."

"My question is this, Dr. Boston: if you knew someone was planning a tour of China, would you tell them anything?"

Boston stroked his chin as he gave the question thought. He looked Glenn in the eyes as he explained.

"There is no legal requirement I know of that compels an epidemiologist to give unsolicited warning or advice. That's particularly true if the information is sketchy. Just like politicians, we epidemiologists might have reasons not to create unnecessary anxiety or fear. We also don't want to create a 'boy who cried wolf' problem where we give a warning where there is no danger, and so we don't have credibility the next time. Experienced epidemiologists know when it is time to warn the public health experts and the public itself. We have no hesitation when warnings are necessary. If we are directly asked, there is an ethical and I believe a legal obligation to answer truthfully so as not to endanger or mislead a layperson. You're the lawyer, so you would know the legal part better than me. I believe scientific ethics would encourage warning people of known dangers, and that includes instances where the physical evidence is lacking, but all signs point to a potential and deadly pandemic. We may not yet be at the level of information where a warning is needed, but under the circumstances here, I would indeed tell someone planning a trip to China that there's evidence of a potential pandemic, a potentially deadly virus. I'd advise waiting until we see the whole picture before going to China."

Glenn absorbed the epidemiologist's explanation. "Thank you, Dr. Boston, you've been most helpful. Have a safe flight and say hello to California for me."

"I will as well," a voice called from behind Glenn. He turned to face the tall, athletic African-American man who said those words. Rodney Snapp smiled at Glenn. He wore a suit and carried a briefcase

"We meet again, my friend. This time you've broken open the case of the virus China is covering up. Not too long ago you broke open a North Korean heroin ring and turned over a North Korean spy. A few years ago, it was a Russian gangster wanted in America. Why not take our offer of employment with the CIA? You seem to enjoy the work."

"Not like you do, Rodney," Glenn replied.

"Sorry to hear that, Glenn. I know you well enough to accept you understand why I am here."

"I sincerely hope it has nothing to do with my legal client, Dr. Thomas Boston, who is also under the protection of the Thai government, as evidenced by the presence of Major Parhat."

Rodney smiled at the Major.

"Stay safe down South," he said. "Even I get nervous going up against those terrorists down there."

Parhat did not respond.

"Didn't fall for the bait," Rodney said. "He's obviously been trained not to openly respond to surprises. You'll do well down there. Glenn was the same. First time I confronted him with all I knew, things he thought I didn't know, he was as cool as you. That's why I've been begging him for years to come work for us."

"It's a great honor to be compared to Khun Glenn," Parhat replied.

Rodney looked to Sleepy Joe.

"Sorry to learn about your injury, Joe. If you need anything, be it doctors, meds, physical therapy, I'll have the best in Bangkok at your service. Just tell Oliver. He knows how to reach me."

Joe said nothing.

"Another pro," Rodney said. "It's a pleasure to be around people on the same wavelength as me."

"We're not on the same wavelength as you," Glenn said.

Rodney arched his eyebrows.

"Really, Glenn? You think your friend Sleepy Joe and your admirer Major Parhat are not on my wavelength? Do you think the Major has any compunction about killing to protect his King and his country? Does Sleepy Joe have any issues with killing to carry out the General's assignments? And you Glenn, as I've told you before, had no problem killing three North Koreans who came to murder you. Everyone is on this wavelength, like it or not. Not just us, everyone in the world. We'll all kill to protect and defend what we hold dearest. In the case of the Major and I, it's for our country. For Joe, it's what honorable people do when they accept danger. For you it was just self-defense. Who is to say which of us has the better justification?"

"None of us have to justify ourselves to the CIA," Glenn said. "You didn't come here to talk about the moral justification for homicide. What do you want from us?"

Rodney scanned the area around him, containing Parhat and the General's men as well as Joe and Glenn.

"We want nothing from anyone except Dr. Boston, and all we want from him is information any patriotic American would want his government to know."

"That government didn't want to know," Tom Boston said. "It did all it could to cut off contact, and it was left to the private sector to investigate. Notice that I'm here, representing the private epidemiological world, but the only person the government sends is a CIA agent."

"You're not going with him," Glenn told Boston. "Major Parhat, please understand that this man has no interest in using Dr. Boston to help protect people. Instead, this American government will do all it can to keep it quiet, just like China. Remember what we told you before: the President is up for reelection in eleven months. If word gets out about a possible deadly virus sweeping the world, all economies will suffer, America's included. I doubt Mr. Trump wants to run with a bad economy."

"And as a result, people will die," Boston said.

"That won't matter to him as long as he gets reelected," Glenn said. "Losing the election could mean serious trouble, maybe even jail. No, this information will never see the light of day."

"It really doesn't matter what you think, Glenn, and Major Parhat has no choice. Please examine this document, Major," Rodney Snapp said as he handed the Major a sheet of paper with a seal at the bottom left corner. The Major read the document.

"It is a directive from the Office of the Prime Minister, cosigned by the Foreign and Defense Minister as well as the head of Immigration at this airport. The American, Dr. Thomas Boston, is to be escorted from Thailand under the protection of the U.S. government, in the person of Rodney Snapp of the CIA. Thailand and America guarantee his safe passage home. It's genuine, not a fake like Flanders used."

"Once in America, the doctor is free to talk with us or not," Rodney said. "We assume any patriotic American would help protect the health of our people."

"The term 'any patriotic American' does not apply to Donald Trump," Glenn said as he glared at Snapp. "That's the man you work for, the man who gives you your marching orders. Since he doesn't want you investigating Russia, you have plenty of time on your hands to kidnap scientists who might save lives."

Rodney Snapp ignored Glenn's stare and looked at Major Parhat.

"Kidnap? Taking an American home, where he wants to be, with an order from the Thai government authorizing me, is suddenly criminal?"

Glenn didn't let go. "If this is just an American going home, why you, why the need for an order?"

"Glenn, you know as well as I why I'm assigned to protect Dr. Boston and why both governments think it's necessary. Why else would Wang and Sleepy Joe be here? If it will allay your fears, let me remind you that an agent of my standing takes illegal orders from no one, not even the President. Dr. Boston will be home in twenty hours, and if he is the kind of American I know he is, he'll tell our experts all he knows and go on his way. If he decides not to help us stay safe, it will be on his conscience, and he'll be free to go."

"There's no choice, Khun Glenn," Major Parhat said. "There's no getting around this order. If Khun Rodney had evil intentions, he would not be so foolish as to show his face to us in this airport with all its cameras."

"I agree," said Dr. Boston. "Now that I've heard from Mr. Snapp and seen that the Thai government has found him legitimate, I'm actually kind of relieved to have a CIA agent on board to watch over me."

"You shouldn't," Glenn said. "He's not doing this for the reasons you think," Glenn said.

Rodney shook his head. "Come to work for us Glenn, and voice your criticism. Now I must bid you farewell until we meet again."

"Which I hope is never," Glenn answered.

∽

Glenn watched Tom Boston and Rodney Snapp walk through the gate onto the plane. Neither one looked back.

"Do you think Boston will be okay?" Glenn asked.

"I think so, mate. Too many saw him get on the plane with Rodney, and there is a paper trail thanks to that order. My guess is they either keep him out of sight for a while or throw out so much disinformation that no one will believe him."

"That's reassuring, Joe."

"Well, it doesn't get better, so take what you can," Joe said.

When the last passenger boarded and the gate closed, Boston's bodyguards dispersed. Wang said he was taking the Airlink train back to the city and the Club. The General's men took cabs to wherever the General had instructed them. Major Parhat apologized for not being able to offer Joe and Glenn a lift back to Bangkok, but he had to drive to his barracks and prepare for his trip South.

"And may you stay safe," Glenn said as they parted.

"I will," Parhat said. "And by the way, since Khun Oliver sent the tape of Doctor Boston's thoughts to experts in Thailand and Australia—and I'm certain the U.S. as well—Khun Rodney was, as Americans say, a day late and a dollar short." He gave Glenn a wai and headed to the parking garage.

"Stay safe," Glenn called out to Parhat. "Come on by when you get leave. There's a seat for you at the NJA Club, and Lek knows to always send you up." He couldn't tell if Parhat heard him.

∽

Glenn preferred the Airlink train, but Sleepy Joe insisted upon a taxi.

"I can smoke a joint in the cab. The drivers always let me," Joe explained.

"No, they don't," Glenn said. "You just threaten to hurt them if they complain."

"But they do let me," Joe countered.

As Glenn and Joe walked through the airport on their way to the taxicab line, they saw two familiar figures coming out of a restaurant. Phil Funston and the General's son were so deep in conversation they didn't notice they were about to collide with Glenn and Joe.

"Watch where you're going, you stupid oaf," Sleepy Joe said when Funston and the son realized who they were about to crash into.

"Who are you calling an oaf?" Phil yelled.

"Both of you," Sleepy Joe replied.

"Call us what you like," the General's son said. "We are on our way to China. I was able to get Phil a tour where we're going to make some money. I'm his manager for this tour. You and your little friend were holding him back."

"You are going to China with Phil?" Glenn asked.

"Just to set things up, make sure they know who they're dealing with if they try to cheat us. I'll be back in a week, after New Year's."

"We were lucky to get last minute tickets this time of year," Funston said. "My new manager has clout."

"Where are you flying to?" Glenn asked.

"The best we could do on short notice was to get on one of these discount Chinese airlines. They all land in Wuhan, and then we change planes to Shanghai."

"Well, no hard feelings, guys," Glenn said. "I wish you the very best of luck. Enjoy China."

"And you enjoy your little waitress. Because next time I see her, I'm hitting her twice as hard as last time."

Glenn moved an inch from the General's son. He looked down at him with blazing eyes.

"Thanks for the warning, because the very next time I see you, I am going to beat you to within an inch of your life. I don't care whose son you are."

"No, you won't," the General's son said. "You don't do things like that."

"But I do," Sleepy Joe said softly. "And to be blunt, your father needs me more than he needs you."

The General's son flinched and stepped back. "Let's get away from these maniacs," he said to Phil. They walked toward the security line.

"You forgot to warn them," Joe said.

"Oh, darn it. I'm always forgetting things," Glenn said.

Twenty-Nine

NJA Club, December 26, 2019

As soon as Glenn was seated, Kit came over and took his order. When written down, she sat next to Glenn.

"This is a good day for me," she said cheerfully.

"Why is that?" Glenn asked.

"Biggest reason is Edward told me last night Phil Funston will be in China for three months. Even better, General's son is taking him. I guess that means you don't manage him anymore. I think that is also happy news."

"How does Edward know all this?" Glenn asked.

"The General's son asked Edward to set up secret bank account in Laos so Thai government does not see the money he makes in China. Edward made me promise not to say anything about money or trip to China. The son told Edward his father didn't know about the trip. So please don't tell."

"I thought the General knows everything," Glenn said.

"Why don't you ask the General? He is your good friend."

"I think it is better if I don't bring that up," Glenn said.

"I think you know the General better than me. Anyway, maybe we will be lucky and they never come back here," Kit said.

"Don't say that," Glenn said. "We don't wish bad things on anyone, not even Phil Funston." *Though I'm not so sure about that anymore.*

"Oh no, Khun Glenn, I don't wish for bad things to Phil Funston or the son. I just hope I can never see them again."

"What's the other good news?" Glenn asked.

"I will be at the farang New Year's party on Koh Phangan. Edward invited me as his date. Not really date, you know, Edward like men, not ladies. But we are good friends."

"That's very nice," Glenn said. "It will be really nice to see you there." *Didn't I just make a date with Kai for when I get back? Now Kit's coming to the party, and I know why. How do I deal with this?*

"Wait till you see me at the party," Kit said. "I will look very beautiful for Khun Glenn."

"I'm looking forward to seeing it, but you're beautiful all the time."

"*Pak wan,*" she replied, the Thai term meaning "sugar-mouth." It was one of the Thai expressions Glenn understood.

"No, just truthful," he replied. He spied Sleepy Joe walking to the bar. He told Kit he had to speak with him.

"What'll it be today, Counselor?" Ray the bartender asked in his lilting Irish brogue. "Since you're done with that Funston jackass, let me serve you one on the house. Thank China for taking him off my hands."

How is it that everyone but the General knew? Glenn told Ray he had something to discuss with Joe. Ray said Kit would bring their drinks.

When they were at a table, Glenn told Joe that the General was unaware his son accompanied Phil to China.

"If he finds out we knew he was flying to Wuhan and said nothing, we have a problem," he said.

"No, we don't," Joe replied. "Even if the General wasn't told and didn't have the chance to warn his son, there's nothing to worry about. If they catch that virus and die, he'll never know we met him and Phil and said nothing. If they come back, I doubt the son is foolish enough to tell his old man he threatened to hit Kit again. In case you are the only one at the Club who hasn't figured it out, he values you more than Sonny Boy. But before you bury those two in China, let me remind you we don't know for certain there even is this special kind of virus, or how contagious it is, or how deadly it might be. Let me say again, mate, based on what we know, there's not a chance in the world they were ditching this trip. So just forget we saw the creeps and everything will be fine."

∽

December 29, 2019

"Hurry up, Glenn, or we'll miss the plane," Sleepy Joe called out to Glenn, still in his bedroom, packing. "I thought you were packed a few days ago, like the Glenn we all know and love."

"I was," Glenn replied, "then I found out Edward is bringing Kit. This was going to be several days of beach casual, but now I have to look good for my fan club."

"What about that masseuse you said you were going out with when we get back from the island?" Joe asked.

"Am I now limited to one woman?" Glenn asked.

"You're starting to sound like the General," Joe said. "What's gotten into you?

"One last number for the trip," Joe said as he lit a joint. They sat on Glenn's couch listening to *Thick as a Brick* by Jethro Tull. Glenn and Joe marveled at the notion that they regularly listened to music made around the time they were born. In Sleepy Joe's case, he had little use for music released after 1990, although he reluctantly admitted to a fondness for Nirvana, The Foo Fighters, Green Day, and Rage Against the Machine.

They sat in silence, passing the joint between them.

"I know you, mate," Sleepy Joe said when they were done. "You're still thinking about those two dirtbags we ran into at the airport. You're flagellating yourself over not warning them."

Glen said nothing.

Sleepy Joe continued. "Let me ease your conscience again, Glenn. You need to hear it once more, hopefully the last time. The General's son could have told the old man he was off to China for a week or so. Someone has to run those clubs each day he's gone. If he didn't tell the General, no issue for you. If he decided to go behind his father's back for any reason, then everything that follows is on him, including missing a warning about a potential danger. If the General did find out about the trip beforehand, from his son or elsewhere, and didn't warn him, why are you the bad guy?"

"Even if the General told his son, that doesn't mean Phil knows," Glenn said. "Maybe the son would want the tour to go on and was afraid Phil would not."

Sleepy Joe laughed. "You're way overthinking this, mate. Once more, do you think there's a chance in the world that chickenshit son or Funston would want to cancel a money-making tour based on what we could tell him? If we did warn them, and they decided to cancel the trip, that creates a whole other set of problems. Dr. Boston wants this information to get into the hands of people who will use medical and scientific methods to protect millions of people against a possible deadly threat, many right here. Don't forget China is just next door. We feared they would grab Dr. Boston to prevent him from spreading the alarm like your Paul Revere. We learned why governments try to hide these things as long as possible. If Funston or that loudmouthed punk knew about Dr. Boston, would we feel confident that we could keep Boston and our friend Mick safe?"

He's right, Glenn thought. *No way Funston can keep his big mouth shut if he can open it and look like a big shot with inside information. The son would probably tip off China for money.*

∽

PHIL FUNSTON lay on his bed, sniffling and wheezing. The General's son gazed down at him, a worried look on his face. Two days until the big New Year's Eve show where Phil was lead guitarist for the main act, and he was coming down with some bug.

"I feel like crap," Phil croaked.

You look and sound even worse, the son thought.

"It's probably a flu. Comes around every fall and winter. If the hotel can't get a doctor, I'll call the American Embassy. I'm sure they have a list."

"I'd appreciate it," Phil rasped, and fell asleep.

He must have picked it up at the horrible airport in Wuhan. We were stuck there for hours with no place to sit, hardly any services. And all those Chinese coughing in our faces everywhere we went. It's a miracle I didn't catch it.

To the son's relief, as soon as he told the concierge about Phil, a doctor was summoned. The son went back up to Phil's room to wait for the doctor. Ten minutes after he returned, there was a knock on the door. Expecting the doctor, the son opened it. Three men wearing white hazardous material protection, the kind called hazmat suits, rushed into the room. They ordered the son to remain where he was. The men reminded the son of astronauts in spacesuits.

One of the men drew a blood sample and a nasal swab from the son while a second did the same to the unconscious Phil Funston. The third collected all of Phil's personal belongings—cell phone, wallet, passport—and placed them in a large plastic baggie. He then demanded the same from the General's son, speaking English.

"This is outrageous," the son screamed. "We have a sick man here and all you can do is harass me? I'm a respectable businessman."

"This is a public health matter," the demander explained. "We wish you no harm. To the contrary, we wish to help you. Your friend is very ill, and if you have been in direct contact with him, we suspect you will soon be as well. We are taking you to a hospital where you will be treated and cured. A few days at most."

"What if I refuse?" the son asked.

"You have no choice," the man in the white hazmat suit said. Two more men entered the room and each gripped one of the son's sides at his forearm and shoulder. They lifted him up and carried him away, the son squawking like a chicken slated for dinner.

～

COLONEL SOMCHAI stopped by the NJA Club for an end-of-the-year drink with the General. The General had been catching up on business that had piled up while he was focused on protecting some people and stopping others from killing or kidnapping. No one had seen him for two days. The following day, Somchai would be with his wife, grown children, and grandchildren in his village a few hours south of Bangkok. The General would be enjoying Oliver's hospitality by the beach, his latest mia noi at his side while he waited welcoming the farang New Year with his farang friends. The Colonel was forever amazed at how the General weaved between the world of the farang and the Thai universe. The Colonel respected many farangs, especially the friends he made when assigned to Australia, honorable people whose word was always good and whose insights were always worth hearing. He felt the same about Glenn and Oliver but had doubts about Sleepy Joe. *He's not quite right in the head, but he gets the job done, and he's fearless. But any military man knows someone like that can get beyond control very easily.*

"I hope that whole mess with your son and Glenn has resolved itself," Somchai said.

The General looked into his martini glass, then at the Colonel. "I haven't seen or spoken to him since that day. I know he expected me to leap in and take his side, but how could I? He struck a woman in public, a woman who works for Wang, one of the dearest friends I've ever had. It happens to be a woman who loves Glenn, the farang I am closer to than any other non-Thai on this planet. Besides, Glenn did what any decent man would do. My son acted like a bully and a thug. I can tell you this, Somchai, since we are such good friends, but please never utter a word of what I am telling you."

"I am a retired military intelligence officer," Somchai replied. "Secrecy is embedded in my bones. My mouth will be forever closed."

"As I thought," the General said. "The truth is, I wish I had a son like Glenn or Parhat. Unfortunately, we do not get to choose our offspring. It's karma. In a prior life I must have brought shame to my father. I hardly know my son, since I never laid eyes on him before he was twenty-one. I may have moved him along too soon. He's not even thirty and he's running a half dozen of my clubs. He had no background in business. From what I gather, he was little more than a street thug who relied on others to do the fighting. Sounds right, because he talks tough, but we saw what a coward he was when Glenn confronted him. From what I hear, and I hear it all, the only reason we drew patrons was because Glenn perpetually booked Phil Funston, who is supposedly as good a guitarist as he is bad as a person. And that kid Rong not only kept Phil in line, but also is a bass player, and he booked a few bands on his own to play the clubs. I'm thinking about asking Rong to accept a position that looks like it is subordinate to my son, but actually has more authority. I'm told my son argues with customers, musicians, and even the police. He tried to negotiate the gratuity he pays them to forget about parking and crowd size rules. Can you imagine such a thing? How does he expect to operate nightclubs in this city if he doesn't make the police happy?"

"Unthinkable," Somchai said. *This is where we differ. My General thinks of the right way to bribe police, and I'm thinking about being back home with my family. Time to change the topic.*

"Your farang friends like Rong," Somchai said. "I must say, they are hardly your everyday farangs."

"I'm not an everyday Thai," the General said.

They spent the next half hour reminiscing about comrades in arms, many no longer alive. When they finished their second round of drinks, Colonel Somchai stood, gave the General a wai—he was the same age, but of higher rank—and promised to stop by for a drink in a few weeks when he returned from the province.

Thirty

December 31, 2019 (New Year's Eve)

GLENN WAS enjoying Koh Phangan. Oliver's spacious home was set on a half-acre right along the beach, not more than a kilometer outside Tong Sala, a pleasant little city with every amenity a farang would want. The house had four bedrooms, plus a guest cottage with two more. Oliver and his new girlfriend occupied the master bedroom, and Glenn, Edward, and Kit each were given one of the others. The guesthouse went to the General and his mia noi. Sleepy Joe was offered Oliver's office, with its sofa bed, but Joe opted to sleep in a hammock on the back porch. He explained that he liked sleeping amidst a sea breeze.

There were no structures between Oliver's house and the ocean, and there was at least seventy-five meters between the adjoining properties on both sides. Traffic on the road running past the house was sparse. In the early morning and late evening, Glenn heard the sounds of the ocean, the wind, the birds, various species of croaking reptile and chirping insects.

On Koh Phangan, the pace of life was slow, the air clear, and the ocean breeze soothing. The island was a favorite of farangs and was unusual with its outsized and pleasant French influence. True, once a month the island was overrun by young Europeans getting drunk and disorderly for Full Moon parties, but that was only a small stretch of the island, and since the coup in 2015, the parties were less frequent and less rowdy. There were no high rises; Glenn was willing to bet there wasn't even an elevator to be found. Most of the island was actually protected and preserved under Thai law. There were many fine places to eat, drink, and hear music. There was no movie theater or airport, but there was decent medical care, and the more developed and more populated island of Koh Samui was a short ferry ride away.

For two days, Glenn began his day with a seven a.m. dip in the Gulf of Thailand followed by a shower and a walk into town. The first morning he discovered a French bistro serving omelettes and croissants and, even more importantly, first-rate coffee. This would be his third breakfast there.

Glenn remembered to turn right at the Chinese temple. As he did, a woman called him from behind. He recognized Kit's voice and heard her hurried footsteps. Seconds later she stood next to him. She wore a pair of shorts and a halter top, and her hair was let down, touching her shoulders. Before this trip, Glenn had never seen Kit in anything other than the NJA Club waitress uniform, which Wang selected because he thought it would keep down the number of hoots, whistles, and unwanted touching that all too often results from a combination of men, alcohol, and vulnerable attractive women. *Her body is nicer than any of the ones before. Even nicer than Kai.*

"May I walk with you please?" Kit asked Glenn.

"Of course," he replied. "It's nice to have company early in the morning. All of our friends like sleeping as late as possible. They miss so much beauty."

"I saw you go walking early in the morning yesterday. I have not been to town and want to see it. "

"In that case, please join me for breakfast. I hope you like French food, omelettes, croissants, brioches…"

Kit interrupted him.

"I never tried them," she said. "So today is my lucky day."

Glenn looked at her and smiled.

"Mine too."

⁓

"Easy to remember where I put them when there's fewer customers," Glenn said as he unlaced his sneakers and left them outside the bistro door. Kit slipped out of her sandals. When they were seated and handed menus, she asked Glenn what he recommended.

"Try an omelette," he said. "Everyone likes eggs. Then add a chocolate croissant. Everyone likes chocolate." He recommended she try a mocha coffee, but she declined and ordered a tea.

Seated across a table from Kit, she was in his sight at every second. The first time he saw her at the Club, he knew she was attractive, but seeing her outside the harried work environment, free from impatient customers, drunken leches, and Phil Funston, and dressed for the island, she looked even younger and infinitely more at ease. Glenn was not surprised when she smiled at him and patted his hand.

"I am very happy to spend even a little time alone with you. I can never stop to thank you for how you helped me when the General's son hit me."

Glenn smiled in turn. "You don't have to thank me. It was an honor and a pleasure to help you. Oh yes, it's not 'I can never stop *to* thank you.' You say, 'I can never stop *thanking* you.'"

Kit laughed and squeezed the hand she held.

"I can never stop thanking you for teaching me good English," she said. "You want me to teach you some Thai? You live in *Pateet Thai*," she said, using the Thai term for the Kingdom. "Your good friend Oliver speaks beautiful Thai. If Thai person will not see him, only hear him, they will think he is Thai."

"You are right, Kit," Glenn said, enjoying the warmth of Kit's hand as it gripped his. "You came to Bangkok a few months ago not speaking any English, and now you are doing just fine. I can help you speak as well as the General or Major Parhat. And you can help me learn to speak Thai as well as Khun Oliver."

Kit laughed. "Oh no, Khun Glenn, I am not so good a teacher to make you speak like Khun Oliver. He speaks Isan also. Very few farang can speak Isan. We Isan people cannot have secrets from Khun Oliver."

Kit released Glenn's hand when the waitress brought their coffee and tea.

"Teach me Thai first," Glenn said. "Then we'll worry about me learning Isan."

"Let me start by telling you the Thai words for what you eat today," she said. When she told him the word for egg was *kai*, to him it sounded like the word *gai*, or chicken, which in turn reminded him that he had a date with a very attractive Thai woman, however her name was pronounced. *When it rains, it pours, as my father used to say.*

⁓

By the time Glenn and Kit walked back to Oliver's property, he knew most of her life story. It wasn't all that different from dozens of similar accounts, but this time he was actually interested. Unbearably hard farm work, coming to the big city to make money and help those back home. In America, Glenn encountered people who dropped out of high school, but until he came to Thailand he hadn't met any who never even started. It was supposedly becoming rare these days, but Glenn had no idea what was true. Kit's story engendered the same sympathy as always. He liked hearing her voice.

To his surprise, in the leisurely half hour walk, he disclosed more about himself to Kit than he had revealed to any friend at the NJA Club. That even included Oliver, the only person aside from Glenn and his lawyer friend Charlie who knew the criminal source of Glenn's Thailand seed money. It included Sleepy Joe, the only person who knew he had seen Phil and the General's son at the airport and failed to warn them. Not the General, with whom Glenn had on several occasions swapped accounts of life-changing experiences. None of them knew that Glenn's former wife told him she didn't love him anymore and refused to have sex with him, or that he had never recovered from his father's death in a car accident, or that he wished he could really believe in some religion and find comfort. Perhaps it was that Kit was such a good listener that encouraged him to open up in ways he hadn't done in his years in Thailand.

∾

IT WAS not yet nine o'clock when Glenn walked on the porch where Sleepy Joe had spent the night. His friend was awake, sitting at a small round wrought iron table, enjoying his first coffee of the morning. Glenn had a mug of his own in hand and joined Joe at the table.

"Saw you and Kit coming back from a morning stroll," Joe said. "If this keeps up, there could be an actual bedroom for me."

Glenn literally waved off the comment.

"Let's focus more on what we're going to do about the General's son being in China, passing through Wuhan, and we didn't warn him."

"We've been through this twice already, mate," Joe said. "I have since come up with a foolproof excuse just in case. You were brought into this mess because the General wanted you to represent him and his business at that ridiculous meeting with the Serbs and Mr. Sun. In other words, we were all within the attorney-client privilege because we were all working for the same guy, the General. His son might have his DNA, but no basis for allowing you to breach that attorney-client privilege."

"Since you're such an expert in American legal ethics, can't that privilege be waived to save lives?"

"You don't need to go there," Joe replied. "When someone is talking to a lawyer, they have a legal right to know whatever they say or hear will be totally confidential. No one outside the privilege gets to hear a thing. The son was outside the privilege. Far as I'm concerned, it doesn't matter if it's a deadly virus or a pie in the face. Dr. Boston and the General didn't want this getting out. Certainly not until we had more answers, as Dr. Boston explained. I don't think lawyers can go around breaching the privilege on suspicion or because they feel bad."

"You would have made a fine law school ethics professor had you not elected to become a professional assassin," Glenn said. "And I mean that with the highest degree of respect."

"Thank you, Glenn, but I prefer the term 'troubleshooter.'"

"We can't shoot this trouble," Glenn said. "I'm talking about this mystery virus."

"No, we can't," Joe agreed. "We can get more detail, and I've asked Oliver to find out what he can and let us know what he thinks will happen. I didn't tell him anything about us seeing those two at the airport. I told him you needed to get in touch with Phil to see what he wants done with some fees coming in because big a dirtbag as he is, you wanted him to get what was due him. Anyone who knows you would believe this. I added you wouldn't mind if he could also find out who he got to manage him after he canned you. Oliver says congratulations on getting rid of Phil. He'll be dropping by after we're done."

"Done with what?" Glenn asked. "Oh, I should have known," he said as he watched Joe light up a joint. Joe passed it to him just as Oliver came onto the porch.

"A little early?" Oliver asked.

"Never too early," Joe replied. "What do you have for us?"

"The facts," Oliver said. "Just the facts. And the facts are that Phil Funston was hired for a tour in China. It's not hard to find that out, because every performer has to register with several state agencies. The surprise is his manager. It's none other than our friend, the General's son."

"I'm amazed!" Sleepy Joe said loudly. "You think he did it to get back at Glenn, not knowing Glenn wanted out from Funston?"

Oliver shook his big shiny shaved head.

"No, it was the money. If he thinks it hurt you, that's probably comforting to him, but he wouldn't do it without making some dough."

"Do you think they are in any danger over there, based on what we learned?" Glenn asked.

"I'm not a scientist, and even our own scientist can't say for certain what lies ahead. I can tell you I would not go to China right now, definitely not Wuhan. They did change planes at Wuhan, by the way. That can't be good."

"Has anyone heard from them?" Glenn asked. "Maybe they found out something."

"That's the strange thing," Oliver said. "Once they got off the connecting flight to Shanghai, they've fallen off the face of the earth. The tour was canceled, they are not registered in any hotel, they haven't flown out. All of those records are easy to obtain. I drew on every contact to see if they were arrested, and no, they were not. No reports about them were made to or by the American or Thai Embassies."

"If my mate Oliver can't find them, no one can," Sleepy Joe said.

"I didn't say I couldn't find them," Oliver said. "I told you there were no records of their arrival or presence. That doesn't mean China doesn't have them, it just means China doesn't want anyone else to know. The information is available to those who know where to look."

"You being one of those who know where to look," Glenn commented.

"Indeed," Oliver said. "Even in the People's Republic, dedicated to the memories of Mao and Marx, money talks. I have a contact in the Chinese Embassy here and another in their Embassy in Canberra. When these commie diplomats spend a little time in a civilized place like Bangkok or Australia, they often develop a taste for the finer things in life. A man like me, who traffics in information, can often exploit that taste."

"Blackmail or bribery?" Glenn asked.

"It all depends upon one's point of view," Oliver said. "In any event, I was able to learn that our General's heir apparent is being treated for a serious respiratory infection in a military hospital near Shanghai. He is expected to survive and be released from the hospital in a week, but he won't be returning here for some time. Not until the health threat is under control."

Glenn put the joint in an ashtray, clasped his hands, and formed a triangle with his elbows on the table. He stared at Oliver as he spoke softly.

"So there really is a dangerous virus in China," Glenn said. "Everything Dr. Boston heard and reported to us is true." He dropped his arms, took another puff off the joint, and handed it to Joe.

"There's something going on, that's for sure, and it seems to be very much what Dr. Boston and his colleagues speculated. I'm not qualified to say if this is a new type of coronavirus, or any virus for that matter. All I can report is highly credible information corroborates Dr. Boston's conclusions that there is a very contagious disease originating in Wuhan. The intense Chinese secrecy tells me they haven't come close to controlling it, not even understanding it, and they are very afraid of where it is heading. They tried to abduct Dr. Boston to find out what was known outside China, and to stop or slow the inquiry as best they could while looking for a solution."

"Well, they sure sent a collection of knuckleheads to do the job of grabbing the doctor," Sleepy Joe said through a cloud of ganja smoke. Oliver took the burning joint from him.

"Mick and the late Mr. Harper would fall into the knucklehead category," Oliver said after he took a drag and exhaled a cloud of smoke. "Their job was to follow Dr. Boston, and if they were caught by anyone, there wasn't much they could tell. Flanders and Sun, the two non-Chinese citizens of the PRC, were by no means knuckleheads. They were highly trained and skilled special agents, Sun with personal combat skills near Joe's level. They would have handled the abduction and participated in the interrogation. They would have kept him here in Bangkok, in one of their secret hideouts. They have them just like our side does."

"I killed a real superstar, didn't I?" Sleepy Joe asked. "A top-of-the-line guy?"

"I'd say so, mate," Oliver replied.

Sleepy Joe gave a thumbs up.

"You haven't told us what you learned about Phil Funston," Glenn said.

"I learned nothing from my sources because there's neither an official record nor any unofficial information, like with the son. The Chinese know who his father is, and being pragmatists when it suits them, they found a way to keep the lid on their problem but not make an unwanted enemy. That's why my contact inside the PRC web so cheerfully assured me Sonny Boy will recover and repatriate when the time is right. The General will understand and maybe even appreciate their gesture. They are trying to take over Thailand, we all know, and so far they are trying to do it by acting nice. You know, promising all kinds of things they'll never give the Thais. Our General is as pragmatic as the Chinese, and he understands them totally. He is part Chinese, along with sixty percent of Bangkok. Now you know he can read and write the language."

"Back to Phil Funston," Glenn said. An uneasy sensation roiled his stomach, and he didn't think it was the strong coffee.

"Phil Funston does not have a powerful father," Oliver explained. "We've never heard about any family. He doesn't even have a real friend. If there's anyone who would be watching out for him, it would be his manager, and the General's son would throw his mother under the bus to save his own skin. I explained why it is worth China's trouble to keep the son alive and get him back in one piece, but that doesn't extend to a jerk everyone hates. Who would even bother to report Funston missing? And if anyone did, how much effort's your country going to exert on his behalf? Does America know he's still around? He's been living here for over twenty years, and I bet he hasn't voted or filed a tax return in all those years. He renews his passport every ten years, and that's the extent of his contact with the government of the United States."

"Lucky bastards!" Joe cried out. Oliver then continued.

"If Phil never got sick, or if he recovered, my guess is the Chinese would do the same with him as with the General's son. They realize that if he was working for the General's son, sooner or later someone will inquire about him, someone the Chinese can't shrug off. If word got out he died under suspicious circumstances in China, the troubles to come would be worse than any that might come from keeping him alive. Think of what would happen to the American appetite for cheap Chinese goods were it to come out that Americans were disappearing in China under mysterious circumstances, followed by rumors of a deadly virus. It might give some of your anti-trade politicians an excuse to impose tariffs or sanctions.

"The way I interpret the facts are that Phil got whatever disease the son has, but Phil didn't pull through. The Chinese don't want the body leaving the country, and they don't want to be issuing any death certificates or notifying any Embassy. Right now, they are desperately trying to keep a lid on whatever is going on, and a Phil Funston killed by a mystery disease is not how they accomplish this. I think they did an autopsy to see what this virus is doing to humans, and when they were done, incinerated the remains and purged any and all records from the second he approached Immigration in Bangkok. If we are able to do things like that, don't you think the Chinese can as well?"

There was a pause before Glenn spoke. "Then you're telling us you think he's dead."

Oliver nodded. "Yes, Glenn, that's usually a prerequisite for an autopsy or a cremation."

Another brief silence followed.

"How are we supposed to be sure?"

Oliver passed on Joe's offer for another hit of the joint.

"When enough time has passed without his return and without a word from or about him, that's a safe conclusion. Don't you lawyers declare someone legally dead after a certain period of time? In the case of an American who disappears into the bowels of China, whatever the period is, we don't have to wait that long to make that finding."

"Our American friend is feeling guilty for not warning those two what they were heading into," Sleepy Joe said. "Phil fired him and said he was off to China when Glenn knew everything Tom Boston told us." He didn't tell Oliver about the airport encounter where the son was also present.

"Nonsense," Oliver replied. "Phil wouldn't have stayed home and he would have told his new manager. The asshole son would have surely sold this information to China, and our late friend Phil Funston would have announced it in every bar he entered. No, Glenn, to the contrary, you made a wiser and more difficult choice. You might be feeling some guilt right now, but rest assured, mate, your silence enabled us to get Dr. Boston back home instead of in a Chinese interrogation room."

"I couldn't have said it better myself," Sleepy Joe said. "I did try."

"What if it was not an act of principle, not a carefully weighed decision, just the act of a man who was pissed off?"

Oliver and Joe looked at each other and smiled. Oliver answered him. "Still a wise and more difficult choice, mate."

The door to the porch opened and the General walked through. He was wearing a pair of shorts and a tank top. Glenn had never seen the General in anything other than a suit or smart casual dress. The beach garb showed off his physique, which appeared as good if not better than Glenn's own. No bulges, no belly, muscular arms and legs. Glenn did not know the General to work out, and it had been many years since he'd lived a life of military regimen and exercise.

He's always telling me those mia noi keep him young. Give the man points for truth. It is sort of exercise.

The General took a chair from the other side of the porch and carried it over to the table, where he sat.

"I imagine Oliver had told you about my son and Funston," he began. He continued without waiting for their response. "My son will survive, as Oliver must have told you. Unfortunately, Phil Funston appears to have succumbed to the virus. You aren't going to see either one again. My son will not be returning to Bangkok. When the Chinese release him, I'll send him to where he grew up, with a small stipend, and a stern warning to avoid all trouble."

"Not that it breaks my heart to hear this," Sleepy Joe said, "but what did your son do that caused this change of heart? Last week he was running your entertainment businesses. Now it sounds like he's *persona non grata.*"

The General did not frown, and his eyes remained dry, but his voice revealed his sadness. "I thought I could make up for lost time. I didn't realize that the clay had been molded and baked in the kiln already. I thought my heir could be a man like Glenn, or perhaps like our Major Parhat. Instead, I wound up with someone who acts like a thug, hits women, insults good people, cheats my friends in business, and wound up trying to take all the money Glenn had worked so hard to arrange. How do you think Funston came to the attention of these Chinese promoters? Who did all the work and had to suffer over two years of Phil Funston? I am so sorry for this, Glenn."

He's telling me it was the son who insisted on ripping us off for that ten percent. He's letting me know he's sorry he let it happen. I don't think he realizes I was delighted to be rid of Funston. I just didn't want him to die.

"Don't feel bad, General. None of this is your fault in any way. I was already trying to dump Phil. I tried to get my new friend and assistant, Rong, to take over, but he's a real smart kid and he said no. He's got a good career ahead as either a bass player or a manager, and any further association with Phil Funston would be counterproductive."

"A smart young man indeed," the General said. "Now that he's no longer in your employ, do have any objections to me offering him the job my son just lost?"

"Just don't underpay him," Glenn said.

Thirty-One

Oliver's New Year's Eve Party, Koh Phangan

THEY WERE gathered on the beach just beyond Oliver's property. The General, Oliver and Mick sat on beach chairs, the rest sat or lay on blankets. Kit was engrossed in conversation with Oliver's girlfriend and the General's mia noi. Mick was a last-minute surprise, announced by the General a few hours before, just as the big Serb walked into Oliver's house.

Now I understand why there was one empty bedroom, Glenn thought.

Glasses of champagne were passed around, poured by Oliver's housekeeper. Several plates of comfort food sat on a small table. The revelers munched on French canapés, mini hot dogs and pizzas, barbecued chicken, and som tam, the ubiquitous spicy papaya salad.

"He has no place to go," the General later explained to Oliver, Glenn, and Joe at the time of Mick's arrival. "He doesn't really have a country to go home to. He was a Yugoslav, then he was involuntarily made a citizen of Serbia, and now he's right to worry he is seen by many in Serbia as a traitor because he wouldn't kill innocent people. Considering all the influence China has in Africa these days, he can't go back to work there. He has no legal right to return to America. His best friend in life was just murdered and he himself is alive only because Australians make better killers than Thai-Chinese. I'm putting him on my payroll."

"After his performance on behalf of the Chinese?" Oliver asked. "What could he possibly offer you?"

"He looks big and tough, and sometimes that's all it takes to do the job. He is a farang, and aside from Joe, I have no others on permanent staff."

"You're going on a real hiring spree," Glenn said. "First Rong, then Mick."

"I always had an eye for talent, Glenn," the General said. "You're the perfect example."

∞

THE SUN set and darkness blanketed the beach. The only light came from the sliver of moon visible and the lights in Oliver's house. The group headed back there by silent consensus, leaving the housekeeper to pack up after them.

Oliver had a feast awaiting them in his living room. Thai cuisine was represented by *pad thai*, *tom yong gam*, fish in lemon sauce, and chicken larb. Western food included a roasted leg of lamb, hamburgers, spaghetti with red sauce, and fish and chips. The beer was Singha, Heineken, Foster's, and San Miguel. Bottles of single malt scotch and American whiskeys filled the rolling bar cart.

Glenn wasn't very hungry, being full from grazing on the beach. He knew after smoking with Joe he would be. He saw Joe walk to the porch and was about to follow when a hand touched his arm. It was Kit.

"Can I get you any food, or something to drink?" she asked. Glenn smiled at her.

"You're not working tonight," he said.

"I know," she replied. "I don't think it is work if I am nice to you."

"I agree," he said. "I'd be delighted if you would bring me a little sample of everything, just a taste. It all adds up to one full meal."

"Your drink?" Kit asked.

"Diet coke with a lemon." Then Glenn hurried out to the porch.

Joe was already smoking a joint. He passed it to Glenn.

"Take a few quick hits and scurry back to your girlfriend," Joe said as he patted Glenn on the back.

"How could you see us? You were walking and facing the other direction." Glenn asked.

"Eyes in the back of my head," Joe answered.

Two hits later, Glenn was walking back to the living room, where Kit had reserved space on the couch and on the coffee table, where Glenn's meal awaited him. He sat down next to Kit.

"I've never been in such a beautiful house," she said.

"Me either, before Oliver bought this place," Glenn replied.

"Oh Khun Glenn, you went to the General's house. Edward says you have a very beautiful condo. And you come from America."

"But this is still the nicest house I've been in. Even nicer because you're here."

"Pak wan," Kit said. Glenn blushed.

"Americans make wishes for New Year, is that right, Khun Glenn?" When he explained they were really promises to one's self, it was true, Kit asked him for his. He said it was to learn Thai.

"Great. When do I give the first lesson?"

"After the ball drops," Glenn said. Kit gave him a puzzled look.

"That means after midnight, when the New Year begins." Glenn explained. She looked at her phone to check the time.

AT ONE minute to midnight, Oliver banged a wine glass with a fork and called his multitudes to order. He told his housekeeper to hand a glass of champagne to each guest. The television was tuned to a Bangkok station which had its own clock ready to ring in the farang New Year. When the clock hit midnight, onscreen fireworks along the Chao Phraya River were broadcast. The partiers at Oliver's downed their champagne. Glenn stood next to Kit and watched her swallow her glass in one swill. He sipped his until empty. When the glass was empty, he saw the General and Oliver embracing and kissing their respective significant others, assuming the General's mia noi was all that significant to him. He put his arm around Kit and drew her close to him. She turned her face towards his and they met in a kiss. A brief kiss, but a kiss nevertheless.

When Glenn opened his eyes, he saw Edward looking at him. He had avoided the Welshman since arriving on the island and hadn't said a word to him. *I was angry at him for inviting Kit. Now I need to thank him*, Glenn thought. *But not now.*

Oliver and the General disappeared with their consorts, Sleepy Joe fell asleep in his hammock, and Mick drank one glass of vodka too many and retired to his room the instant the New Year began. The only people left in the living room were Glenn and Kit and Edward. Edward smiled at them a from across the room and went upstairs to his room. In the quiet of the house, Glenn heard the door close.

"Time for my first lesson," Glenn said to Kit as he took her hand and led her to the stairs leading to his bedroom.

On New Year's Day, Glenn found an open motorcycle shop along the road facing Oliver's house and rented a shiny new Honda 150 cc. For the island, that was a powerful little machine. With Kit sitting behind him, he drove as far north as possible on the mountainous road above the coastline. All signs of civilization disappeared, and the view was endless ocean, sand, sun, and green hills. They stopped when Glenn estimated they were at the northernmost point on the island and enjoyed the lunch Oliver's housekeeper packed as they watched the sun bounce off the blue ocean. Glenn took a small thermos of coffee and a bottle of water from under the bike's seat. He handed the water to Kit. They remained there for half an hour, eating, watching the ocean, periodically embracing or kissing, and somehow, Kit taught Glenn five new Thai words.

Thirty-Two

Bangkok, January 4, 2020

Two things changed at the NJA Club: the calendar and the permanent absence of Phil Funston. Everyone knew the former; most learned the latter during the first week of the new year, and few expressed any sorrow. When Wang asked Glenn to prepare a notice he could distribute, Glenn was surprised, but Wang explained.

"He was a hard man to like, but he was a good and loyal customer," he explained to Glenn. It was to say Phil died in a car accident and, in accordance with his self-proclaimed Buddhist faith, was cremated. There would be a drink on the house for all who attended a very brief memorial for Phil that evening. Glenn asked Rong to help him design a memorial flier for the occasion, as the young man was far more well-versed in computers and graphic options. Glenn and Rong selected a headshot photo Glenn had made for promotion; it emphasized Phil's shiny dome and downplayed the ever-present sneer. The text described Phil as "Bangkok's greatest blues guitarist" and "A longtime member of the NJA Club community." Rong suggested adding that Phil would be "sorely missed," but Glenn decided on the less controversial "RIP." They'd hand out a flier and give out the drinks, but nothing more. No one could think of anything good to say about Phil since the day he'd arrived in Bangkok, and nothing was known of his prior life.

There wasn't any need to call people, as anyone who might attend was a club regular. Ray poured their drinks with a big smile Glenn thought might be due to Phil's demise. No one at the event looked the least bit sad.

Glenn took his free vodka martini with an olive and joined the General, Oliver and Sleepy Joe at the General's usual table. The General's bodyguard sat behind him.

"I propose a toast to the memory of the dear departed Phil Funston," Oliver said. No one spoke nor did they raise their glasses.

"He was a horse's ass," Sleepy Joe said to break the silence. "But even a horse's ass deserves a toast. Here's to Phil Funston, the biggest horse's ass we've ever known."

The men raised their glasses and clinked them in a toast to the man none of them could stand or would miss.

"I am concerned about Dr. Boston," Glenn said when the drinks were drained. "The holiday is over, and I suppose I could call his employer, but I doubt he's there." Turning to Oliver, he asked if there were any ways to find out about the doctor.

"It may take a few days, but yes, I am fairly confident I can find out where he is," Oliver replied.

"And what should we do with the information we learned about this virus?" the General asked.

"Not much," Oliver replied. "Pay attention to news reports, call your doctor if you're not feeling well, don't go to China, stay away from these zero-baht Chinese tourists," he said, referring to those who book tours with companies in the PRC and stay in PRC-owned hotels and eat at PRC-owned restaurants.

"All we can do is watch the news and keep our ears open for things that might not make the news," Glenn said.

"Que sera, sera," Sleepy Joe said.

As Glenn was leaving the Club, Edward walked in. They passed each other a few feet from the entrance before Glenn walked through into the street. Edward looked at Glenn like a puppy begging for affection.

"Thank you, Edward," Glenn said as he walked past him.

BACK AT his condo, Glenn put down the latest issue of the *New Yorker* magazine, which Lek had handed him in the lobby earlier that day. He set his phone to play a blues album in honor of Phil. He chose *Blue & Lonesome*, the Rolling Stones 2012 album where they delighted Glenn and Joe by returning to their roots as the world's best blues band, covering Howlin' Wolf, Little Walter, Jimmy Reed, Willie Dixon and other blues giants. A joint awaited him on the balcony. He walked out into the night air, sat down, and smoked the joint as he emptied his mind and stared at the lights of the buildings across this section of Bangkok, occasionally looking down at the headlights snaking their way along Sukhumvit Road. The ringing of his phone cut through the music. He answered and the music stopped.

"Hello, Glenn," Rodney Snapp said. "I understand you've been wanting to talk to me."

"That's not true," Glenn said. "I told Oliver I wanted to know that Dr. Boston is safe."

"You mean you wanted to make certain he was safe from us," Rodney said.

"Do you blame me?" Glenn asked.

"Not at all," Rodney replied. "I'd feel the same were I in your shoes.

The purpose of this call is to allay your fears. I'm on your side, Glenn. I understand why you think our own government might not take Dr. Boston's information as a call to action, but instead might try to cover it up."

Why is he telling me this? Glenn thought. He asked Rodney.

"Because you are right. If this information is brought to the attention of the current occupant of the White House and his enablers right now, it will be suppressed or Dr. Boston discredited, whatever it takes. Elections are eleven months away. We need time to gather more proof and get out the word to the scientists and doctors who are free from political influence. That's our only hope if we want to save lives."

"You sound like me," Glenn said.

"I'm an intelligence officer," Rodney said. "I see what he does with the intelligence we give him when it's something he doesn't want to hear. No reason to think he'd ever put America's interest above his."

Glenn was still uncertain he could believe Rodney. "You work for the bastard."

"Wrong, Glenn. I work for you and every American citizen."

"When can I speak to Dr. Boston?" Glenn asked.

"We are unofficially entertaining him in comfortable quarters for a few weeks," Rodney said. "His employer thinks he's doing a special project for the Thai government, something with dengue fever. The White House has no idea he even exists. We're trying to get his information and whatever else we learn to scientists in the government agencies we know we can trust. By the beginning of February, he'll be back in his lab in California. It will be safe for him to call you then."

Glenn drew on his joint, held it in for a few seconds, and exhaled.

"You still there?" Rodney asked.

"Affirmative," Glenn said. "I hope I can trust you."

"As if you have a choice," Rodney said. "Needless to say, this conversation never happened." The line went dead.

∼

"STARTING THE New Year with a bang, as we said in high school," Oliver told Glenn as the waitress at Au Bon Pain in the emporium brought their food. "From no women to two, very impressive. Looking forward to your big date with Kai? Don't worry, I won't tell Kit."

"Do you think Rodney told the truth about Dr. Boston?" Glenn asked.

"Without a doubt," Oliver said before taking a bite of an everything bagel with cream cheese.

"I'd like to believe that's the case," Glenn said. "But we're talking about a CIA guy who openly admits to killing people."

"Exactly my point," Oliver said. "Rodney doesn't lie to you."

"Will his actions make any difference?" Glenn asked, looking at Oliver.

"I'm no scientist," Oliver replied. "I have to think that the more information gets out quickly to the right people, the easier it will be to stop a pandemic before it gets out of hand. No doubt that's also Rodney's thinking, and Dr. Boston's of course."

"Will our saving Dr. Boston make a real difference?" he asked.

"Que sera, sera," Oliver replied.

Acknowledgments

Bangkok Blues is the third book in the NJA series, but the first written in the third person. I was fortunate to have a professional editor, James Osborne, whose able assistance and sharp eye for detail (and error) sharpened my own skills and made for a much better book than would have resulted without his input.

Special appreciation is owed the Center for Disease Control (CDC), whose website contained a wealth of information enabling a fiction writer to describe the COVID virus in terms understandable to reader and author alike. An immeasurable debt of gratitude is due the men and women of CDC for the countless lives they saved in the face of unceasing political interference and misinformation from the highest levels of government. Appreciation is also due Congressional Representative Lloyd Doggett (D-Tex), whose "Trump's Coronavirus Timeline" on his website provided a necessary fact-check on the chronology used in the novel.

It goes without saying I must again thank the Kingdom and people of Thailand, who provide this author with an endless string of intriguing tales and kindness.

Once again, a deep appreciation to my wife, Josie, who had to endure yet one more novel from her writing-obsessed husband.

About the Author

Stephen Shaiken practiced criminal law in for more than thirty five years, the first four in Brooklyn, and the rest in San Francisco. His decades as a criminal trial lawyer are often reflected in his writing. He is a graduate of Queens College and Brooklyn Law School, and earned an MA in Creative Writing from San Francisco State University. He currently splits his time between Bangkok, Thailand, and Tampa, Florida. (When the current pandemic permits.)

Bangkok Blues is Stephen's third NJA novel and features the same characters as the first two, while introducing several more. It's also the first of the three written in the third person, so readers learn what the other characters are thinking and what they are doing when not with Glenn, who narrated the first two novels from his point of view.

Stephen's three NJA Club novels are best described as exotic noir thrillers, but he also writes historical fiction, humor, literary and science fiction. Several of his short stories in these genres were published; those and others are posted on his blog.

Stephen will soon release a different kind of novel, set in New York City in the late sixties era, against the backdrop of a young rock and roll manager struggling to break from the second-tier Queens rock scene to the glamor and stardom of Manhattan.

When he isn't writing, Stephen enjoys travel, gardening, yoga, guitar, and following politics and current events with a passion. He's a voracious reader of fiction and non-fiction in too many genres and subjects to list.

Follow Stephen on his blog at www.stephenshaiken.com and on Twitter @StephenShaiken, and sign up for his newsletter to receive advance notice of Stephen's future novels and short stories.

Made in the USA
Las Vegas, NV
21 October 2024